THIS IS NOT A HORROR MOVIE

M/M New Adult Rom-Com

SARA DOBIE BAUER

D1607790

COPYRIGHT

Cover Artist: Natasha Snow Designs
This is Not a Horror Movie © 2021 Sara Dobie Bauer

ALL RIGHTS RESERVED

DEDICATION

To Cheryl for all the love.
(Teenage you is fangirling right now.)

To Isabel for believing in me.
(And I'll always believe in you.)

CHAPTER 1

"Emory." My twin sister says my name in that annoyed way of hers that means she's been saying it for a while, but I'm halfway through *Salem's Lot* and don't have time to listen—not when I'm high on Florida sun and horror.

She says my name again, louder this time, followed by "Hey, princess, I think your boyfriend's here."

I look up from where I'm sitting at our kitchen table and throw the book, which could be considered a deadly weapon. Stephen King doesn't mince words. Liz is practiced enough to duck. Sure, we're both eighteen and headed to New York University in the fall, but we've never outgrown the need to pick at each other.

She's right, though; I hear a car in the driveway next door. The Nichols family has arrived, which means Connor has arrived. For the record, he's not my boyfriend. Exhibit A: I'm pretty sure he's straight. Exhibit B: For the past four summers, he's treated me like some little kid whose name he can't quite remember.

All right, that's not true. Connor and I are "friends" for

two weeks of every year, but not, like, good friends. He mostly ruffles my hair and "play wrestles" me when he's not charming *every other person* on Longboat Key. He doesn't know I have a crush on him.

I hope he doesn't know I have a crush on him.

Mom and Dad are out walking the beach since we only arrived yesterday. We Joneses like to soak up as much saline and sun as we can as quickly as possible. That means Liz and I are the lone greeters. Usually, we would walk over as a family and welcome our two-weeks-of-June neighbors, but we don't have to. Before Liz or I can move, I hear Connor's heavy feet on our patio—yes, I know the sound of his feet. Don't mock me.

Liz tosses *Salem's Lot* back, and it nails me in the stomach. I grunt and bend over at the waist, hoping she didn't rupture my appendix. Then, I stand and run my fingers through my stupid hair. God, why didn't I get it cut? Thanks to an earlier swim, it probably looks like a dead animal pelt.

"Stop fucking preening," Liz hisses.

"I'm not," I growl. "Do I look okay?"

"Of course you look okay. You're the male version of me." She disappears around the corner and toward the big back patio that overlooks the Gulf of Mexico. The screen door slides open and shut, and she shouts, "Connor" like it's a war cry.

His voice is a low rumble that I feel in my skinny chest. Great, I'm in nothing but swim trunks. As if ex-football star Connor Nichols needs to be reminded that I'm the human equivalent of an under-stuffed scarecrow. It's even worse now that I shot up five inches my senior year of high school. A horrifically late bloomer, I'm now six feet tall and have trouble controlling my appendages. Running into walls is my newest hobby. I'm a pro.

The screen door slides open and shut again, and the

rumbles turn to words. "Where's my favorite book nerd?" he says.

Yes, that would be me. I have the urge to raise my hand like I'm back in school.

He turns the corner into the kitchen, and there is no way he got better-looking. How did he get better-looking? I mean, why? How? Someone tell me how this golden god of a man could get better-looking. His blond hair is a little bit longer on top. He's still a big tower of tan muscle. The glitter of his grin actually makes a *ding* sound in my head. I'm a microwave dinner that's done.

I open my mouth to say something—*say something, stupid*—but catch my sister making a funny face at Connor. Liz makes funny faces at me all the time. I can usually read her precise level of Emory-exasperation based on eyebrow curvature alone. Connor doesn't exasperate her usually, but right now, she's staring at him like he's a math equation, and Liz sucks at math.

"Emory?" Connor says.

I let out the breath I'd been holding when I start feeling dizzy. "Yeah?"

His whole forehead is a staircase of creases, and his mouth hangs open like he's a hungry fish. He hasn't shaved in two days—two. I'm an expert at Connor's facial hair. He has ambitious chin follicles that could blossom into a full beard if he wanted.

I'm waiting for him to cross the room and put me in a headlock, because that's what he started doing last summer when I was seventeen and Connor, nineteen, was a student at some community college in New York State. I swear his life purpose last summer was embarrassing me. But Connor doesn't move, and this is some *Invasion of the Body Snatchers* shit right here.

"Dude." Liz grabs his upper arm and shakes. Of course

she's totally confident in nothing but a red bikini because she's *Liz* and has confidence and *boobs*. "Earth to Connor. What's the matter with you?"

He clears his throat but looks like he's choking on a golf ball. "You look different," he says to me.

Liz nods. "Oh, no shit, right? He shot up a million inches this year, but you should see him walk. He's like drunk Gumby."

I lower the dark unibrow I refuse to let my sister wax.

Connor flashes those white teeth. *Ding! Ding!* "No, you look like a grown-up," he says. "What's up with your hair?"

I reach up and squeeze the probable disaster that is my head. Back home in Ohio, Liz told me to grow it out over Christmas. What was once a frizz ball, short on the sides and long on top, is now a thick, tangled veil of brown that falls past my ears and often into my eyes. In social situations, I have literally hidden behind my hair. I'm sure the addition of Florida humidity has made it a sea anemone.

I vomit some consonants before finding actual words. "It's stupid, I know. I should have got it cut."

Liz squawks. "Everyone loves the hair. What are you smoking, Emory?"

She's right; everyone does love the hair. The girls back at Perrysburg High School spent our final semester petting me like a pony. Sadly, I did not get the same treatment from guys.

Connor talks a lot. Always. He'd be a fabulous talk show host, lulling guests into telling him their deepest, darkest secrets all with a wink and a smile. He's not talking now at all.

"So how was the drive down?" I hear my voice, so I assume I'm the one who asked this boring question.

He's still swallowing around that golf ball when he nods. "Fine. No, your hair looks... good. I'm gonna..." He points in the direction of the beach and leaves.

Liz's chin is down around her toes. "What the hell was that?"

I shrug. "The blinding paleness of my skin ate away at his frontal lobe?"

"Where was the headlock? I love when he puts you in headlocks." She holds her hands up, a T-Rex mimic, and shadow boxes. "You look like a praying mantis being eaten by your mate."

I scoop *Salem's Lot* from the floor and sigh. "Maybe if he's weird and avoids me for the next two weeks I can stop being desperately in love with him, go away to college, and pretend he didn't set the bar ridiculously high for the rest of my adult life."

I can feel her eye roll from across the room—that weird twin thing of ours. "Drama queen. Speaking of your paleness, let's go lay on the beach. It's time to start on that tan."

By the end of our Florida vacation, I'll resemble a different race. Our mom's family is Italian, so I have enchanted tanning genes. One second, I'm the color of snow; five minutes later, I'm an Olympic bronze medal.

I walk past her into the mudroom. "Fine. You can shave my head later."

She jabs me in the arm. "I'm not spending our time here wading through shit piles of self-loathing, princess. This is our last summer before we enter the adult world—"

"Pretty sure college is not considered the adult world."

"And I want to have fun, fun, fun 'til her daddy takes..." She stops talking, then moans. "You're the writer. Say something clever."

I quote *Army of Darkness*, obviously: "Gimme some sugar, baby."

"It's too early for incest jokes."

I make a loud gagging noise. This is how we are, all the time. I feel bad for people forced to spend time with us.

I leave my book on the patio. Liz saunters down the three steps to the sand while I take a flying leap. I'm still excited by my newly acquired long legs, so I do a lot of jumping nowadays. Half the time I end up a groaning pile of mangled limbs. Nobody calls me "Grace."

Once we reach the warm ocean waves, I spot Mom and Dad coming toward us. It's hard to miss my dad's bright white hair or my mom's huge red sunhat. She and Liz share a sort of old Hollywood movie star style; Dad and I share an obsessive love for scary movies. He started me watching Vincent Price films when I was a fetus.

Dad gives Liz's long hair a playful tug, and Mom puts her arm around me.

"The Nichols clan has arrived," Liz says. "Although I'm not sure who was more of a spaz this morning: Emory or Connor."

I kick at the sand. "I wasn't a spaz."

"My beautiful hair is stupid, blah, blah." Liz mimics me so well that I'm terrified of ever truly pissing her off. Lord knows how many embarrassing phone calls she could make.

Mom finger-brushes my curls. "What's wrong with your hair?"

"Nothing. I don't know."

Mom smiles that infuriating smile of hers that screams, "Isn't it horrible that I can read your mind?"

Liz kicks at an incoming wave. Water sprays from the tips of her painted toes in a crystalline arch. "What's the gossip, Pops? I know you talked to Roberta already."

My dad smirks, and I get a clear picture of what I'll look like in thirty years. "Just wait until you see the shell sculpture right now. She's outdone herself."

"Yeah, yeah," Liz says. "The gossip! Who's dead? Divorced? Got a new mistress?"

Having been coming to Longboat Key for the past six

years, we're practically part of the community now. The same people are here the same time of year every year, so we've formed a mishmash vacation family, the Nicholses included. It's hard to keep secrets on this beach, small as it is, and Roberta is the unchallenged gossip guru of Gulf of Mexico Drive.

"Some real estate developer finally bought the Outpost," Mom says. Her white linen cover-up blows in the breeze.

Dad nods. "It's going to be hell to renovate after eight years empty."

"Oh, no!" Liz bellows. "But that's where we all go to—"

I clear my throat. My sister is the queen of not keeping her mouth shut.

"That's where we all go to... pet rats," she says. "Lots of rats. Brush 'em and stuff."

I suck my lips into my mouth. I know it's my nervous giveaway, but I really hate my lips. They're too pink. I know I'm gay, but why do I have to have Barbie's mouth?

My dad snorts, and Mom shakes her head.

I'm pretty sure they know what we really do at the spooky, abandoned Outpost Beach Resort. We party. Most nights, you'll find a smattering of teenagers down there with pilfered beer and cigarettes. Sometimes, we even get bottles of cheap liquor. Once, we got weed. Couples sneak off and have sex in abandoned rooms, still stacked with old furniture, beds, and linens like everyone left in a big hurry.

Liz isn't kidding about the rats, though; there are so many rats. They're the size of Volvos.

"Well," Dad says. "I guess you'll have to find a new place for your rat brushing, hmm?"

"Let's not make that into a euphemism," I mutter.

Liz shoves me in the shoulder, but I duck a slap by running into the waves. There's a big dip a couple steps in that's important to avoid. The breaking waves dig a sort of trough, filled with broken shell pieces and the occasional baby stingray. I dive headfirst into the water, flap my arms and kick, kick. I'm a lifeguard in the summers at home, so I've always been a strong swimmer. Ever since watching *Jaws*, Liz won't come out farther than waist-deep, so I know I'm safe from her attacks once I can't touch. I tread water and look back. My family waves from the beach in front of our big, yellow house, so I wave back.

The Nichols residence is to the right: a modern, green beach monstrosity, even bigger than ours—and our bit of Longboat Key real estate is not small. I think I see Connor on the screened-in lanai, but it could be his dad. They're both tall guys.

It'll be easy to avoid Connor if he keeps up his act from this morning. Liz is right; where was the headlock from last summer? True, since the day we met, Connor and I have had a weird... *relationship*. Is that the word for it? More accurately, we've had a tumultuous give and take that has involved two literal fights, one crying fit, and a leg massage.

Jesus, the leg massage: What the hell had Connor been on that night?

Anyway, avoidance is key. It's time for a fresh start, away from the small town bullies of my Ohio high school and the social nightmare that was my teen years. I'm headed to the Big Apple in two months. There is no room for looking back —or for fruitless pining over Connor Nichols, the man I'd like to climb like a tree.

My big, shiny gay life starts in Manhattan. All I have to do is live through the next two weeks on Longboat. No problem.

CHAPTER 2

The Outpost gets grosser every year, although I guess that'll end soon, since some real estate developer bought it for a gazillion-million dollars. Okay, so I don't have the exact figures, but I skimmed the article in the *Longboat Key Observer*. A hotshot financial group out west did the buying, but they don't have any concrete plans yet. They knew they wanted the land, so they bought the land. Probably a good investment, considering Longboat's waves roll green with new money.

Case in point, I glare at the fancy-dressed girl dancing with Connor across the empty bean-shaped Outpost pool. Her name is Tiffany. She probably spells it some funny way, like "No, Tiffany with a double E." Every year, she's the welcome wagon for new kids. She knows everyone, and everyone knows her. It's annoying, although I'm safe since she ignores me.

My bad mood is not her fault. I shouldn't pick on her for her social prowess and fancy clothes. If we're being honest, my family is rich. Dad started a landscaping business decades ago that now has seven locations throughout Ohio. Mom can wear whatever designer threads she wants, and even though I got a full academic ride to NYU, paying for Liz's tuition will be no sweat.

No, my bad mood is a culmination of two things.

One, Connor is being his usual friendly, handsome self. He's smiling and joking with everyone while drinking some liquor concoction from a red cup. I haven't seen his camera yet. Last summer, Connor showed up with a fancy digital thing and snapped pictures of everything—except me. Now, he's talking to everyone—except me.

Two, I've been forced to retreat to a bench overlooking the empty turquoise soybean because girls keep staring at me to the point of me having paranoia. I realize I'm not super stylish, but my navy-blue polo doesn't have mustard down the front (I've checked), and I don't have a big booger on my face (I don't think), so why am I getting all these weird looks?

The air smells like salt, fish, and wet moss with the occasional whiff of cigarettes or cologne. There's about twelve of us at the Outpost tonight. There'll be triple this number for the big summer solstice party, which usually marks the end of Liz's and my time on Longboat. It gets really pagan. Last year, a bunch of fellow hoodlums danced naked around a fire, Connor included. I swear I didn't look. Much.

Condensation from my beer drips down my wrist, so I wipe my hands on my skinny jeans and kick at some leaves. There's a sand-covered sucker, too, decorated with crawling ants. When I kick the discarded candy, probably left behind by some little kid on a dare, it bounces over the edge of the empty pool.

Liz dragged me here, of course. I'd rather be home reading *Salem's Lot*, or *The Exorcist*, or *The Haunting of Hill House*. I'm always reading multiple books at once. Liz says I have ADD, but I like having options depending on my mood. Maybe I don't want to read about vampires tonight, okay?

I'd say it's about time for me to go. I've put in my requisite social time. Liz will yell at me, but I might be able to sneak away without her noticing. She's talking to a hunk in swim trunks and disturbing large black earring gauges—kids these days—so should be sufficiently distracted, although she keeps reminding me: "You're going to have to make new friends in college! You can't hide behind books forever!" She's right, but I can hide for now.

I crush my empty beer and stand but almost trip when one of the Outpost's rodent tenants runs past my feet.

I apologize. To the rat.

He acknowledges my apology by stopping and staring up at me with a big piece of bread in his mouth. Lucky little guy — Where'd he find bread around here? He holds his snack in his pointy rat fingers and chews. Is he expecting small talk? I don't think this is what Liz had in mind when she said "new friends."

There's jam on the bread. There is red jam on the bread.

I lean over, closer, but since a couple battery-operated lamps are the only illumination around the abandoned pool, it's hard to see much. Just bread, but...

Does that piece of bread have a fingernail?

My mouth drops open, and the rat stares up at me, all friendly like. I can practically hear his squeaky rat voice: "Want some, mister?"

He closes his tiny jaws around his treat and runs. I drop my empty can and follow, but he scurries around an overgrown palm—and beyond that, there's nothing but black. I swear I can barely hear the music from over here, almost like all the overgrown trees and lifeless Outpost buildings are starved for sound. I reach for the phone in the back of my jeans before remembering I didn't bring it. No flashlight for me then. I'm about to follow the, well... finger, when a hand lands on my shoulder. I suck a panicked gasp in through my lips as Connor says, "Sorry! Sorry."

I put my hands on my knees and relearn breathing.

He stands there, backlit like some kind of hot angel, and shrugs. "Maybe you should be thanking me."

"What?"

"You like to be scared."

He's right. Haunted house in the neighborhood? I'm first. Spooky cemetery? Coming through. Maybe that's part of the reason I always let Liz drag me to parties at the Outpost. It feels like being in a scary movie. I'm waiting for Leatherface to show up and murder the morally reprehensible youth. Of course, if horror movie rules are true, I'm totally dead. I lost my virginity at sixteen and more often than not spend "happy hour" sharing malt liquor with Longboat's famous homeless dude, Leland.

"What are you doing over here?" Connor asks.

"Befriending local wildlife." I glance over my shoulder into the dark. It couldn't have been a finger, right? Just a trick of the light. I shove hair out of my face—a nervous tic I've acquired since growing it out. Because I needed another nervous tic. "What are *you* doing over here?"

"Talking to you." He grins, but I can feel a disconnect.

Connor and I have always had a mutually agreed upon rhythm. He's the big, gorgeous straight dude who puts up with me, the skinny, little gay kid.

Well.

No one knows I'm gay down here. Florida is for family, not fu— Anyway.

In summers past, Connor wrestled me and tickled me, and I pretended not to like it. We talked about some things, mostly scary movies, but kept an emotional distance. He accepts me being a drama queen, and I never let him know I would climb Everest for his kiss.

Staring at me with a dumb look on his face is not our rhythm.

I finally lose my shit. "Jesus, am I bleeding from my eyes?"

He coughs out a laugh. "What?"

"You're looking at me funny."

He looks away. "Oh."

I cross my arms. I have, in fact, filled out a lot since last summer—and the lifeguarding helps—but I'm still self-conscious about my small frame and will probably never forget the jocks calling me "Tinker Bell" from seventh to tenth grade. I press my lips together and side-eye the kids dancing to some club beat on Liz's phone. "Everyone's looking at me funny, actually."

Connor clears his throat and plucks at the front of his tight, white T-shirt. He looks like he wants to dive headfirst into the empty pool at his back.

"You don't have to talk to me, you know."

His blue eyes flit back my way. Even in the dark, I know they're blue. He says, "But I like talking to you."

I hug myself tighter and lift a shoulder. "Seen any good horror movies lately?"

His smile is back. "Tons. I saw this French one called *Raw.*"

I bounce up on my toes. "Cannibals! Oh my God, that movie was so good! The writing." I tear at my hair in euphoric bliss.

He nods. "And the scene with the roommate."

"And the ending!" I poke him in the chest. "Dude, I tried to get Liz to watch it. She's all vegetarian now because she dated this hippie dude senior year. She said she gave up meat for her health, but I think it's because he said he tasted death in her mouth."

Connor does the silent open-mouth laugh thing that happens when my storytelling reaches peak levels of absurd.

"She made it thirty minutes into the movie before she had to leave the room and vomit. Meanwhile, I was sitting there eating, like, spaghetti."

He puts his hand on my shoulder as he keeps laughing. I smell his deodorant: sporty man stuff. "I can't believe I almost didn't come this year."

That steals the air from my lungs. Sure, I should be avoiding the guy, looking forward to the future, but all of a sudden, I can't imagine a summer without Connor Nichols making me blush. "Why wouldn't you have come?"

He shakes his head, levity leaving his face. "My dad is being a dick. It's—" He looks down and takes a deep breath, in and out through his nose. "You know what? It doesn't matter." He slings a beefy arm around my shoulders, but I'm not short anymore, so I have to slouch forward for it to work. "I'm at the beach with my favorite writer." He squeezes, and my face shoves into his armpit.

"You've never read any of my work." My voice comes out muffled, my mouth full of his shirt.

"Well, if it's anything like the way you talk, I'm going to like it." He starts walking back toward the other kids—shudder—and I have no choice but to follow as he drags me along.

CHAPTER 3

A wicked witch cackles at 8:27 a.m. Don't be scared: it's my cell phone alarm.

I have this creepy... thing. Well, I have several creepy things that I do and am into, but I feel like my Florida morning routine is the creepiest.

See, I know what time Connor gets home from his morning jog pretty much to the minute.

No matter that he was probably out drinking way later than me last night—I escaped dreaded socialization at the pool by midnight—I know he'll still be out running this morning as he does every morning we're in Longboat Key. I don't know his route or anything, mostly because I would die of a heart explosion if I tried running with a buff dude like Connor. But I do know he gets home at 8:30 a.m., all sweaty and huffing breath and... freaking gorgeous.

I roll over in bed and fruitlessly try to brush hair out of my face. I forgot the humidity down here is way worse than up in Ohio, and although my hair doesn't frizz (Liz hates that my hair doesn't frizz), it feels thicker than usual. I kick my legs out of my sheets; well, try to. Thanks to my growth spurt, I first get tangled before cussing and kicking like my sheets are sharks chewing my toes. In nothing but boxer briefs, I hustle—quietly—to my window and peek outside.

My window looks right at the Nichols residence, so I have a perfect view of the driveway we share. It's silent out there, a bit too early yet for families to be on the beach. I hear breaking waves and smell what might be remnants of rain. Then, I hear the telltale sound of his feet hitting pavement. He doesn't stomp; he floats like a professional marathon runner. Take my word for it, the guy is in excellent shape. I don't know what he's majoring in at school. According to my dad, Connor is supposed to take over his pop's sealcoating business someday. Whatever his future entails, Connor works out—a ton.

Below me, he appears, petering out at the end of a sprint. He wears gray running shorts and holds a white T-shirt in his fist. Sweat glistens—seriously, *glistens*—in his chest hair and makes his broad shoulders shine. He slows to a walk and wipes his face with the T-shirt before huffing out breaths through his open mouth and walking down toward the Gulf.

I already had morning wood, but this? I forgot how much I love this. Best part of my vacation? Probably best part of my vacation.

Jesus, I have to get to New York and away from this stupid crush.

Because I'm not actually thirteen and have gotten laid before, I don't require a cold shower before going downstairs. I put on my swim trunks—my favorite pair, the ones with three big, horizontal stripes in red, white, and black. No, my mom didn't— Okay, yes, my mom picked them out for me. Anyway, I throw on my swim trunks and a tight white tee and gallop down the steps toward the kitchen where I smell coffee and hear Mom talking on the phone. The ear-splitting volume and breakneck pace of delivery means one thing: she's talking to our New York family.

The Angellis are a clan of crazy Italians with black hair, permanent five o'clock shadows (even the women), and too much eyeliner (just the women). Don't believe me? Liz is in a constant battle with her chin hair. She uses tweezers to pluck her face sometimes and would kill me if she knew I knew.

Mom keeps scream-talking into her cell phone but finds time to kiss my cheek and hand me a mug of espresso blend. She loves the strong stuff. All the Italians do. I once tried putting creamer in my coffee when I was, like, twelve, and my New York uncle Frank slapped me upside the head.

The *Longboat Key Observer* sits alone on the dining room table, which means my dad is golfing. He always golfs while we're in Florida but never back home in Ohio. He says golf is for vacation only. I assume he's pretty bad at it, but he always comes home relaxed.

Liz, as expected, is on the back patio, balanced on her head in skintight workout gear.

"Morning, loser," she says.

I stand but tilt my body over so my head is upside down. "Morning." I almost tumble when I stand up straight. I really need to get a grip on this new body.

Liz—who did not grow practically half a foot in the past year—gracefully lands on her toes and immediately goes into some other weird yoga pretzel in the middle of her purple mat. She's balanced on her hands, knees on the back of her elbows, when she asks if I had fun last night.

I'm about to answer when the Nichols's screen door slams open and shut. I look up in time to see Connor's dad storm outside. I sort of lift my hand in greeting and expect the same in return. Instead, he looks like he ran into a brick wall.

He says, "Emory? Jesus, kid, I'm glad you finally started

using 'roids, but cut your hair. You look like a goddamn drag queen." And he keeps walking.

This is how Mr. Nichols talks—abrupt and without excuse. Although I am impressed that a sixtysomething white guy from upstate New York who owns a sealcoating company actually knows what a drag queen is. Entrepreneurial skills and an affinity for cigars and scotch are the only things Mr. Nichols and my dad have in common, considering Connor's dad word vomits all the time and is kind of a douche, while my dad is quiet, unassuming, and polite.

I slouch into an Adirondack chair and sip coffee as Liz does warrior shit behind me. Mr. Nichols—he always tells us to call him "Lou," and I never have—stalks his son down the beach. There's no other word for it.

"Duke," Liz says.

"Huh?"

"The guy last night. His name was Duke, and he was an excellent kisser."

I stretch my arms over my head and yawn. "Okay. Gross."

"Did you know coffee is bad for your adrenal glands?"

I groan and stretch my legs out in front of me while watching Mr. Nichols get ever closer to his only child.

"I'm serious, Emory. Caffeine puts your body in a state of fight-or-flight when there is literally nothing to fight—"

"I'd like to fight you."

"So eventually you'll have adrenal fatigue, and then where will you be?"

"Hopefully, far away from my sister."

"Pfft." She pulls my hair. I've been too busy watching Connor to notice my sister is no longer doing yoga but looming over me like a spandex monster. "You could never live without me. Never."

It's annoyingly true—the curse of twins. When it came time to apply for college, there was no way we were going to separate schools. It would have been like chopping off my favorite arm and beating myself with it.

Liz nudges me with her elbow. "What's up with Lou? It looks like he's flailing. Is he flailing?"

He's only just now reached Connor, and even from this distance, it's obvious the Nichols men are not happy with each other. Mr. Nichols does indeed flail, and his face is all squished up. Connor is doing a lot of head shaking. His hands are balled into fists.

"How did it go with your boyfriend last night?" she asks.

"Don't call him that."

"I saw you two chatting." She sits cross-legged on the patio next to my chair, which is a terrible idea. We're in Florida; there is sand everywhere, no matter how many times my dad busts out the broom. "You looked cute together."

"Correction: he looked cute. Because he is always cute."

She grins up at me with those familiar eyes. Can I tell you how off-putting it is when someone else has your eyes? Obviously, Liz and I aren't identical, but we have the same eyes— these green-gold orbs that change color depending on the light.

I sigh. "What?"

"Nothing."

"You have the face."

She shrugs. "What face?"

I point. "That face. The one that means you think you're so smart."

"You're the smart one, princess. I'm cheeky and adorable." She pokes me in the knee. "But, seriously, did you have fun last night?"

I lean back in my chair. Connor and his dad are still talking with wide, angry mouths and gesticulating all over the beach. "Yes. I had fun. Kind of. Although I think the rats at the Outpost are eating people now."

"Wouldn't be a bit surprised. And your adrenals will be too tired to fight back."

I sputter out a laugh.

"You'll be worthless, so me and Connor will have to kick some rodent ass." She looks out at the ocean. "He seems shy this year, though, right? Or am I mental?"

"Are the two mutually exclusive?" I finally pay attention to my neglected coffee. It's still warm and tastes smoky in its strength. "I feel like he looks at me funny. Everyone does. Like I have plants growing out my ears."

She scoffs.

"What?"

"Nothing."

"You've got the face again."

"Stop talking about my face!" She stands and shoves me in the shoulder before rolling up her yoga mat.

Connor and his dad are still on the beach, although they're now walking in different directions. I can see Mr. Nichols coming toward us. He's beet red and mumbling to himself. Connor is moving away from us, but his steps are jerky, uncoordinated for a guy who's usually a tower of muscular grace. I'd like to go after him, maybe ask if he's okay, but I don't because I'm a big wuss.

It's that in-between time after dinner but before sunset, so the beach is cleared out for now. I'm still in my T-shirt and trunks from this morning, since I spent the afternoon swimming and reading with my fam. I'm about halfway through *Salem's Lot*, and everything keeps getting more and more ominous.

Connor was out on the beach today with his mom, and let me say, Mrs. Nichols is hot. As a gay dude, even I can vouch for this. She's not as hot as her son, duh, but she's a blonde, Southern bombshell who struts around in bikinis and lacey cover-ups. She reads bad romance novels (the classic kind with Fabio on the cover) and, according to my mother, makes the best sangria ever. Her name's Maud, and I'm way more likely to use her first name than Connor's dad's. Maud screamed when she saw me and actually scurried through sand to latch onto my hair and croon, "You look perfectly adorable!" She might be delusional—but very nice.

Connor had his digital camera on the beach. He asked Liz and me to pose for a few. When Liz and I take photos together, it's basically me hiding behind her while she smiles and pouts her lips. I swam a ton. Mom says I'm half fish. Connor got in the water a couple times, but he mostly took pictures of people and surf.

Now, I'm off to see Roberta, since I am her official dog walker in June. I kick at sand and amble along. The sun's at that level where it's staring you right in the face. Liz always bugs me, says I should get sunglasses, but I don't like the way they filter the light. It's visual censorship, and I don't have to take it.

A group of college kids plays volleyball closer to the water. They laugh and hug each other. I've been the weird, smart kid my whole life. Liz is my best pal, and I've never had an official boyfriend. I wonder if all that'll change at NYU or if I'll still be the kid who'd rather hang with professors than other students. Will my entire romantic experience be wrought with hot one-night stands? Sigh.

Does Connor have a girlfriend? The first summer we met, I would never have asked such a question, but I was only fourteen at the time, and he was sixteen. I already knew I was gay but didn't care because I was too interested in school to think about sex. See, late bloomer in every way: sexually and physically. While other boys were falling in love with their right hands, I was taking upper-level English. Pretty sure I was invisible to Connor that first summer, but it wasn't like we had anything in common—or so I thought.

The second summer was when shit got real. I was alone, reading on the beach, when some older guys came by and stole my book and started shoving me around. They called me names and tore my book in half. They'd probably been drinking. Looking back, I was a freaking dumbass, because I tried to push them and throw wussy punches. They laughed at me until one dude actually knocked me over and knelt on my chest so I couldn't breathe. I was never so scared in my life.

Next thing I knew, I heard a familiar voice: Connor's. He was shouting, and he punched one dude right in the face. I remember being able to breathe again. Then, those assholes were up and running. I didn't blame them; Connor was already big by then. He pulled me to my feet and asked if I was all right. He pretended I wasn't crying. He walked me to this peaceful area down the beach where there's a cove of trees and an old hammock. It's right near the Outpost. I went there to read by myself sometimes—still do—but didn't know he knew about it.

We sat in the sand as I watched him try to piece together the torn pages of my book: Stephen King's *The Shining*. He looked at the movie edition cover with Jack Nicholson smiling back. "Isn't this a little old for you?"

"I like to read."

"Yeah, but doesn't it give you nightmares?"

"I'm not a child." It would have sounded so much cooler if I hadn't still been sniffling and wiping salt from my eyes.

"I know that," he said. "So have you seen the movie?"

"Of course I've seen the movie." I grabbed the destroyed book back from him. I didn't know why I was mad at Connor

—maybe because I was embarrassed he'd been there to see my ass get kicked, a normal occurrence in my life since birth.

"Well. What did you think?"

I flipped my thumbs through pages. "It's Kubrick's masterpiece. Excellent cinematography. The score makes that movie, man, and Shelley Duvall never gets enough credit."

He nodded. "Did you know Kubrick purposely treated her like shit on set so that she'd feel alienated and dig further into her role?"

I didn't know that, but it made me like Kubrick a whole lot less. I looked away and felt bad about being angry with Connor. I honestly couldn't figure out why he was still sitting with me, the dumb, crying kid with an attitude, but he kept talking.

"So do you like scary movies?"

"What is this, the opening sequence of *Scream*?"

And that, folks, was the first time Connor Nichols smiled —big and bright—at me. For the first time in my little gay life, I understood why guys were best friends with their right hands and why there were so many sappy songs about love.

He only made things worse by putting his huge hand (seriously, he has Hulk hands) on my shoulder and leaning close. "Hey, you look funny. Are you going to be sick? They didn't punch you in the stomach, did they? Or hit your head? Did they—"

I ducked and rolled away from Connor searching through my hair. "Uh, no, I'm good. I'm—" I wasn't good, then or now.

I thought the crush would go away, but it never did.

We watched scary movies together that summer—old classics like *Rosemary's Baby, Nightmare on Elm Street*, and *Psycho*. We sat on my parents' couch and talked Hollywood trivia and cinematography. Liz never joined us, but my dad sometimes did.

I never thanked Connor for stopping those bullies on the beach, and he never brought it up. We've still never talked about it, not once, but I can't watch *The Shining* without feeling bad for Shelley while remembering my proverbial knight in shining armor.

I'm almost to Roberta's condo. It's a fifteen-minute walk from my family's place to hers, but I like to walk. Gives me time to think and not usually about Connor. Usually I make up stories in my head or invent characters. Speaking of characters...

"Emily! Emily? Is that you?"

Leland is a seventysomething-year-old alcoholic war veteran who lives on park benches—or, occasionally, at the Outpost—and thinks my name is Emily. I corrected him the first couple times but have since given up.

"Yeah, Leland, it's me." I give him a little salute.

In exchange, he shoves his paper bag of booze in the sand and wraps me in a hug that almost picks me up off my feet. It would have, if not for the recent growth spurt. "Come sit." He gestures to a dirty towel in the sand. Back in the brush, near a path, I spot his shopping cart full of random shit. "I have a story for you." He has so many stories—part of why I love the guy.

"As much as I'd love to, I have to walk Ella."

He slumps down into the sand and extends his thick, old man legs in front of him. Leland is a big dude, which is sort of a wonder. I guess he eats really well for a homeless guy? I know my mom makes him food sometimes that I hand deliver, and he pays me in stories. He could tell stories for thirty years straight. Scheherazade went for 1001 nights? Weak.

He picks up his paper bag and extends his hand to me. "Well, take a slug for the road."

Not only does Leland possibly think I'm a girl named

Emily, but he also thinks I'm thirty. I don't turn away offered booze, though. I take a big gulp, and it tastes like warm lake water with a burn.

"I got some 'shine you'll have to try. I bartered. You know how bartering works—give a little of yourself, and somebody does the same." He pulls at the front of his worn Hawaiian shirt to get some air and adjusts his huge, straw hat. He wears red plastic sunglasses tonight as he squints toward the surf. "You remember I was in 'Nam, and when I was over there, well, it wasn't all bad. There were some nice folks that welcomed a handsome soldier like me." He puffs up a little at this before taking a hit from the bottle. "This kind lady made me a dish, called it 'bun cha.' Some sort of soup with noodles and spices like you ain't never had before. And a salty meat, so tender."

God, I hope it wasn't dog.

"But this lady, she let me into her home and made it for me when the world was blowing up all around us. And I remember she touched my hand; don't remember why I remember that, but it was so tender in that moment." He shrugs. "So anyway, I made my buddy down the beach some ramen noodles yesterday in his microwave, and he gave me some 'shine. That's bartering, Emily."

Some days, I need a road map to follow his train of thought—an intricate one with underground tunnels and shit.

"Did you hear some rich folks bought the Outpost?" he asks.

I nod. My eyes follow the silver back of a dolphin out in the surf. The sky is turning a bright shade of orange as another dolphin surfaces close behind.

"The most comfortable bed of my life is in room 306, Emily. They're going to get rid of my bed."

"That sucks, Leland." I know he sleeps there a lot of the time. Apparently demolishing the Outpost is going to affect more than just partying teens. Good for the local economy; bad for our homeless guy's sleep. "I really do want to catch up, but I need to get over to Roberta's. She's expecting me."

He nods and lifts his bottle again. "Of course, of course. I'll save that 'shine for a night when you and I can chew the fat properly. Tell Roberta I say hello, and get on out of here."

"Yes, sir. Thank you, sir." I salute him again, and the sound of his husky laugh follows me down the beach.

I get to Roberta's not long before sunset. I always know when her condo is coming up because the shell shrine begins. Roberta works on the shell shrine every day. The fancy spread should be in a museum. I know she spends tons of time walking up and down Longboat Key, even hitting up Beer Can Island on the northern tip for the prettiest shells she can find. She brings them home and builds this art in the sand—carefully crafted lines and swells of shells creating shapes like huge mermaids, hearts, and crosses.

She's at work right now, in fact. In a big, white muumuu disaster, she waves when she notices me. I've grown accustomed to everyone commenting on the new me this summer, but I still have the same dark hair, too-pale skin, and gangly appendages that make me look (I imagine) like a skeleton in a bowler hat from far away. I'm surprised I don't scare small children.

"Why, Emory Jones, don't you look handsome this fine evening?"

"Cut it out, Roberta." I give her a hug. She's all soft, warm skin and big, white teeth. I could probably sleep comfortably on Roberta and she wouldn't even notice I was there. "Leland says hi."

"Oh, I'm sure he does."

"How's Ella tonight?"

She waves her hand as though wafting a bad smell. "She's fine. Been missing you, child."

I follow her small, quick steps up the beach to the back steps of her tiny condo where Ella waits impatiently by the screen door, tail doing a jig. As soon as Roberta opens the door, Ella is in my arms, hopping and trying to kiss me. I scratch behind her ears before grabbing her leash.

Ella isn't technically supposed to be on the beach, so I mostly walk her down the wide sidewalks of Gulf of Mexico Drive where the most dangerous things are bikers, buzzed from happy hour. We almost got run over once. Seriously, we were knocked into some bushes; Ella landed on her back, whimpering. I thought about calling the cops, but Roberta didn't want to get them involved. She has a thing about police.

She and her husband used to rehabilitate ex-cons and young gangbangers up at their church in Detroit, and the cops were never very nice to them, no matter their noble cause. When Roberta's husband died in a gang-related drive-by shooting, I guess the investigation was weak. They never did catch his killer, and Roberta moved to Longboat soon after.

Tonight, Ella and I walk past a bunch of resorts, including the abandoned front gates of the Outpost. Expensive cars zip by as big, blue herons and swans fish for food in the little ponds off the road. Ella is basically prancing. Good girl likes her nightly walk.

We arrive home right at sunset, which means Roberta will be down on the beach. I put Ella inside and kiss her head before joining the amassed crowd. Sunset means bagpipe guy. Even though I've been coming here for six years, I've never met bagpipe guy. I stand there, watching the sky change, and listen to him play with his feet in the breaking waves. He always starts with a couple Irish numbers but ends with "Amazing Grace" just as the sun tucks itself into bed.

Standing by her shrine, Roberta puts an arm around my

27

waist and tugs me close while humming along to her favorite hymn. Some nights, she goes full gospel and sings every word. She's got a voice that makes Adele sound like a shrieking mouse.

Responsibilities done for the day, I promise Roberta I'll be back tomorrow and head home. Once I get near my family's house, I see a lone, shadowy figure sitting in a folding chair down the beach. Connor sees me as I try to sneak inside. Damn my lack of invisibility.

I really don't feel like saying anything embarrassing right now. It's been a good day, and I've acted like a semi-normal human. Can't I have *one day?*

Apparently not, because he waves me over. I step up next to him, the sky a shade of purple you'll never see anywhere else. Stars are like sky freckles in the opposite direction.

He looks up at me, and only then do I notice the camera in his lap. "Oh, excellent," he says, smiling in a way that makes me want to dive headfirst into the surf. I know that look; it's the "I've got the perfect shot" look, although he's never directed it at me.

"No." I start walking up to my house but stumble, of course, which allows Connor to catch me—of course.

"Dude, the lighting is perfect with the glow from the houses and the sky behind you. Come here."

It's not worth fighting him. I allow myself to be turned around so my back is to the ocean and make the grumpiest face I can manage. I slump my shoulders and almost dart away when he plucks a big curl from the center of my forehead and folds it in with all the rest.

"Don't look so miserable." He stares at the glowing display on the back of his camera.

"I don't like having my picture taken."

He quirks an eyebrow at me. "It's your fault you're photogenic."

"I am not."

"Are, too. I would know. I'm a professional."

I cross my arms in defiance. "A professional what?"

"Har-har. Smile, Emory."

"Nope."

"A census taker once tried to test me. I ate his liver with some fava beans and a nice Chianti." The Hannibal Lecter impression is so spot on, I spit laughter all over the beach until I'm practically bent over, hiding my face behind my hands.

When I get control over my sick sense of humor, Connor is smiling.

"Well?" I ask. "Did you get the shot?"

"Eh, maybe." He shrugs and hangs the camera strap over his shoulder. "Where are you coming from anyway?"

I throw a thumb over my shoulder. "Roberta's. She's this older lady. I walk her dog."

"That's nice of you."

"She has stories."

A sea breeze blows at the collar of his shirt and the front of his hair. "And you like people with stories."

"What are we without stories?"

"People." He puts his hands in his pockets, and I mirror the gesture.

"Boring people," I say.

A man's scream rudely interrupts us, and I'm glad I'm not the only one startled. My heart is beating fast, but Connor's eyebrows are so high, it looks like he got a bad face-lift.

"What the hell was that?" he asks.

We both look up and down the beach, but it's dark. I even check the ocean, expecting some dude to run up with a shark attached to his head. Nothing.

"Probably just drunk kids," I say.

He nods, but I see his Adam's apple bounce like he can't swallow right.

Then, a woman screams and appears, laughing and being chased by a guy in khakis and a blue button-down. He's cute and they're only playing, so that's good and normal.

Connor and I smile bashfully at each other. I'm surprised we don't share a rough back slap and caveman grunts to cover the fact that we were both quaking in our metaphorical boots.

Instead, he glances at his house. I think I see the orange ember of a cigar watching us from the lanai. "Look, I don't want to go home," he says. "Have any new movies for us to watch?"

"Um, yes? Movies—um." And here is the Emory everyone knows and loves.

Why is he still standing there waiting? Most normal people would have walked away by then, deeming me unfit for friendship.

"Um...I've been meaning to watch *Neon Demon*? Have you heard of that one?"

His face lights up. Seriously, it's like the sun is in his mouth. "Hell yeah! I've already seen it, but I'll watch it again. I can't wait to hear what you think."

I feel myself physically caving in. Liz says I do it when I'm nervous: my shoulders curl, and I clasp my hands in front of me like I'm praying—to the God of Awkward Losers probably.

"Let's go." With his big, runner legs, he starts walking toward the house—my house—so I guess I should follow. It's my house and my movie and my dad will want to join us and—

"Right. So, yeah...um." Would you listen to that shit? I'm supposed to be a writer, and Connor Nichols does this to me every freaking time.

CHAPTER 4

I'm dreaming about Elle Fanning covered in blood. Don't be alarmed; it was a scene in *Neon Demon*. Connor and I did indeed watch it and totally geeked out. Sure, the symbolism was a little heavy-handed, but the creep factor was fabulous. So now, here I am, dreaming of a hot chick covered in blood (it's not a metaphor, okay) when someone whispers my name from the window.

I'm on the second story, so I assume it's one of the vampires from *Salem's Lot*—don't let them in!—but I soon recognize the voice as Connor's.

I mutter a quick "What the fuck" before grabbing my cell phone.

It's two a.m.

"Connor?" I whisper back. I kick at the sheets. As usual, I can't escape due to my newly acquired calves and actually fall out of bed, landing with a thump on the floor. I cuss some more.

"Are you okay?" he asks.

I mutter to myself and crawl toward the open window.

Through the screen, his profile is lit by a red light on the

Nichols's patio. The red light keeps the baby sea turtles from going the wrong way once they hatch. It also has the effect of making everything look like something out of a John Carpenter flick.

"What are you—"

"Does the screen open?"

I stand and rub my eyes. "Yeah." I press two buttons on the bottom of the screen and push up. The screen slides easily, and Connor army crawls through my window and lands with a graceful roll on my bedroom floor.

"How did you—?" I look out the window, and like I thought: there isn't a trellis or a ladder—just a drain pipe. "Are you Spiderman?"

He stands and shoves his hands through his hair. He paces once, twice, fingers curled into fists. He's still fully dressed, wearing the sexy collar shirt and shorts from earlier. Meanwhile, I realize way too late that I'm in nothing but gray boxer briefs and bedhead. I do a running dive back into bed and pull the covers up to my chin. Connor apparently takes this as an invitation, because he lies down next to me, on top of the covers, thank God, and folds his hands behind his head before staring at the ceiling.

"Uh, you got bedbugs or something?"

"I shouldn't have come to Florida," he says.

I sit up, again panicked at the thought of him not being somewhere on Longboat Key while I'm on Longboat Key. "What?"

"I thought it would help. My dad and I..." He shakes his head. "Things aren't good right now. As soon as I got back from watching that movie, he cut into me again. We've been fighting for hours. I had to get out of there."

"What were you fighting about?"

He takes a deep breath. "I got into film school."

"Holy shit, that's awesome!"

He sits up a little and shushes me. Right, it's two a.m., normal people sleeping time. But he's smiling, at least. I see the shine of his teeth in shadow.

I cover my mouth and speak through my fingers. "Sorry. I guess I didn't know you wanted to go to film school."

"I've kept it under wraps for a long time. I mean, not from my mom. She helped me buy my first video camera when I was thirteen." He smacks me in the arm. "My first movie was called 'Tree Monster.' It was terrible; you would have loved it."

I snicker. "Are you saying I have bad taste?"

"No." His head droops, and he doesn't say anything.

"I don't understand what your dad's pissed about."

"I've ruined all his dreams for me." He pokes at my thin, cotton comforter. "I played football in high school."

"I know."

"Of course, you know. You know everything."

"The ignorance of that sentence is astounding."

At least he's smiling again, but he stops when he starts talking. "I got offers from colleges to play quarterback. Good colleges. Dad was upset when I turned them down, but I said I wanted to go into business."

"Sealcoating."

"The family fortune," he mutters. "But I was biding my time. CUNY doesn't accept film students until their junior years, and even then, they only accept something like twenty-five people. I wasn't getting my hopes up—but I got in, Emory." He laughs once, shocked as though hearing the news for the first time.

Even though I want to hug him, I don't. No, I do not. "That's awesome, man."

"I really can't believe it. And neither can my dad. He keeps using words like 'ungrateful' and 'betrayal.' I think 'creative queen' was even thrown in the mix at one point."

Again, I'm impressed by Mr. Nichols's knowledge of gay culture, but... "You have to do you."

He nods. "I know. Mom's so proud. She keeps calling me Spielberg."

"So you want to direct?"

"I think so. I guess it could change once I get to CUNY. Maybe I'll fall in love with cinematography. I've always loved that shit, but directing? Yeah. I want to tell stories. I guess you and I have that in common, huh?"

Holy shit, we have something else in common, too, something that makes me want to swim to the bottom of the sea and live there. All this time, I thought New York City would be where I could finally forget about Connor Nichols—and instead, the sexy bastard is following me there for school. I try to swallow around the lump of dread in my throat. It takes three tries before I finally manage, "We'll be neighbors."

"What do you mean?"

"Liz and I are going to NYU in the fall."

"What?" He practically shouts the word and sits up straight in my bed.

It's my turn to shush him.

"Sorry," he whispers. "NYU? That's... Wow. That's a great school." He runs his hand over his face, and I can practically feel his fingers catch on whiskers. "Why'd you pick NYU?"

The bed creaks when I lean against its frame. "Beyond the fact that their creative writing program is ridiculous, we have a lot of family in Brooklyn. The crazy Italian side. They're not actually mafiosos, but they wear a lot of velour tracksuits and gold chains. I think my one uncle actually has a chest-hair wig." I hold my hand up in front of my naked chest. Even though the hair on my head is 100 percent Italy, I obviously got my dad's British genes in the sparse body hair department. "I once watched my aunt melt her eyeliner over the kitchen stove and then put it on her face. I still don't know what that was about."

Connor giggles silently. "God, Emory. What would summer be like without you?" He ruffles my hair like he used to before he showed up this year acting weird—although he's not acting weird right now. Except for saying weird shit like *that*.

I can't imagine he wastes a thought on me once he leaves Longboat, no matter how many times throughout the winter I pause and wonder, "How's Connor Nichols today?"

He slowly scoots to the bottom of my bed. "I should probably let you sleep. Italian princes need their rest."

"I'm not a prince. A viscount maybe."

He stands and holds his hand out to me. We share a quick slap of palms before he swings a leg over the windowsill. "Hey, thanks for listening. Not everybody would."

I shrug. "Thanks for scaring the shit out of me. I thought you were a vampire."

"I have been known to bite."

And doesn't that make my toes curl?

I stand as he ducks out the window. I barely hear him climb down the drainpipe—just the quiet slap of his shoes on concrete when he jumps from halfway down. He gives me a quick wave, and I put the screen back in place.

I fall back into bed. Connor is going to be in New York. He's going to be in *my* city, the city where I wanted to start all over and be, like, loudly gay and meet tons of hot dudes and fall in love without the constant distraction of my first stupid crush. I stumble into sleep feeling like the world's punching bag.

CHAPTER 5

"You're being such a whiny bitch," Liz says, loudly, in the middle of Harry's Continental Kitchen, which is a super-small takeout place with yummy, high-carb food. In other words, ten people with white hair and two young parents with kids turn to stare at my sister and her potty mouth.

I shove her toward the coolers. Her shoulders are still warm with sun, and she's beating me on the tanning front because I hid behind foliage today. I took my books and went to that shady tree area near the Outpost—the place with the hammock—and spent the afternoon avoiding everyone.

Okay, avoiding Connor mostly.

I swear someone was even moving around in the Outpost. I didn't think anyone ever hung out there during the day. I didn't see an actual person, per se, but I assume it was construction dudes scoping out the new digs? I'm not sure how real estate works, but with the condition of things at the Outpost, I guess they need to demolish and start over. I don't even want to think about the ghosts of sperm that float around the place—plus the empty beer cans, cigarette butts,

36

broken doors and windows— Who knows what else? I would burn it to the ground.

I finished a good chunk of *The Haunting of Hill House* before passing out in the shade and only waking when my sis eventually found me and flipped the hammock, shouting, "Why are you hiding?"

Twin science is magic. I don't know why I try hiding things from her. Maybe that's why she tells me everything— because it's not worth wasting stealth that should be used on our parents. They're having a romantic dinner in St. Armand's Circle tonight at Café L'Europe. A drink there costs more than a new car. Liz and I have been left to fend for ourselves, hence Harry's—which isn't a punishment. Harry's makes awesome pasta (well, not as good as Mom's), crab cakes, and salad. It's a restaurant both locals and tourists visit regularly.

I'm eyeing a huge vat of cheese-covered lasagna when Liz sticks her pointy elbow in my rib, and I yelp.

"He doesn't own the city."

"No, but"—I open the cooler door and grab the lasagna plus a side of garlic bread—"he'll probably want to, like, get coffee. I don't know, be friends?"

Liz does a silent movie scream and claws her face. "Not that!"

I chuckle and shove past her. "Are you getting anything?"

She reaches for a Greek salad, and I glare.

"If you get any skinner, I'm going to lose you to a stiff wind."

She makes a fish face but does pull another serving of bread from the cooler.

"I'm not good at being friends with Connor because I pine. I get distracted, and he makes me say dumb shit."

Someone nearby gasps at my cuss word, so I scurry to the register. We have to get out of here before things escalate. I use the cash my dad gave me to pay for my pasta and Liz's

rabbit food. The clerk is nice enough to bag it up. He probably recognizes us by now after six years of takeout and
knows we walk from our family's beach house. He rings us up
and winks at me. I feel Liz's eye roll behind me—feel it—and
have no clue why some dude being friendly irritates her. Girls
are weird.

Outside, she walks on ahead, red swimsuit cover-up
blowing in a light breeze. "You're right," she says once I catch
up. "You are a moron when he's around."

"Thanks."

"You know you are. But then you're not. It's like your
moron switch is busted. One minute you're funny and smart,
and the next—" She holds her palms out in front of her. "—
you're insane and mousy like Eleanor."

Dear God, my sister made a literary reference. "How do
you know about Eleanor?"

"You leave *Hill House* sitting around sometimes. I *can* read,
you know."

"I know." I press my lips together.

We cross Gulf of Mexico Drive at a slow trot. Half the
drivers on the key are either drunk or long-time retired. It's
better not to take chances.

"This is what's going to happen." She spins around and
walks backwards, half her long, brown hair blowing in her
face. "We're going to move to Manhattan in August, and
you're going to meet some studly bartender or barista.
Someone super suave, right, and he'll be a student at NYU,
too, and you'll fall in love and forget all about Connor."

"Yeah. What's this bartender or barista going to look
like?"

"Tom Brady." She twirls back around, obviously pleased
for bringing up my biggest celebrity crush.

"Uh-huh."

She curls her arm through mine as we walk side by side. "Let's cut down to the beach."

I see Leland's famous shopping cart before I see the famous Leland. Liz always circles the thing like it has fleas. Maybe it does. I touch Leland's mound of stuff and then touch Liz, which makes her scream and slap at me. Then, his head pops up from the tall grass, complete as always with his straw hat and sunglasses.

"Emily!"

I nod. "Leland."

"Emily's sister!"

Liz nods, accustomed to my nickname.

Leland looks up and around as though he's only now realizing the day has gone by and it's almost dinnertime. "You in the mood for that 'shine?"

Oh my God, yes, absolutely. This is what I need to erase the Connor Nichols-New York debacle. I waggle my eyebrows at Liz. "I'm hanging with Leland for a while."

"Don't you have to walk Ella?"

I swing the bag of food at her. "I did that early today."

"Oh, right, I wouldn't know because you were hiding all afternoon. One of these days, a rogue wave is going to drag you in, and your sorry skinny corpse will be eaten by bottom feeders."

That's Liz's way of saying she worries about me.

She hugs our food to her chest. "It's way early for drinking, princess. Mom and Dad will totally know you're drunk when they get home."

I'm already stepping through knee-high grass to get to Leland's blanket. "Then, I won't get drunk."

"Yeah, says the guy who's about to drink moonshine. You'll probably go blind."

I groan and raise my hands to the sky. "Give me a break, Liz!"

She sticks her tongue out at me but turns and starts walking home. "I'm not covering for you!"

"You always cover for me!"

She flicks me off, so I wave at her retreating back before slouching down next to Leland, who's picking his nose. "She talks a lot," he says.

So does Leland, which is awesome.

He passes me the 'shine. It's in a big, green bottle with a swing top that bops me in the nose when I take my first sip. It's surprisingly okay. It tastes sort of like burning but maybe apple cinnamon too? I've heard people add apple slices and cinnamon to moonshine.

Leland takes his own huge gulp and rests back on his hands, legs extended out in front as he watches the waves down shore. "I fell in love on a beach once. Did I ever tell you that?"

I shake my head and settle in.

"I was down near Miami with my family, probably around your age."

I don't think Leland has any idea how old I am.

"I was a gymnast before the war. I was doing these back-flips and cartwheels on the beach, and there was this girl. Nice pair of lungs, if you catch my drift. She kept making eyes at me, so I started doing handstands in the surf. You should have seen me, like a circus performer. I was one proud peacock. Look at my feathers, gorgeous!" He extends his arms high. "I couldn't find her the day I was supposed to leave, so I left a note near where she'd been sitting with my phone number. Sincerely, the Gymnast." He nods. "Would you believe she did call? She called to tell me she was already engaged." He clicks his tongue and hands me the 'shine. "Damnedest thing."

"What was her name?"

"Elena. It's French for 'great jugs.'"

I cough. Some 'shine gets in my nose and burns, but I'm laughing too hard to care.

"How come I never see you with a pretty girl on your arm?" he asks.

I pass the bottle back and pick at the cuffs of my jeans. "Um, I—"

"Or boy." He winks in the way Santa Claus would probably wink.

"How did you—?" I shake my head and stare at the sea. The waves are so tiny, it looks like a mirror. "How do you know stuff like that?"

"I've got a fifth sense." He taps his forehead.

"Yeah, I'll bet you do."

"You look at boys and girls differently is all. You look at girls like they're abstract pieces of art. You look at boys like they're the Sistine Chapel." He glugs the 'shine and hands it back. "I'm not blind."

No, he isn't. I'm pretty sure Leland sees a lot more than people give him credit for.

"So you got a boyfriend back home then?"

I shake my head no.

"And why not?" He adjusts his hat so he can look at me better. "Good-looking guy like you? They should be banging down your door."

Leland is not the person I ever expected to have this conversation with, but the 'shine is doing its work. "Guys my age always seem too immature. Annoying." I shrug. "Most of them only want to go clubbing or talk about sports or celebrities. I'd rather talk about books or *life*, you know. Just stories about real life."

"Real life?" He snorts. "Aren't you the guy who's always reading those crazy books about ghosts and vampires? What's real about that?"

"Well, that's escapism. I'm living my life here." I shove my finger in the sand. "When I read, I like to go away. Read about things that could never happen in real life. Go on an adventure and escape the mundane."

Leland shakes his head. Thanks to the 'shine, he's taken on an orange, hazy glow. "There ain't nothing mundane about real life, kid." He tips his head to me. "And yeah, Emily, I do know you're a kid. I don't mind because you say interesting things, but you're wrong about life being mundane. Something outrageous happens every day." He tries to poke me in the nose but almost hits my eye. "You just gotta find it."

I think I have, sitting in the beach grass with Leland. He might be the most outrageous person I know.

Two hours later, I'm stumbling home. And giggling. Holy shit, I am drunk—but not blind. Hooray! Take that, Liz! I halt and almost fall over when I realize there is no way I can hide this level of inebriation from my parents. They're going to take one look at my (probably crossed) eyes and know I'm wasted.

No, it's okay. I can fake it. I shake my hands out at my sides and keep shaking them because it feels good. Wow, that feels great. I don't remember finger shaking ever feeling this good before. Christ, what was in that 'shine? I take a big deep breath and giggle again because breathing feels amazing. Everything is amazing!

Come on, Emily, get it together.

Oops, your name is Emory.

Em-o-ry.

Okay, now that we've got that under wraps...

Families are walking up the beach, heading home. Leland and I listened to the bagpipe guy before I left him to probably pass out. I need to pass out. No, I need to eat. Lasagna! I have lasagna! My salvation is down the beach!

I start walking faster but stop again because my parents

are also probably back from their fancy dinner and down the beach.

Shit, think, Emory! You're usually so good at thinking! Did I break my thinker?

Someone is saying my name. Is someone saying my name?

I look up, and Connor is right in front of me. I smile and give him a big hug. Hugging is the best.

"Dude." He leans back, holds me by the shoulders, and stares into my face.

Uh-oh, there's three of him. That's not good.

"Are you drunk?"

I grab him by the shoulders too. "I am drunk. So drunk."

"Where were you drinking?"

"With Leland, the homeless guy." I'm sing speaking now. I must be stopped. I don't like to drink too much because the more I drink, the more flamboyant I tend to become. Liz says my inner drag queen escapes. Right now, we're at critical mass. "I should go home." I try to walk around him, but my feet don't want to work. My ankles have turned to Jell-O.

"No, no, no, you are not going home like this. You'll be grounded for the rest of vacation."

"Grounded? I won't get grounded. I'm eighteen."

"Yeah, I know. Legal drinking age is twenty-one, remember?"

I'm honestly not sure I do. At least there's only one Connor now, though.

"Let's go sit on the beach for a while."

What an amazing idea! Why didn't I think of that! The beach!

Connor keeps his arm securely around my shoulders as we walk down to the surf. As soon as I hear the quiet sound of waves, I lean down to roll up my jeans but fall on my side instead.

"Oops."

Connor scoops me right-side-up like a spilled vase. "What were you drinking? Shit, tell me it wasn't that 'shine he was talking about."

"It was! Do you— Do you know Leland?" I have to lean forward and back to keep Connor in focus.

"Everyone knows Leland."

"Yeah, yeah." I nod and then shake my head. "No. I don't think that's true because people think he's just this drunk homeless guy, but he, like, sees things, you know?"

"Are you trying to tell me Leland is psychic?"

"No, well, maybe." Connor is sitting with his legs folded in front of him, his tan forearms resting on his knees. I stare at his cute blond arm hairs before turning to face him, cross-legged. "I mean, like, nobody down here knows I'm gay, but Leland knew. He said something about Picasso and Michelangelo, I think."

"Wait? What?"

"Michelangelo?"

"No."

His mouth is hanging open— Why is his mouth hanging open?

"Emory, you're gay?"

"Oh!" I reach out and close his mouth. I think he looks surprised I did that, but I'm not clear on facial expressions right now. "Yeah! I took Nick to my eighth grade dance. It was sort of my coming out in Ohio. Nick and I had fun, but see, the basketball players used to call me Tinker Bell, so they pushed us around a little bit." I press my lips together. Where'd I been going with that? "So yeah. But they didn't call me Tinker Bell this year, though." I stare down at the sand, contemplating... the meaning of sand, I guess.

"Emory, maybe we shouldn't talk anymore. Maybe we should sit."

I claw at his arm. "Oh, God, did I say something bad?"

"No! I just don't want you to regret anything you're telling me right now."

I try to remember what I told him. Nope, it's gone. "I wonder if there's a party at the Outpost tonight. We should go. No, I don't want to go. Why would I go there?"

"You are definitely not going there."

"No. The other night, there was this rat with this finger and— But everyone was looking at me funny." I tumble onto my back, and wow, nothing has ever felt better than the warm sand against my back. "I know I got taller, and I have this hair." I pull on one of my many wild curls.

Connor leans down next to me on his side, head propped on his arm.

"I feel like people stare at me lately. Like I have something on my face."

"You have your face on your face."

I scrunch up said face. "Would that make sense if I were sober?"

"Emory, all the girls were staring at you because they wanted to make out with you."

"What? Gross. What?"

Connor laughs and falls onto his back. He stares at the sky while I stare at him. Then, epiphany!

"Holy shit, dude, this feels so much like the opening scene of *Jaws*." I rise up onto my knees. "The lighting is perfect!" When I start to take off my shirt, Connor's hand closes tightly around my wrist.

"You are not going swimming right now."

"But! You know the lighting is perfect! I can flail around, and you can take pictures. Where is your camera anyway?" I start making the *Jaws* music sound. "Duhn-duh, duhn-duh, dun-dun-dun-dun."

"Emory, no."

I try to crawl away from him, yes, still singing the *Jaws*

song. He manhandles me before I get any closer to the water, and I'm too drunk to do much more than wiggle like a cat about to pounce. However, there is no pouncing. I end up with Connor half on top of me with my face in the sand.

"So. Much. Sand," I mutter and start giggling.

Connor bursts out laughing behind me. Remember how I thought the sand felt good on my back? Nope, this is much better. So much better! My teenage crush is wrapped around me, laughing on a beach in Florida. This is the best ever—better than any best in the history of bestest.

We're still laughing as we sit up, and I keep rolling until my head thumps against his chest. Why is my head so heavy?

"Because of your big brain," he says.

Apparently, I asked that question out loud.

"Yes, you did."

Danger zone! There is now no filter between Emory's brain and his mouth!

Connor starts laughing again, and his jittering chest vibrates my skull. I think I'd like to sleep here, but Connor says that is not a good idea. And so it continues: I am now saying everything I think, so I try not to think anything bad.

Connor tells me to stop thinking, but I don't know how.

I feel his hand in my hair, and I stop thinking. Oh, so that's... *hmm*.

Things get hazy after that. Well, hazier. I'm pretty sure Connor uses my phone to call Liz because I remember seeing Liz. Our parents, bless them, aren't home yet, still out on their date. I think I remember lasagna. I remember tomato, pasta, bed, Connor laughing... Yeah, bed.

CHAPTER 6

There's a knock on my door, and the door opens before I say anything because no one in this house respects my privacy. I wank in the shower for that very reason.

"Hey, sleepy head." It's Mom. My mom has a sweet voice most of the time, unless she's talking to her Italian family or screaming at Liz about curfew. However, this morning, her voice might as well be a banshee cry.

I shoot up in bed—and regret it. Oh, God. I cover my face with my hands.

"You're not sick, are you?" she says from the doorway.

Mom, I am so hungover. Please hug me and bring me Gatorade. I will never drink again, promise.

"Emory?" She's got a concerned wrinkle on her forehead, and she's coming closer, already dressed for the beach in her one-piece retro bathing suit and designer cover-up.

I hold up my hands to halt her forward progress, considering I probably smell like alcohol and death.

She holds her hands up as a mirror. "You good?"

"Yep." I sound like a frog that's been stepped on. I probably look like one too; I have got to be green in the face.

"It's almost nine. You've been sleeping forever. Time to get up?"

"Yeah. Sorry." I nod. I never sleep this late. No wonder she thinks I'm sick.

"Okay. Love you."

"Love you too."

She closes the door. Her Yves Saint Laurent sandals click down the hall. Dad bought her those for Easter; they're her favorite.

I resist every urge to tumble back into bed because I fear I will never walk again if I do. Gremlins are trying to dig out from behind my eyes. There's one in my stomach, too, doing a tap dance. I would probably feel better if I threw up, but there's no way I'm making myself throw up. I think I remember lasagna last night, and I do not want to relive the experience in the opposite direction.

Coffee. I need coffee.

Shower first. That will help. And ibuprofen. Liz has ginger pills somewhere. My sister taught me the ginger trick. She first learned about ginger supplements to help with her menstrual cramps while dating that hippie guy but soon came to realize they cured hangovers, too—something about the little suckers being anti-inflammatory and anti-nausea. A perfect combo. Need some now.

The shower helps, and since Liz and I share a bathroom, it's child's play digging through her stuff for ginger. I pop the pills and drink an entire glass of water. I brush my teeth twice because I can still taste the sugary aftereffects of too much liquor on my tongue. I blow a breath into the palm of my hand and sniff to make sure I'm not breathing booze.

I don my second favorite bathing suit: navy blue with white piping from Hollister. I picked this pair out by myself, thank you. A soft gray tee completes the look. I finger-brush my damp hair before taking a couple deep breaths. The ginger will kick in soon, and I'll have coffee and soak up some sun. Thank Christ, I'm only eighteen; I can't imagine what hangovers are going to be like in my thirties.

As if my mother read my mind, she has a mug of steaming black coffee ready when I step into the kitchen. Dad is at the table reading the *Observer*, so no golf for him today.

He says, "Hey, Thing One, you feeling okay?" I was born five minutes before Liz, so Dad sometimes refers to us as the famous Dr. Seuss pair.

"Yep. Needed sleep, I guess." I take a sip of dark, smoky goodness. "How was your date?"

Dad looks at mom and lifts his eyebrows. She turns away blushing. So they had a good time, then. I know it's gross, but I'm glad my parents still get laid. I'm glad Dad still looks at Mom with googly eyes. I'm happy they're happy.

Liz is probably on the back patio doing her morning yoga routine, so I head in that direction to get the playback of last night. I hope I wasn't too much of a mess for her to deal with —although I've covered for her drunken ass too many times to count. She was the one who went to high school football games to party. I was the one who only went to meet older guys from other schools.

She is indeed on the patio in the middle of a headstand, but she's not alone. Connor is out there with her, trying to copy her moves in his running shorts and shoes—no shirt— but he's mostly just laughing as he tumbles over next to her. Liz lands with a swan's grace on her toes and wags her finger at him, smiling.

Because my brain has flatlined at the sight of Connor shirtless and upside-down, I don't notice the sliding glass door is only partially open and slam right into it, spilling half my coffee on the mudroom floor. I shift the mug to my other

SARA DOBIE BAUER

hand and wave my scalded one in the air like an injured seagull.

Liz opens the door all the way and grabs my wrist. "Shit, princess, are you okay?"

"Yeah, I—"

Connor appears behind her, hands on his hips. I look up at him and remember.

"Oh my God," I squeak and recoil back into the house.

I hear Liz make some excuse. The glass door slides shut, and her feet follow. I dump the forgotten coffee in the sink and run cold water over my hand, willing the tears to go away. I'm mostly successful. Only one sneaks out, and I brush it away on the shoulder of my shirt.

Liz grabs my arm. "What's wrong?"

"Emory?" Dad's still sitting, and Mom watches with her own coffee in hand.

I trudge to the table and fall into one of the sturdy, wooden chairs before looking at Liz. "I came out to Connor last night."

"Oh, damn," she says.

"Well," Mom says. Then, she doesn't say anything for a couple moments. "That's okay, isn't it?"

"Not particularly!" I don't mean to sound so panicked, but I cover my face with my hands. "He didn't need to know. I didn't want him to know."

Dad asks why in that infuriatingly calm way of his.

Mom has his back. "Emory, you've been out for years. Why wouldn't you want Connor to know?"

"It's not like you've ever hidden it before," Dad says.

"We always want to support you, honey."

They keep on going with platitudes and after-school-special bullshit, but they're circling round and round like a clueless hurricane and Liz is the eye. Except she is not calm—at all. I can practically hear her temper rising, so I'm not

50

surprised when she suddenly shrieks, "Connor is the jock, and Emory is the gay kid!"

The collective freeze-frame would be funny if not for Liz's horrible truth.

My sister sighs as though our silence is annoying. "Mom, Dad, truth time. The big jocks at school were not always very nice to Emory. In fact, most of them were assholes. And he never told the school and never told you because he didn't want to look like a victim."

"Shut up, Liz!" I yell across the kitchen.

"How many times did you hide bruises so Mom wouldn't get upset?"

My parents sputter out queries as I dig my hands in my hair and pull. "I am way too hungover for this shit."

My parents now both shout my name, which, excellent, that helps.

"Emory, is this true?" my mom asks.

"Yes, I'm hungover."

She clicks her tongue and looks away.

"Yeah, I got bullied in school, but it doesn't matter. It's over now." I poke at a placemat. "And senior year was better."

"Yeah, it's time we talked about that." Liz crosses her arms in all her sweaty yoga glory and frowns while I groan toward the ceiling.

Mom puts her hand on my shoulder. "I don't think Connor is a bully, honey."

"You don't know that," I mutter.

"I think Mom's right, princess. He seemed pretty worried about you last night even though you are a"—air quotes —"homosexual."

I squeeze my eyes shut. "I hate everyone right now."

"Well, we love you," Dad says, and okay, what's with the waterworks this morning? Maybe I should lay off depressants for a while. I wipe my eyes and look toward the beach. I could really use a long swim.

Of course, Liz won't let that happen, not yet. "Mom, Dad, would you kindly buzz off?"

My dad actually makes a buzzing sound, which makes me laugh, as he grabs my mom's hand. They walk into the mudroom, and the glass door slides shut as they step outside.

Liz sits across from me and folds her hands on the table like she's about to tell me I have cancer. She doesn't say a damn word.

"Liz?"

She puckers her lips and presses them to the side. This means she's thinking. "There's a reason you didn't get picked on as much senior year."

"What, you sell your soul to the principal?"

"No, and this is not an incest thing," she says.

"Might want to rethink that opener."

"You got hot."

If I had a hearing aid, I would turn it up. "Come again."

She rolls her eyes. It's a big roll that probably has the power to alter tides. "Last fall, something happened, and you got hot. And everyone at Perrysburg High School was talking about it behind your back. Like, *everyone*. It was fucking disgusting."

"Everyone? Who everyone?"

"Everyone, Emory. Like, all the popular girls were bitching about what a tragedy it was that you were gay. And Mrs. Simmons."

"Mrs. Simmons?" I sound like a strangled mouse. "The gym teacher?"

Liz shudders. "I'm pretty sure the jocks stopped picking on you because they didn't want to piss off the popular girls who were crushing on you. Plus, you grew ten feet, and your chest is no longer actually concave."

I open my mouth and move my lips, but no sound comes out.

"Emory, are you breathing? Breathe, dude."

I think back to what I can remember from last night. "Oh my God. The girls staring at me at the Outpost. I seriously thought I had a booger on my face."

"No, they all wanted to fuck you."

I make a barf noise.

"That's why I went off with Duke. I had to get out of there." She plants her elbow on the table and points her finger in my face. "And another thing! You ruined my senior year!"

"Oh, come on, Liz!"

"Okay, fine, you didn't ruin my senior year, but"—she pouts—"it's not easy when, all of a sudden, your brother is prettier than you."

I slide out of my chair and take the one next to her. "Liz, no one is prettier than you."

"Go wash your mouth out." She laughs, but it's not for real. Something is still bothering her, but I don't ask. I give her space. It doesn't take long. "I gave up meat."

"For your hippie boyfriend."

"No." She leans her shoulder against mine. "I didn't want to get fat. And you had, like, *blossomed*, and I didn't want you to leave me behind for all the pretty people in New York."

"Come on." I wrap her in a side hug and press our heads together. "Stop being mental."

She snuffles, but Liz doesn't admit to crying, so we both pretend it's allergies. "I know you had a hard time sometimes, princess, but that's all over now."

"Because I got hot."

We both snort laugh.

"I don't feel hot."

"I know." She wipes her nose. "You're clueless. When you look in the mirror, what do you see?"

"A skinny kid with too much hair."

"I would scalp you for your hair."

I lean back and look at her. "Liz, we have the same hair."

"Nope." She grabs one of my curls and pulls. "Mine doesn't do this Shirley Temple shit." She finger-brushes my mop before grabbing my chin. "Listen to me, Emory Jones. By the time we get to New York, I want you to feel better about yourself, okay?"

"I'll try." I give her shoulders a squeeze. "Same to you, huh?"

"Bitch, I'm fabulous."

I notice her eau de yoga. "Bitch, you stink."

She scoffs and shoves me away. Before going upstairs to shower, though, she gives my hair another tug. "You're going to hide today, aren't you?"

"Oh, yeah." I can already picture my hammock in the shade.

"Well, just today. You're going to have to face the music eventually."

CHAPTER 7

Ah, quality time with a demon-possessed child on a lovely, sunny afternoon in paradise. I couldn't ask for much more than *The Exorcist* and me.

Earlier, my parents allowed me to sneak away. They knew I was doing it, but they also know I always come back and talk to them eventually. Well, except about the bullying thing. It's not quite as simple as what Liz said.

No, I never wanted to be seen as a victim, but it also felt so damn trivial. So the jocks called me "Tinker Bell." So I got crushed into a few lockers. So I learned how to take a punch to the ribs without any serious damage. It wasn't mass genocide or our country's acceptance of Crocs as footwear, nothing horrible like that. Just me dealing with some ignorant assholes for a hot minute.

I don't think I fully grasped the lingering psychological effects until this morning, though, when the thought of Connor becoming a bully almost made me sick. I can't picture Connor's lips twisting around words like "faggot" or "fairy."

Butt pirate—that's my favorite. One year, Liz forbade me

from buying an eye patch and being a butt pirate for Halloween. I was going to get a hook for a hand and everything! Of course, I would have ended up getting my ass kicked, but sometimes I get so tired of people's bullshit, it's worth getting beat up. Later, when they look at their bruised knuckles, I hope they wonder, "Why did that make me mad? What dark part of me could let something so stupid get me so upset?"

Maybe some of the jocks at PHS look back and think that about me: *What was it about Emory Jones that made me want to hurt him?* Or maybe they don't think about me at all.

Two summers ago, Connor actually scared me, and not in the fun jumping out from the bushes sort of way. He'd been different two summers ago—angry. He'd always seemed like a nice guy. The only time I ever saw him irate, actually, was when those bullies tore my copy of *The Shining* and tried to squeeze the air out of my chest. That was anger I understood; he was protecting me. But the anger two summers ago came out of nowhere.

I should have noticed something was wrong. Connor was drinking way too much at The Outpost. He was kissing every girl in sight—but not Liz, thank God. We were only sixteen at the time, while Connor was eighteen and newly graduated from high school. You'd think he would have been excited. I know I am, flipping the finger at four years of sheep and the teachers who tried to herd them.

I remember there were some newbies at the Outpost this one night—a group of girls and boys of different ages but all pretty drunk and obnoxious, playing rap music too loud and grinding at the empty pool's edge. I was sitting on my usual overgrown park bench, so I didn't hear anything untoward, but something untoward was said, some inappropriate whisper between Connor and a guy dressed like Eminem—if Eminem shopped in a Florida dumpster.

As soon as the shoving started, I moved. Fists were flying when I stepped between Connor and another dude way bigger than me. I'm pretty sure Eminem thought I was a girl, because he backed up right away. Connor grabbed onto my hoodie and dragged my ass from the gathered crowd.

"What the fuck did you think you were doing?"

I smelled the liquor on his breath. "Saving you from going to jail, asshole!"

Apparently my irate reaction gifted him a level of sobriety. He rubbed his hand over his face. "Emory, you are way too small to be breaking up fights."

"Well, it didn't look like anyone else was going to!"

He glanced back at the party. Liz had already left to kiss some guy in an abandoned Outpost condo, and Eminem was back to dry humping his girl. "Let's take a walk," Connor said.

We walked for a long time that night, never saying anything. Eventually, Connor sat in the sand, so I joined him. Despite all his anger, the flying fists, what scared me most was his unexpected crying because I didn't know what the hell to do. These were not the secret sniffles of my sister; these were manly, wrenching sobs that made his chest curl in like he might vomit. I didn't touch him or say anything. I sat there with my skinny arms wrapped around my skinny legs and watched the black of nighttime ocean, broken only by the white of cresting waves.

Clouds covered the moon, so I didn't feel self-conscious when I stood and unbuttoned my jeans.

"Emory, what are you—?"

I pulled my hoodie over my head. "Let's go swimming."

"Right now?"

"Yeah, right now." I didn't know if he would follow me into the warm waves, but he did. We swam out together side by side past the sandbar. I couldn't touch, but Connor could. I treaded water near him until he put a hand on my waist.

"Here. Climb on my back, you little shrimp."

"Little shrimp?" I grabbed onto his shoulders and hooked my legs around his waist. What a squandered opportunity, but I was too young, I guess, to enjoy that comfortable intimacy. "Who you calling a little shrimp? I saved your ass."

Connor turned so we were staring farther into the endless water. "I could have taken that guy."

"So what? Fighting is stupid."

After a couple seconds of silence, he agreed. "Fighting *is* stupid."

I jumped off his back and swam around. We splashed each other like little kids. I didn't realize until later I was trying to make him laugh.

We watched a movie at my place that night, *Evil Dead II*. We sat on the couch together, but I couldn't get warm, so Connor kept stacking more blankets on top of me, tucking them in around my body until I felt like a mummy.

He ruffled my hair when he went home later. If memory serves, it was the first official Connor-Emory hair ruffle. Then, he thanked me; maybe it was his way of saying, "Please don't tell anyone about me fighting and then crying on the beach." I never did tell anyone—not even Liz.

Considering his age back then and knowing what I know now, maybe Connor didn't want to go to community college to get a business degree so he could work in sealcoating with his dad forever. He wanted to make movies, and now, he can.

I rest *The Exorcist* on my chest and stretch out on the hammock with my arms behind my head. I close my eyes, hangover almost gone. God bless you, ginger pills.

I inwardly groan at the sound of a camera click.

Maybe he's taking pictures of the Outpost nearby or the ocean. He probably can't see me where I'm hidden. But then I blink one eye open, and he's standing right there.

"Did you just take a picture of me?"

"No," he says and smiles. "Maybe. You looked happy."

I sit up and cautiously put my feet in the sand since hammocks are wily creatures. "Did Liz tell you where I was?"

"No." He hangs the camera on its strap over his shoulder. "I searched the whole beach for you before remembering this place."

"How'd you know about this place?"

"I've always known about this place, and we've been here together before. Remember?" He rests his hand on a tree branch and pops his hip out.

Oh, yeah. After those bullies stole my book and Connor chased them away, we came here. I stand and feign nonchalance by stretching my arms over my head. "It's no big deal if you don't want to talk to me anymore."

He sighs.

"I don't want you rethinking the last few years and, like, hoping the gay didn't rub off." I'm regurgitating things mean guys have said to me. I know all their lines.

"Jesus Christ, Emory," Connor murmurs, but there's definitely something like anger there.

I take a step back and prepare to be destroyed.

He doesn't punch me, though. He takes a step closer and runs a hand through the front of his hair, blue eyes staring out at the Gulf. This is it. He can't even look at me. He—

"I don't know why you never said anything. Maybe I should have noticed. I don't know." He looks at me, teeth chewing at the inside of his lip. "I'm not like the jocks at your school, okay? I'm not going to call you names or push you around. I like you. I've always liked you."

My shoulders start to droop; I hadn't even noticed they were up around my ears.

"Why did you never tell me?"

I hug myself. "It didn't seem to matter."

"Of course it matters. It's part of you, like bad horror

movies and scary books." He gestures to my head. "And fluffy hair."

I chuckle. Some weight I didn't even know was there is lifting. "You're really different this summer."

"Maybe because I'm happy."

"You were never happy before?"

He smiles. "Not like I am right now. But will you stop hiding from me, please?"

I nod but am wholly unprepared for the hug. Connor goes for it with enthusiasm. He pulls me in by the front of my T-shirt and gives me a hug that would have crushed my bones last summer. Now, we're almost the same height and I grew muscles, so this works. It's quite manly—and yet isn't. This is a lengthy, silent, chest-to-chest hug. I can even feel Connor's breath on the side of my neck until he takes one big inhale that would make me think he was *smelling me* if that wasn't so weird.

He clears his throat as he pulls away, and I hope my eyes are not literally in the shape of hearts right now.

I must hear the nearby rustle of leaves first, because when I look up, Connor is still looking at me like I'm saying something interesting. He jumps when the sound gets louder, like something's flailing around in the dried, dead grass just through the Outpost fence.

"Did you—"

I put a finger to my lips. I get the spooky feeling we're being watched, so I go into stealth mode, half bent over as I take large steps toward a wide-trunked tree covered in green leaves. Connor is right behind me. We stare at the abandoned property, but the sounds have stopped. The only sound now is ocean waves and the occasional seagull scream.

He pokes my spine. "Is that Leland's shopping cart?"

I mimic his gaze and see the back of a tarnished shopping cart filled with Leland's random shit. Half of it is hidden in foliage, and I assume the same of its owner. My hands drop from the gnarly trunk. "Shit, it was probably Leland. I should see if he's okay after the 'shine incident."

"I'll go with."

I leave my bag of books, water bottle, and sunscreen by the hammock as we navigate our way over hot sand. I'm wearing flip-flops, but that sneaky stuff has a way of getting between your toes. Connor, who I just noticed is barefoot, practically dances from one patch of shade to the next.

"Don't laugh at me," he says.

"I'm not." I am.

"This is your fault. I came on a rescue mission to find you and, in my distress, forgot shoes."

"Distress, huh?"

"Distress. Yeah."

I press the tip of one finger to the shopping cart and hiss; the metal is scalding, so it's been sitting here for a while. From beyond overgrown trees, broken windows glare. I've never set foot inside The Outpost during the day—I never wanted to see how gross it really was—but desperate times.

I sigh. "Better go find him. I hope he's not passed out in the sun."

Connor winces at the thought.

We make our way around to the secret place where the fence has a hole that comes up to my waist and duck through. A sudden wind whips sand in my face. "Shit." I close my eyes in time but do get a mouthful of sand, which I spit onto the ground.

The earth moans.

Connor and I freeze and look at each other.

As if on cue, we laugh and say, "Nah," before walking farther inside. The waterless pool is blessedly empty of a drunken senior citizen. Thank goodness, because I have no idea how we would have pulled Leland from the bottom of a ten-foot deep concrete hole. Past the pool, there are dirt paths that were once roads. I assume there's still concrete under there, but eight years of ocean storms have turned the resort into a desert. The empty path yawns out before us with stacked condos on either side. There's a decrepit, faded "Restaurant" sign to our right.

"Jesus," Connor says.

"What?"

"I don't know, man. This place feels—" He lifts his shoulders and shudders them down while making an oogie-boogie noise. "I never really thought it was creepy before, but—"

"Pussy."

He shoves me in the shoulder, laughing.

"Leland?" I call his name, and it bounces back at me like we're in a cave. "Why'd my voice echo?"

"I don't think I want to be here."

Yeah, I get that. I won't say it out loud, but Connor's right: this place is actually creepier during the day. "I'm not leaving Leland." I keep walking—otherwise, I might not.

"Well, I'm not leaving you."

"Leland? It's Emily!"

"What?"

I roll my eyes. "Leland thinks my name is Emily."

Connor giggles but stops suddenly as that sound also echoes.

When we turn the corner of a busted-up gray building that, I assume, used to be nice, a tall woman is standing there, staring at us. I lurch backwards, right into Connor, who catches me before I fall ass over teakettle.

The lady is all sorts of fancy. She's in this to-die-for tailored business suit and red-soled shoes—Jesus, who wears Louboutins to an abandoned resort?—with striking red hair swept up in a perfect modern beehive. The little queen in me screeches with delight. I try not to flash celebratory jazz hands.

"Oh." She smiles, and her teeth are like shining stars.

"I'm sorry," I stutter. "I know we're not supposed to be here, but—"

She takes two steps toward us, and I have never felt more hunted in my life—and I was bullied in school. Her eyes, some pretty shade of gray, burn a path from my sandaled toes to the top of my head. "Aren't you a teaspoon of yum?"

"Uh..."

Connor actually shoves me behind him like this lady has fangs. "I'm Connor."

She grins up at him. "Are you now? And your adorable friend?"

"We were just leaving." He grabs my arm and tugs, but I tug back.

"Wait! We're... Look, we know we're not supposed to be here, but we're looking for a friend. Old guy. Hawaiian shirt. Straw hat, usually. Might smell like vomit."

She clicks her tongue and blinks long eyelashes in thought. "I haven't seen him. I didn't catch your name, sweetheart." She extends a perfectly manicured—French tipped! —hand.

It'd be super awkward if I didn't take it, so I clasp her hand in mine. "Emory."

"Emory?" She does not let go of my hand. "German origin, isn't it? Strange, you look so exotic."

I want to tell her my mom is Italian, but then, I also don't want to.

"I'm Tabitha Crown." She still has my hand, but she looks at Connor for a beat. "Of Keebler and Crown, the real estate agency. I've flown in from New Mexico to inspect our new space. You young men seem to know your way around; perhaps you could give me a tour?"

SARA DOBIE BAUER

I slowly, politely slip my hand the hell away from hers. "We really need to find our friend."

"Mm. Of course. Do be careful." She winks.

"Okay, thanks," Connor says. His voice sounds deeper than usual, which would be sexy if I wasn't keeping an eye on Tabitha as one might a hungry lion.

She turns to walk away, back toward the front gates, Louboutin soles flashing like red dollar signs—but stops and turns profile. If I were into chicks, I would notice her banging body. Hell, I'm gay, and I notice her banging body. "Oh, and Emory? I hope to see you again."

"Uh... yeah." I press my lips together until she finally turns and traipses back to what I assume is a super expensive Lincoln Town Car or limo.

"Wench," Connor whispers.

"Dude."

"Sorry. I didn't like her."

I push windblown hair off my face. "She was like Cruella de Vil's evil little sister."

"Yeah, and she wanted to turn you into a coat."

I laugh, happy that Tabitha has disappeared from view.

"Do we even know for sure that Leland is here?"

"No. Nobody knows what Leland does. He's like the wind."

Connor lifts his camera and takes a couple shots of the sand-covered road and condos with busted roofs before snapping one of me.

"Cut it out."

He smiles from behind the lens and takes another, right in my face. "You don't like having your picture taken."

"Does anyone?" I hold my hand over the lens.

"Models, I guess."

"Connor, focus! We need to find a sweet, old man who is possibly melting like butter in the sun."

"Okay, okay." He puts the camera back over his shoulder. His forehead glistens with sweat, as does the spot of chest revealed at the top of his V-neck tee. Mm... wait, what was I talking about? Right, Leland. "Where does he hang out?"

"Well, all over the place," I say, "but he wouldn't leave his shopping cart. That's like you leaving your camera in a trash-can. Or me leaving a Stephen King book literally in the ocean."

He tips his head. "Point taken. So he's here somewhere—but where?"

I flip through the filing cabinet of my brain, back to all the conversations I've had with Leland and am sad to say half of them are fuzzy, thanks to my underage alcohol consumption. I'm about to cuss, maybe kick a rat or something, when I remember. "Room 306. It's his favorite room."

"Why didn't you say that earlier?"

"I didn't think of it earlier."

"Well, where's room 306?"

I turn in a circle, studying nearby buildings for faded numbers. I see a couple twos and a three, so I point farther up the road. "Maybe there?"

He puts his hand on my upper back. "Okay, princess, let's go."

I point up into his face. "Hey, only Liz is allowed to call me that."

"Sorry, I didn't mean—"

"No, it's fine. Old habits."

"I really am sorry that guys like me picked on you."

"Well, they weren't guys like you. Obviously." I gesture to myself as if to say, *Look at the homo you're hanging with.*

"No." He bumps his shoulder into mine. "Not guys like me. True."

We start walking, and although I'm on a mission, I don't walk too quickly. I'm enjoying myself, so I stretch out the moment by taking smaller steps, regardless of my Gumby legs.

"How long have you known that you're...?"

I glance over at Connor. "What?"

"Gay."

"I dunno. Since, like, week ten of conception?"

Connor snorts and bumps me in the shoulder again.

"Have you ever looked at a goat and thought, 'I want to have sex with that goat'?"

He pauses with one foot in the air and sways in the sun. "Are you comparing women to goats?"

"I'm a writer." I shrug. "It's a metaphor."

"Huh. Well, no, I've never looked at a goat and thought about sex."

"That's how I feel about girls. They're cute, and I like being around them, but I would never have sex with one."

"Don't knock it until you try it," he says as we near a big empty building marked three.

I gesture back the way we've come as though my words linger like a rolled-out red carpet. "Goat metaphor, remember?"

He winces. "Goat metaphor. Got it."

"Building three." I march toward the rickety wooden steps, covered in moss and probably black mold, but a big, strong hand wraps around my wrist and tugs. I look back at Connor, and he's gawking at the building like it's Poe's house of Usher. "Dude, what?"

"Are you sure it's safe to go inside?"

"Leland does."

"Yeah, but Leland—" He blows a breath of air out through his mouth. "You're fragile."

"Fragile? I grew muscles this year!"

"Like, two."

I scoff but can't help smiling as I pull my arm away from him. "Fucker."

"Fine, but I'm going in first."

He goes to move past me, and I follow. "Maybe *you* shouldn't go inside, what with your football Neanderthal body."

He laughs around an "Oh my God" before hopping up the steps like the graceful ex-athlete he is. The stairs feel sturdy beneath my feet, albeit crooked, and if they can support Leland's weight, they can support us.

Room 306 is on the second floor, so we pass a bunch of closed yellow doors on our way. One is cracked down the center, revealing a fully furnished condo, decked out in loud, floral print couches and curtains. A wine glass has fallen over on the kitchen table.

"How come these places are still furnished anyway?" Connor asks. "Shouldn't they be empty?"

"I guess. I don't know."

"Apparently the owner wanted people the hell out."

"Three-o-six." I pass Connor in a hallway that smells so much like stale seawater I can almost taste it. The door is shut, so I pause and knock.

Connor looks at me funny.

"What?" I whisper. "It's like his house. Leland?"

"Emily's here," Connor says loudly.

"I should never have told you about that."

Connor grins and pushes past me, opening the door.

Although I don't see Leland right away, he has definitely slept here before. I can smell the booze—which makes me retch immediately. Connor doesn't even have to ask; he crosses the dim living room and opens a window, waving air inside like that'll help dispel months and probably years of a sweaty alcoholic's funk.

He realizes the futility and stops waving his arms around.

"You want to wait outside?"

"Nope." I swallow a belch. "Nope, I'm good." I'm really not. I'm never drinking again.

"I'll check the bedroom."

"Mm-hmm." I keep my lips pressed together and think about nice smelling things like flowers and Mom's coffee and my super-expensive shampoo. (Give me a break. Liz made me buy it when I started growing my hair out, okay?) I linger in the shady foyer, decorated cheap Southwestern chic, and wait for Connor to announce that Leland is here, safe and sound.

Instead, he says, "Emory?" His voice shakes, so I move —fast.

In the bedroom, he stands next to an unmade bed, covered in dirty pillows and blankets. He stares down at the floor around the side of Leland's favorite sleeping spot. I take two big, bounding steps, expecting to see a bloated corpse but, thank God, no; it's just a stain. Well, not *just* a stain. It looks a lot like—

"Is that blood?"

I reach around Connor and tug at the curtains to let some light inside, but the glaring summer sun only makes the probable blood more apparent. "Shit," I mutter. It's a big enough stain to cause concern.

"What do we do?" Connor asks.

I consider a childhood of watching police procedurals—I was a twisted little kid—and point at his camera. "Take pictures. We have to go to the cops."

Connor's blue eyes are all scrunched together. "Do you think something happened to him? Someone hurt him?"

I swallow around a mounting sense of dread. "Pictures."

He swings the camera off his shoulder and removes the lens cap before stepping back. I hear the familiar click of his camera a couple times before he grabs my shoulder and pushes me toward the door. "Let's get the hell out of here."

CHAPTER 8

The sheriff's office is the size of Liz's closet back home in Ohio, probably because nothing bad ever happens here. Well, nothing really bad. I mean, kids get arrested for drunk and disorderly, and rich old people complain about skateboarders, but that's about it. A big bloodstain is, to say the least, unique.

I was hoping for some ditzy front desk girl, but they don't even have that. Connor and I are left standing, his camera around his neck and my hands in my swim trunk pockets. I consider whistling to fill the silence, but with the panicked green tint of Connor's skin, that might scare him to death because whistling is creepy.

"Hello?" I call down a short, wide hallway.

A chair creaks from someplace.

We look at each other and then look back down the hall.

A chair creaks some more.

Connor shakes his head. "Nope."

"What?"

"This is some *30 Days of Night* shit where the vampires kill all the cops, and the police station becomes a death zone."

"You know that movie?"

"Of course I know that movie!" he whispers in agitation.

I hold my hands up in apology, because he's right; now is probably not the time to geek out over how much I love the makeup in that film.

A chair creaks—again. Connor is right, this is some ominous shit, but the creaking is soon enough followed by a friendly voice. "Someone out there?"

"Um, yes?" I say.

Creak, creak, and one final big, long *creak* as I imagine someone dislodges his huge ass from an ancient office chair. It's not fair of me to assume my local law enforcement officer has a huge ass. It's just that I've seen so many eighties horror movies where the kids go to the cops and the cops are fat and lazy and totally worthless and don't believe *anything* until half the town is massacred by a guy in a hockey mask—and then, it's too freaking late, okay?

"Emory, why are you hopping on your toes?"

"What?" I stop hopping. Apparently, my internal rant session poured into a physical tic. "He's not going to believe us."

"Who?"

"Lazy eighties cop."

"What are you—?" He opens his mouth and closes it. "Are you still drunk?"

I sigh just as the authority in question appears at the end of the hall. "I'm sorry, didn't hear you boys." He ambles toward us, and whelp, this guy is not fat. Sweet baby Jesus, he's Tom Selleck, circa Magnum PI. Anyone want a mustache ride? Me. I do. "Can I help you?" he says.

I'm too busy staring at the curly, black tufts of chest hair escaping the top of his shirt to respond—until Connor nudges me. Hard. "Ow!"

Connor clears his throat.

"Sorry. Hi. Um." I don't even know where to start. "I'm, well, I'm friends with Leland. You know Leland?"

"Everyone knows Leland, son." He crosses his hairy tree-trunk arms.

"Right, um, we found his cart down by the Outpost. He sleeps there sometimes in room 306. It's his favorite. Anyway, we wanted to find him to make sure he was okay because he would never leave his cart sitting around, but— This is going to sound totally insane."

Hot Sheriff tells me to "Go on."

I look to Connor for support, and he blessedly gets the hint. "We found a blood stain in room 306. A big one." He moves for his camera.

"Y'all know it's a crime to trespass on that property."

And here we go, eighties horror movie cop step one: wave off the young witnesses as bad kids and ignore their pleas while Freddie Krueger haunts their dreams.

I'm already resigned to failure as Connor fiddles with his camera. "Sorry about that, sir, but we did find a blood stain, and we can't find Leland. Look, I have pictures."

Hot Sheriff looks totally bored. "Leland probably cut himself on a beer bottle and is sleeping it off in another room. It wouldn't be the first time he's disappeared for a day. Nothing to worry about." He flashes a big, toothy grin.

"But," Connor continues. "It's a lot of blood. Don't you want to see the pictures?"

"I'm sure you take very nice pictures, son, but you shouldn't be poking around the Outpost. The property ain't safe, and as I said, it's trespassing. I could write you both up."

"But, sir—" Poor Connor.

"How about this? I take down your names and phone numbers, and once Leland surfaces, I'll give you a call. Would that make y'all feel better?"

I tug on Connor's shirtsleeve until he looks at me, and I

blink up at the sheriff from under lowered brows. I plaster on my creepiest china doll smile. "That would be great, thank you."

Apparently, Hot Sheriff is not good at reading people, because he smiles and nods even though I'm laying on the bullshit real thick. I give him my name and cell phone number and tell Connor to do the same, even when he looks at me like I've lost my damn mind. I even shake Hot Sheriff's hand on the way out and thank him again. Oscars, here I come.

Compared to the weak air-conditioning of the sheriff's office, the late afternoon Florida heat is enough to knock the air from my lungs. Connor paces back and forth once on the sidewalk before freezing and turning to me with a knowing smirk. "Lazy eighties cop."

I make a clicking sound with my cheek. "*Nightmare on Elm Street* all over again."

"This isn't a horror movie," he says.

"Yet," I reply. "Come on." I start walking, pretty sure at this point he'll follow.

"Where are you going?"

"Back to the Outpost."

He spins me around with a hand on my arm. "You can't search the whole property."

"I know, but I was panicked before. I didn't get a good look at the room."

"You want to go back to 306?"

"Obviously. Why are you freaking out?"

"Hey, you know—" He huffs and pulls me off the sidewalk and into the shade of a huge banyan tree, covered in Spanish moss, although I shy away. Banyans give me the creeps. "—if this were a horror movie, you're the one who would live, and I'm the one who would die."

"What? Nuh-uh."

"Yes, huh. Because you would be the smart, virgin lead, and—"

"I'm not a virgin."

"What?" He leans back. "Really?"

I throw my hands in the air. "Why would I be a virgin?"

"I—" He backpedals so hard vocally, he practically moves in reverse.

"You think no one would want me?" And defensive Emory is back.

"What? No! You've always seemed so—"

"Awkward? Clumsy? Spooky?"

"Innocent," he says. "Sweet." He looks down at the ground, which is good because I'm blushing like a ripe peach. "Huh. So I guess if this were a horror movie, we'd both be dead."

"So dead," I agree. "Come on, let's go be dead together." I start walking toward the Outpost and only then realize that joke was probably in poor taste considering Leland is currently missing, and there's a bloodstain the size of a Michael Myers killing spree in his abandoned room.

By the time we get back to building three, we've given up all hope in authority figures because pretty much every horror movie tells us to. Even the trying-to-be-helpful cop in *Scream* ended up stabbed, and parents are obviously worthless. It's always the kids who save the day, so here we are —saving it.

Connor does this sneaky thing where he uses his slightly longer legs to lope ahead of me, all nonchalant like, when we reach the steps. Do I think it's cute that he likes protecting me? Okay, yeah. I'm not even sure it's a wholly conscious decision on his part. Maybe it's a big guy routine.

By the time we reach the door of room 306, Connor has his camera out like he's a professional crime scene photographer. He walks straight for the bedroom, but I take a quick second to look around the dusty living room. There are empty beer bottles on the floor but not much else— "No sign of foul play," as they say. I stare at an off-putting painting of a lonely dude on a nighttime beach and startle at the sound of Connor's panicked voice.

"This is the same room, right?" He sounds like someone kneed him in the balls.

"Yes. What's—?"

In the bedroom, he stares at the floor by the bed, mouth half-open and bright eyes wide.

I step up next to him. "What's the—?"

The bloodstain is gone.

"Huh." I take a little breath. "As a writer, I thought I'd be at least forty before I lost my mind."

He chuckles once, but it sounds more like a cough. "I saw it, too, dude." He lifts his camera and shows me the digital screen. "And I have pictures."

According to ten digital images of the carpet and room, the bloodstain should be here. So where is the bloodstain? I immediately assume the ghost of a maid still drags her cleaning supplies from room to room, moaning and trailing her chains behind her.

Connor kneels and puts his palm right where the stain used to be. For some reason, I have the urge to shriek, "Don't touch it!" But nothing happens, of course. He doesn't get sucked into the floor. A monster doesn't reach out from under the bed.

"The carpet is dry," he says and looks up at me. "What the hell is going on?"

I shake my head. "No idea, but I'd like to get a closer look at those photos you took earlier."

"I have my laptop back at the house. Way bigger screen."

"Perfect."

Outside, late afternoon is turning to early evening. I have

to go back to my hammock on the beach to get my books, and I refuse to leave Leland's cart sitting around for anyone to steal. Connor, bless him, helps me drag the thing to the closest sidewalk. I get a little panicked when I catch a whiff of Leland's homeless guy odor amidst old, shifting blankets. I have a bad feeling, and Leland is a good guy.

I don't know if I make a sound or if my face scrunches up, but Connor puts his hand on my shoulder. "We're going to find him, okay?"

I nod and keep walking.

The moment we reach our shared driveway, Liz starts yelling, waving her phone in the air. "Where have you been?" She's in her frilly blue cover-up today with a hat that belongs at the Kentucky Derby. "I've been calling you! Mom has been calling you!"

Shit, I'd left my cell phone at home. "Sorry, sorry!"

She glares at the shopping cart. "Tell me you didn't rob the homeless guy."

"We think he's missing," Connor says, and he jumps into the grass alongside the driveway to escape the hot pavement. I keep forgetting he doesn't have shoes, which is my fault because he was "distressed" by my early morning disappearance.

"Let's go inside and look at those pictures."

Connor pushes Leland's cart beneath an overhang on the side of his house, and I follow—as does Liz, who asks, "What pictures?"

I tell her, "There was a bloodstain in room 306."

"Are you speaking in code?" she hollers.

The lanai of the Nichols's huge home is covered in succulents, smells like cigars, and feels way too warm, but we're soon through the glass door and drenched in air-conditioning.

"Connor, baby?" I hear Maud's voice from the kitchen, so Connor moves in that direction. A moment later, we turn the corner, and there's Mrs. Nichols in all her middle-aged, scandalous glory. She's not in one of her teeny bikinis but a white lace sundress instead that compliments her tan skin and cork bottom heels. She turns around with a huge watermelon in her hands and grins when she sees me. "Emory!" She walks right past Connor after handing him the watermelon and squeezes my cheeks. "You are the cutest thing!" She's so close, she might rub our noses together. Mrs. Nichols freaking loves me.

"Mom." Connor's embarrassment is palpable, but this is what parents do: embarrass their children.

Maud puts her arm around my shoulders, and I smell her famous sangria on her breath. "You're just in time, Connor. I needed a big, strong man to cut that watermelon. Would y'all like some watermelon?"

"Um, well, we need to use Connor's laptop." I bust out the puppy dog eyes and actually feel Liz cringe behind me. I've been using puppy dog eyes on my parents for years, but she's never mastered the trick.

It apparently works on Mrs. Nichols, too, because she pats me on the head. "Of course, honey. Why don't you go on upstairs, and Connor will be right there after he cuts me some watermelon, hmm?"

I nod and smile as Connor trudges toward the cutting board, camera still hanging around his neck. He reaches for a huge knife and says, "First door on the right."

I grab Liz's hand and drag her through the modern art museum that is the Nichols household. I'm not sure who decorated the place, but there are big, abstract murals all over and super-modern furniture that I'm not even sure how to sit on. I've only been over here a couple times, honestly, and I have never been in Connor's room. I try not to scurry.

First door on the right. First door on the right. It's half-open, so I toe inside.

"Huh."

It's very sparse. There's a bed and a comfy-looking blue chair by the window—a huge window that overlooks the beach and turquoise water beyond. He has a perfect view of everything that happens along the crashing waves of Longboat Key. His MacBook sits closed on a sleek, modern desk in the corner. Liz sinks into a swiveling, black office chair and opens it.

"Liz, don't snoop."

"I'm not snooping." She fingers the mouse pad. "You're the one snooping. I know you're stalking his room for books."

She's right. I judge entire households based on their bookcases alone. Connor doesn't have a bookcase, though. Hell, I don't even have a bookcase down here, because it's not worth bringing my entire massive collection for a two-week vacation. There is, however, a small pile of books on a tiny table by his unmade bed. I lean down and take a glance.

He's reading a graphic novel: Neil Gaiman's *The Sandman*. I might swoon a little. He's also reading something called *Save the Cat* about screenwriting. Hmm, that actually might be up my alley. I'm flipping through the table of contents when Liz makes her WTF noise. She's fine-tuned it over the years. Imagine someone humming "What the fuck," and that's what it sounds like. I can translate the majority of my sister's humming into full sentences.

"Tell me you're not looking at porn."

She slams the laptop closed as I turn around. "Hmm? What?"

"Liz?"

She shakes her head violently and actually picks Connor's laptop up, hugging it to her chest.

"Why are you spazzing out?"

"Uhh."

I put the book down and stand, which makes her hug the laptop harder.

Connor enters the room with a plate full of watermelon slices but freezes when he sees Liz cuddling his MacBook. "What are you doing to my computer?"

"Nothing! Nothing. And nothing that Emory saw." She clears her throat, and it's like six exclamation points fly from her eyes.

What the hell is going on?

I look to Connor, but he's staring at Liz, clenching his jaw.

I wave my hands between them. "What's the matter with you guys?"

Liz's voice is practically a low growl. "I think you and I need to have a little talk, Connor Nichols."

His eyes dart to me once before resting again on Liz, who's basically holding his laptop captive.

"Look, sis, whatever you've been smoking today, I'll have some later, but right now, we need to look at the pictures on Connor's camera."

"Emory." My name sounds like an order. "Tomorrow," he says.

I gawk at him. "Seriously?"

"I need to talk to your sister, okay?"

"You've got to be kidding me!"

At my outburst, Connor looks like he wants to throw the damn watermelon out the nearest window and shake me like a Polaroid picture.

"Hey, dickhead!" Liz is such a lady. "Aren't you supposed to be walking Roberta's dog about now?"

Based on the orange glow of the sun outside, yes, I'm supposed to be doing exactly that—but how can I be expected to leave this Liz-Connor *Twilight Zone* without any answers?

"Emory, go," she orders, and Connor does nothing to help me out. In fact, he won't even look at me.

This day has been so long, and I am still a little hungover. I'm now officially Connor's *gay* friend, and Leland is missing —and cops are stupid. Sisters are stupid. Friends are stupid. I slump and mutter, "Fine. Whatever." I leave Connor and Liz to share their stupid, *stupid* secret. Sure, fine, great; it's not like I've never been left out before. No one ever picked me in dodge ball.

When I go to pick up Ella, Roberta says I look like somebody drank my Kool-Aid. At least the dog is happy to see me.

I know I'm being ridiculous, but Liz and I don't have secrets. None. When I lost my virginity at sixteen to a Maumee High School soccer player, Liz was the only person I told. When she lost hers a month later to some freshman at Bowling Green State, she told me right away. If two siblings can talk about sex, what can't they talk about?

I walk Ella on the beach but up by the grass line so no one gets huffy. I wouldn't mind an evening swim. Water has always been an emotional balm for me. I like being underwater. It's quiet there. I also want to go to sleep. I didn't notice how tired I was until right now, and I'm excited to wake up tomorrow not feeling like a cat pooped in my mouth.

I stop walking when I see Connor and Liz up ahead, sitting on the beach side by side. Liz is smiling. It's the same grin she wore when we both got into NYU, so whatever they're talking about—whatever secret they're sharing—it's a good one. I can't see Connor's face, but he shakes his head, and Liz rubs her hand across his back.

No. Oh my God.

No, please, Liz, you wouldn't.

Did she find a love letter? Was he writing a love letter to her? Liz and Connor have always been friendly. She's not awkward and bumbling like me. She doesn't hide in books like me. Despite her own insecurities, she's always been pretty. People like our dark hair and green eyes. Boys like her boobs and long legs. What is there not to like about Liz?

But she wouldn't. She knows I'm crazy about Connor. She wouldn't do this to me.

I turn away from their quaint scene and walk with Ella back toward Roberta's. I might blink back a few tears as I let Ella eat sea grass and roll around in the sand. Ah, the simple life of a dog.

I could really use a drunken Leland right now.

When I drop Ella off, Roberta asks if I'm okay five times. She offers to make me some tea, but I refuse. I want to walk, so I do. I walk until it's past dinnertime, and then, I swim. I go way past the sandbar and float on my back, daring a shark to come get me. That'll teach them. Liz would be super upset if I was eaten alive.

I hang out by the bagpipe guy and wait for "Amazing Grace" before rambling home. My family is sitting in the living room when I get there, eating delivery pizza and watching game shows.

I grab a tepid slice of mushroom and black olive—no meat for Liz—and give them all a half-hearted wave and some excuse about being tired. When Liz moves to follow me, I shake my head at her, and she sighs back into the couch. *Not now, sis.*

I slump into bed and eat pizza while considering how awful it would be for Connor Nichols to date my sister in New York. Wouldn't they be just precious together?

CHAPTER 9

My wicked witch alarm cackles at 8:27 a.m., but I remain on my back in bed, repeating the mantra, *Don't look, don't look*. A minute later, I hear his sneakers on the pavement outside my open window and resolutely do not look. I roll onto my side and muffle an irritated groan into my pillow as my bedroom door swings open and an overblown beach ball bashes me in the back of the head.

"Wake up, fucker!" My bed dips as Liz sits on the edge and starts bouncing. She continues bouncing until I push hair out of my face to glare at her.

"You should consider knocking."

In her spandex yoga gear, she looks like an overcaffeinated aerobics instructor. "You should consider getting out of bed. Connor wants to see you first thing to look at those creepy pictures he took yesterday."

I roll away from her and mumble obscenities into a pillow that smells like sunscreen and my sweat. "Why don't *you* go look at pictures since you two are so buddy-buddy all of a sudden?"

Liz bounces some more, so I push my foot out and shove

her off the bed. Of course she lands gracefully whereas I would have been a tangle of limbs.

"Are you going to tell me what you two were talking about last night?"

"Nope!" she sings. "Now, wake up and play hero! Save the homeless guy!"

I grumble and mumble some more, but Liz is right: I do want to find Leland. I do want to look closer at those pictures Connor took yesterday. And I can't avoid the guy, even if he does want to bang my sister. When I realized my crush level was at critical mass, I tried avoiding him last summer, and all that achieved was his more focused attention as he made it his job to ruffle my hair, wrestle me, and be adorably annoying.

"Fine," I huff. "But I'm in nothing but boxer briefs right now, and I'm an eighteen-year-old male, so get out of my room."

Her nose wrinkles in understanding, but she does, thankfully, leave me alone.

I take a quick shower and don't even bother brushing my hair. I shave my pathetic excuse for facial hair, which is really just some fuzz on my upper lip that makes me look like trash if I let it go. I put some product in my curls and twist them around the way Liz taught me so they look "extra lush." By the time I'm standing at my closet, staring, I realize I have achieved top marks for procrastination. I never take this long to wash up in the morning.

"Come on, man," I whisper and grab a white baseball shirt with blue piping and khaki shorts. No swim trunks today; I've got work to do. Plus, it looks like it's going to rain. There are dark clouds on the edge of the horizon like a gathering army.

By the time I'm brushing my teeth, my hair has air-dried, and huh. Okay, maybe Liz is right and I do have sort of nice hair. I mean, it looks okay. I look okay—maybe? I'm still not buying Liz's whole "you got hot" spiel, but I'm not, like, a total travesty. I pluck at the front of my shirt, thankful for all the swimming I've done recently because I do have a couple muscles now, but I'm still too skinny. I will always be too skinny. And my stupid lips are always too pink, like a girl's. And my chin is pointy, and...

Here comes my invitation to my pity party.

Before I can sink into a world-famous Emory Jones funk, I slip into my brown flip-flops and leave the room. Mom, as always, hands me a cup of coffee once I get downstairs. She kisses my cheek because she can't reach the top of my head anymore. She says, "You look so grown-up this summer."

I smile down at her. It is weird suddenly having a whole new view of the world. For most of my life, I had to look up at people. I saw up lots of noses. Now, people are looking up my nose, which makes me think I should probably check for nose hairs. God, do I have nose hairs? I scratch my face to hide sudden panic over the state of my nostrils and press my lips together before shuffling away from her and over to the kitchen table where dad left the *Observer*.

My hand rests on a familiar face: Tabitha Crown of blah-blah-blah real estate in New Mexico. Of course, she would look perfect in pictures with that red hair and shimmery smile. In the photo, she stands in front of the Outpost's crooked old entrance, shaking hands with the mayor—some old dude in a pastel suit with gold necklaces and rings on his fingers. He's probably ex-mob. With all the money down here, I wouldn't be a bit surprised.

I slurp down the last of Mom's espresso blend. That last sip is always a doozy, and my eyes shake in my head with caffeine overload. I tell her I'm going over to Connor's.

"Want to help make ravioli tomorrow?"

I nod from the doorway. "Yeah." It's one of our family traditions.

"Love you."

"Love you too." Through the glass, I see Liz in some upside-down pose on the patio. I open the door and shout, "Boo!"

For a second, her legs kick out all funny, and then, she tumbles to the side. She bellows my name the way she did when we were five and I pulled the head off her favorite doll, but I'm now old enough to know when to escape. I rush down the back steps and into sand before she can recuperate and land a punch.

Between our houses, Leland's cart is still safe and sound in the shade, the sight of which makes my mission all the more pressing. Must find Leland. He is more important than whatever dumb shit is going on between Connor and my sister, so I don't hesitate before knocking on the Nichols's side door.

Mr. Nichols answers a few seconds later wearing what appears to be fishing gear: pastel shirt and shorts with a fishing hat and unlit cigar in his mouth. I'm fairly positive Mr. Nichols doesn't fish. His chin mushes back into his neck as he eyes me. "Jesus, kid, you got too tall. You look ridiculous."

"Thank you, sir. Is Connor—?"

He opens the door wide and starts walking away. "Spielberg is in his room."

Right, so, okay, just another normal day with Mr. Nichols.

I close the door behind me, considering there's no one else around to do it. Maud is nowhere to be seen, so she's probably on a morning walk. I take the steps two at a time and say Connor's name.

His bedroom door swings open like he's been waiting for me. Based on his damp blond hair, he must have showered post-run. He's in a tight white tee with Ash from *Evil Dead* on the front, and he grins down at me like I said something hilarious. So I guess I don't have to look down at *everyone*. Connor Nichols will always be bigger than me.

I shoulder past him, hands in my pockets. "Let's look at those pictures."

"Yeah, they're on my MacBook, all queued up." He walks past me, and wow, he smells good. I want to eat his shower gel—but no, I'm pissed at him. I'm pissed at the secret he would share with Liz and not me. I try to stay pissed, but it's not easy when he shoves me into his office chair and messes with his mouse pad while looking and smelling like a cologne ad. "There."

He gestures to the screen, which is when I realize my mouth is full of spit because I haven't swallowed since I walked in the room. I suck saliva down my throat and lean toward the screen where there's a folder named "Leland." I have a Mac at home, so I navigate the screwy mouse pad easily and open the first photo.

Ugly carpet? Check. Floral patterned comforter? Also check. Big bloodstain? Yep, there it is. I zoom in; I zoom out. I go to the next photo—a closer shot of blood. I tilt my head and squint.

"So, like, how can we be sure this is actual blood?"

Connor leans over, so when I turn to glance at him, my face is practically in the crook of his neck. Based on my expert analysis, he shaved right before I got there because not one whisker pokes free from his tanned skin. I'm tempted to nuzzle against him like a cat but clench my fingers against my thighs instead.

He clicks a button and studies the screen. "It looks a lot like blood, and not the movie kind. It looks like postgame-football-broken-nose blood."

I swing the chair in the opposite direction of his body and stand. "I'm going back."

"Don't you want to look at more pictures?"

"Later maybe. We know the bloodstain was there, and then, it was gone. Admittedly, that's weird shit, but I'm more

SARA DOBIE BAUER

concerned about finding Leland. I think he's still at the Outpost somewhere, and he may be hurt." I sidestep to get around Connor.

"Hey, wait up!"

I pause in his doorway. "You don't have to come with me." *You'd probably rather be with Liz.*

"Of course I'm coming with you."

I turn without acknowledging and hop back down what are quickly becoming familiar stairs. The house itself is silent, but I can smell Mr. Nichols's cigar smoke from the lanai out back. Before I head in that direction, Connor tugs the shoulder of my shirt and nods to the side door.

Outside, I notice he doesn't have his camera like usual. I also notice the thunderheads have moved a lot closer. I glare up at them. "Shit."

"Maybe we should wait until later?"

"No." I start walking fast. He's probably right—we should wait until the storm passes—but it feels good to be contrary. I am a very large child.

"Jesus, slow down, Emory."

"It's your fault my legs grew." I regret the words as soon as they're out. I promised myself I'd never bring up the leg massage. Never. With the mood I'm in, I couldn't have picked a worse time. Instead of waiting for his response—wondering if he even remembers that night last summer—I kick up the pace even more until Connor is practically jogging.

The first raindrop hits me as I duck under the busted fence at the back of the Outpost. I look up while waiting for Connor to step through, and we're in some deep shit, folks. In Florida, there are rainstorms and then there are apocalyptic cloud-lettings. Based on the black sky and total lack of sun, we're about to be hit by the latter. I cuss, which makes Connor look up too.

"Oh, boy," he mutters. "We've got to move." He hurries past me, glancing back once to make sure I'm following. We make it to a crooked overhang by one of the big buildings as the quiet water droplets become attack missiles. Connor takes a load off on the back of a park bench, his feet on the seat. "I guess we wait it out."

I inwardly groan. This is so not what I need right now. I'm literally trapped with the dude I want to avoid. The only thing that would make this worse: if he wants to talk about Liz. Storm be damned, I'd make a run for it.

Instead, he says, "What do you write about anyway?"

Thrown by his non sequitur, I blink for a few seconds. "Um... stuff."

"I assume you're more eloquent with your prose."

I roll my eyes and mimic his seated position on the opposite side of the bench. Around us, the scent of rain hitting wood and soaking sea grass intrudes. "Mostly fantasy and horror. Some American gothic stuff. You know, creepy small-town neighbors and husbands murdering wives. That sort of thing."

"Is that why you read horror? Is it research?"

"No, I just like it. I like scary stories. They're comforting."

He snickers. "How?"

"No matter how bad life gets, at least I'm not being chased by Leatherface."

He gives me a wide-mouthed silent laugh above the sound of deluge on a crooked roof. Rain falls off the edge to my right like a waterfall. "So writing is like reading—an escape for you?"

I poke at my sand-covered toes. "I guess."

"Do you want me to stop talking?"

I shake my head. "It's fine. Talking has never been my strong suit."

"I think you're very good at talking."

I stare out into the storm. The rain falls so hard it almost looks like fog. "Writing is so much safer. It gives me time to think about what I'm saying before I say it. I need more space between my mouth and my brain."

He's way closer than I realized when he whispers, "I'm very fond of the space between your brain and your mouth."

I turn to look at him, and he's right there, in my face. And, of course, I fall backwards off the bench—which would have been embarrassing enough, thank you, but I do one better and actually fall through rotted wood that was apparently covering a hole. I keep falling until my head smacks into something, and my body hits the ground. All the air rushes from my lungs, and ouch, that hurt.

I think I hear Connor up above shouting my name, but the storm is so damn loud, as is the ringing in my ears. I curl onto my side on the cold, damp floor before trying to sit up. Something warm drips into my right eye, and I realize my head is gushing blood. Great. Some drips onto the floor below as I try to remember how to breathe.

"Fuck." I groan.

Even though the only light is coming from the hole I busted in the floor, I see the rats staring back at me. There's a dozen of them at least, probably waiting out the storm down here.

"Hey, please don't eat me."

They don't scurry—they're used to humans by now—but their stillness is— I'll be honest: horrifying. Plus, I'm bleeding from my head, and I have no idea where I am. A big boom of thunder makes the rodents jump and scatter. They scream as they run, and, okay, maybe I scream a little, too, as I continue blinking blood out of my eye.

I assume my shattered skull is what conjures a pair of red, glowing eyes in the darkness about ten feet away, but before I have time to embrace my newly acquired hallucinations, there's the pounding of feet from somewhere, followed by the panicked screaming of my name.

Connor appears, blocking the red, glowing eyes. He grabs me by the face. "Emory! Em— Oh my God, your head."

I shove him out of the way, but the red, glowing eyes are gone. All that's left is Connor brushing hair back from my gushing wound while muttering to himself.

"It's nothing," I manage. "Head wounds always bleed a lot. You've seen the movies. It means nothing."

He puts one arm around my shoulders, the other beneath my knees, and lifts.

I cuss once I'm airborne. "You don't have to carry me. I —" Oh, I feel sick. Oh, the room is spinning. Shit. I cling to the front of his shirt and bury my face against his neck. Pride, be damned.

"Emory, talk to me."

The world is shaking too much.

"Emory, please."

"Can't talk. Might vomit."

"I'm going to get you home."

The sound of rain wakes me some. "Did you see the red, glowing eyes?" I ask.

"What?"

Talking is much too difficult, so I lean my head against his shoulder and—

"Emory, please stay awake. We're almost there, okay?"

"Mm-hmm." I clutch tighter to his shirt when he holds tighter to me.

Thanks to the ongoing storm, it's super dark outside, so walking into my family's brightly lit mudroom, covered in blood and rain, is like being smashed in the face by a frying pan. I try to tell Connor to take me outside again, but my voice is no match for Liz's howl.

There are lots of hands and people saying my name as I

feel couch cushions behind me. I'd like to rest, but I shiver. The air-conditioning is no good for my soaking wet clothes. I hear Mom's voice—strong and authoritative. "Connor, give me that blanket! Liz, the first aid kit! Then, call your father."

"'M fine," I mutter and then notice the bloody disaster of my shirt. "But I shouldn't have worn white today."

"If he's worried about fashion, he should be fine," Mom says. "Where were you boys?"

"The Outpost."

Mom turns toward Connor, who looks like a wet, abandoned kitten. "I've said before that place is dangerous."

"Sorry, Mrs. Jones."

She sighs. "Knowing my son, it wasn't your fault."

"Sort of was, though," he whispers, and I'm not sure anyone was supposed to hear.

The moment Liz comes back, she starts wailing again until I tell her to stop. I'm not so sleepy anymore, and the room isn't spinning. I'm still freezing as Mom pokes and prods at my head and eventually sends Liz for a bag of ice. By then, Connor is gone. I didn't notice him leaving. Mom orders Liz to go get me a dry, clean shirt, and Dad comes back from a rained-out golf game, concern curling the edges of his face.

"I'm fine," I reiterate, although they continue circling me like panicked flies until Mom finally leaves to make lunch and Dad goes to shower.

Liz holds a bag of ice to my head, and I stare out the window. The storm is passing. The sky isn't black anymore but a shade of purple-blue. The ambitious Florida sun will be out any second now.

"What the hell happened?" she whispered.

"I honestly have no idea."

"Did you, like, black out?"

"No. I'm just really confused."

"I can probably help with that." I was not expecting Connor's voice; I assumed he'd bailed at the site of the ugly invalid.

Liz's voice brightens, as does her face. "Connor!" My ice bag forgotten, she rushes him and gives him a hug. "Thanks for getting my big brother home."

He hugs her back, laptop in one hand. God, I'm really starting to hate that thing. "Of course," he says and pulls away. "Liz, could you give us a minute? And make sure your parents don't come in?"

She nods and pats him on the shoulder before vacating the area.

Connor pulls a wicker chair up next to the couch, then scoots a little closer so his knees almost touch my arm. I'm quick to drape my hand over my head like a Victorian maiden.

He puts the MacBook across his knees and opens it. He's wearing a different shirt from earlier, and I wonder if I got blood all over the other one. "I need to show you something," he says, "and I hope it doesn't creep you out."

I drop the bag of ice from my head and lean up on the couch. "God, it's not sexy pictures of my sister, is it?"

"What?" He laughs around the word.

"It's... well, you two looked so chummy on the beach last night, so..."

He squeezes his eyes shut, and muscles dance in his jaw. "I am such an idiot. Just... here." He shoves the laptop at me.

There's already a folder open, and it has my name on it. Because I'm so intelligent, I say, "It has my name on it."

His eyebrows are a straight, nervous line. "I know."

I scroll through a couple little thumbnails, all images, before opening one, and it's me. It's me not looking at the camera, sitting by Liz, and laughing about something she said. The next one is a picture of me reading in the shade.

There's even a close-up—he must have used zoom—of my profile.

"They're all pictures of me."

"Yeah, I know that too."

I have trouble swallowing. "Why?" I don't open all the pictures, but I scroll through. There are at least thirty; over half are from the previous summer.

"Look, it started out innocently last year," Connor says. "I'd just bought the new camera, and I'd applied to CUNY. To become a better director, I wanted to practice framing shots and the rule of thirds."

"What's that?"

"It doesn't matter. You... you were always around, so I used you for practice. And, Emory, you've always been—" He looks outside where gentle raindrops frolic over glass. "—beautiful. You've always been beautiful."

I have to search my entire body to find my voice. "I am now more confused."

"I like you, Emory." He sighs. "I *like you*, like you."

I'm not sure what weird thing my heart is doing, so I put my hand over it to make sure it's not trying to escape. "No, that doesn't— You like girls."

"I'm pretty fluid in that department. And, let's not forget, you were straight until two days ago."

My brain can't handle the present, so it time travels back to June twenty-first of last year. "The leg massage last year at the summer solstice party. Was that—? Were you—?"

"I wasn't even sure you remembered that."

"I remember." The very force of my voice makes his eyebrows rise.

Oh, I *remember*, Connor Nichols.

The summer before, I tried to avoid him, and he made it absolutely impossible, showing up everywhere I was until I gave up and smothered all emotion to make it through two long weeks with my unattainable fantasy right next door. Liz was the one who made me attend the last big party at the Outpost's abandoned pool. I may have been "overserved," and when "overserved," I tend to draw away from crowds even more than usual. That was how Connor and I ended up alone.

He found me sitting in the shadows at the far end of the pool all by myself. Pretty drunk, too; he almost knocked me into that big concrete hole when he grabbed my legs and put my ankles in his lap. I'm pretty sure I yelped but was soon silenced by his huge hands massaging up and down my calves with a singular focus.

Voice shaking, I asked, "What are you doing?"

I remember he laughed but didn't look up. "Trying to make your stubby legs grow."

Well, they had grown last fall, but they'd also felt like jelly the rest of that night. Afterwards, I swore I felt his warm fingers on me even while falling asleep. Sometimes, if I tried hard enough, I could still feel them.

Now, in the living room, he pokes my knee. "I didn't mind when your legs were short. I just wanted an excuse to touch you."

My eyes sting, and Jesus, this is not the time, Emory! I despise that I can be so emotional. My teachers always told me it's a good thing for writers to be vulnerable, but I hated believing them. I didn't want to be vulnerable—not ever and certainly not now.

"Hey," he says, and his voice is soft. "Hey, don't do that."

I wipe my eyes with the back of my hand. "Did you try to kiss me earlier?"

"Yeah. I didn't mean to give you a concussion."

I shove rain-damp hair out of my face. "So, what? You're bisexual?"

He leans his elbows on his knees, ever closer to me, and

he smells like laundry detergent. "I'm very Emory-sexual right now."

"Oh my God." I hide my face behind my hands. "Is it because of my stupid hair?"

"No." He chuckles. "Although I like your hair. I like a lot of things about you, not the least of which being we're both in New York this fall."

I peer out between two fingers. "Huh?"

"Look, I've had a lot of flings. I couldn't stand the thought of you being one or, I don't know, of me rushing things and messing up and you never wanting to talk to me again. But then, you said you were going to school in the city, too, and... and you accidentally told me you were gay. Then, Liz may have mentioned you find me attractive—"

I hide my face again. "I'm going to kill her."

"Don't." He wraps fingers gently around my wrists and pulls until I have no choice but to make eye contact or stare directly up. Unlike me, a probable tomato face, Connor is cool and serene with a soft smile on his lips. "She gave me the ultimatum. I had to come clean, or she would tell you about the pictures."

"I'm an ultimatum?"

"No. I was nervous to talk to you."

"But, I'm the nervous one."

"You don't have a monopoly, dude."

I fold my hands in my lap to keep from pulling out my hair. "Why would you be nervous to talk to me?"

"Because you can be intimidating. You're the smartest person I know, and you look like a Parisian runway model. What right do I have to talk to you?"

I sniffle and start crying again.

He puts one hand on my cheek. "I really need to stop doing that."

"I must have hit my head really hard, because this is definitely not happening."

With my eyes closed, I feel the couch dip at my hip, which means Connor is right freaking there. His other hand comes up to my other cheek, so he's cupping my whole face right now, and this would be such an inopportune moment to melt into a puddle.

"Emory Jones. Can I take you on a date?"

I nod, and he kisses my forehead, avoiding my bump. Fireworks explode behind my eyes.

"There's a carnival coming to town this weekend down on Bradenton."

"Yeah?"

He talks with his lips right against my skin, warm breath in my hair. "An authentic, old school circus. There'll even be a haunted house."

I hum an affirmative, and he nudges his nose against mine. I assume my eyes make an audible *click* when they pop open. Oh, Lord, he's going to kiss me. It's going to happen. It's really going to—

I pull back at the sound of barely contained stage-whispers.

"Mom!" Liz shouts, and I sit up straight.

My entire family has their heads poking around the door, watching.

I pull the throw blanket up around my body like I'm naked. "What the—? How long have you guys been there?"

"We were making sure you were feeling okay," Dad says as he basically tugs my mother and sister away by their hair.

Connor is still sitting right next to me, shaking the whole couch with giggles. When I apologize, he waves it off. "Your family is awesome."

"Yeah, right. Try living with them."

He shrugs. "Better than my dad right now."

"Speaking of, does he know that you're... I mean, this isn't going to turn into some after-school special where your dad, like, comes after me with a baseball bat for turning his son homo, is it?"

"Wow, uh, no." His eyes wrinkle shut when he laughs. "My parents are fully aware of my sexuality."

"And it doesn't bother them?"

"No. Well, my dad was a little uncomfortable at first, but he's cool now. My mom's going to be jealous more than anything. She has a huge crush on you this year."

"Stop it." I cringe just as the sun casts shadows across the living room. Storm gone, we're surrounded by nothing but light. "There's an irony somewhere here. Your dad doesn't care if you date dudes, but he can't stand the thought of you directing movies."

"What can I say? The man loves *Queer Eye* and hates Coppola."

I snicker and press the top of my head against his shoulder. As if a previously undiscovered reflex, his hand immediately cups the back of my neck, thumb in my hair.

"So can I take you to the carnival tomorrow night? I have to spend the day with my family first. Mom thinks we need to do some *healing*, I guess, so we're shopping in the city and bike riding—all three of us—but I can be here by seven."

"Okay." I nod. "You realize all those secret pictures would be super creepy if I wasn't obsessed with you."

"You're obsessed with me?"

"Oh my God, shut up!" I shriek. "You're the one who sniffed me yesterday!"

There's a long pause. "I am definitely not as smooth as I thought," he says.

CHAPTER 10

I wake up before my alarm clock, maybe because I'm excited but also maybe because there's a small man swinging a sledgehammer in my head. Holy shit, head wounds are no joke. Mom took me—forced me—to see a doctor after the Outpost incident. Then, during the night, Liz woke me every five seconds to shout, "You in a coma yet, princess?" I roll over and don't even have the fortitude to groan. I lay there, mouth open, trying to breathe.

Yesterday, it was almost like Connor knew I needed some space to process. He gave my hand a squeeze and left, grinning around the word "Tomorrow."

Tomorrow is now today. Today, I have a date with Connor Nichols.

I bet Mom makes me lay around until the exact moment Connor comes over tonight. She was a total nutcase yesterday, forbidding me to even go out on the lanai. Connor offered to walk Ella for me, which was... *swoon*.

Over dinner, Liz took it upon herself to weave the epic story of Connor and Emory, which was really a mere retelling of everything I already knew, mostly about the pictures. I'm still embarrassed about that. There are pictures of me on his laptop—just *existing*. I'm embarrassed, but I'm also a barrel of glee. Someone thinks I'm worth pictures. That someone is Connor Nichols.

My stomach lurches a little, but it's okay. It's okay. This is good. This is what I've dreamt about for three long years.

Saved by the witch cackle, I turn off my alarm and do my usual covert routine of looking out the window, waiting for Connor to run by.

I cuss and lurch back like a stunned turtle when I look down, and he's looking back at me. I hear his voice through the open window: "Morning."

I finger-brush my wild hair before leaning my elbows on the windowpane and returning the greeting.

His eyes crinkle. "Do you know what time I run by your window?"

"What? No." Mortified, I rub my eyes.

Bastard looks like he won a prize. He must have skipped his run because he's already dressed in khaki shorts and a tight blue tee. His hair is, of course, perfect, and even from a floor up, his eyes shine like the Caribbean Sea. "How's your head?"

I nudge at the butterfly bandages near my hairline. "It hurts."

"You going to rest today?"

"Yeah, Mom will probably have me on house arrest again." I press my lips together and feel a mixture of power and crippling fear when I realize his gaze moves to my mouth. "Uh... thanks for walking Ella last night."

He nods, hands on his hips. "No worries. Roberta's nice."

"Just don't get her talking about jazz."

"Ah." He glances toward the ocean. "Ella. As in Ella Fitzgerald. Got it."

The Nichols's side door opens, and out pops Mrs. Nichols

in bright-white capris and a low-cut pink top. I can practically see all the way down her shirt to her bellybutton from up here.

"Morning, Mrs. Nichols." I hold up a hand in greeting but feel practically naked knowing I'm in nothing but a well-worn T-shirt and boxer briefs with bed head.

She flaps her hand up at me. "Enough talking, you two. You'll have all night together. It's family time!"

I gulp at the idea of "all night." Pretty sure I'm nowhere near ready for *that* yet. Not that I don't want to, but I need to get well and used to the idea of Connor *like*-liking me before anything resembling an overabundance of oxytocin.

"Lou!" Mrs. Nichols bellows.

I must wince, because when I look at Connor, he's watching and laughing.

"Christ's sake, Maud, I'm coming!"

"You move slower than molasses in winter!"

It's too early for all this shouting, and let's not forget the sledgehammer in my skull—but this is how Connor's parents talk to each other. It's a constant contest to see who can hit higher decibels.

Mrs. Nichols climbs in the passenger seat of the huge family SUV as the side door bangs open and shut, and there's Lou dressed as Crocodile Dundee. Where the hell does this man buy his clothes? He walks toward the car and doesn't look up at me. At least, I don't think he does, until he shouts, "Nice hair, pretty boy! Friendly neighborhood madman—" He gets in the driver's side and slams the door before I can respond, so I lift an eyebrow at Connor.

"Say goodbye, Connor," Maud singsongs.

We say, "Goodbye, Connor," in unison and share a look before he salutes and disappears into the back of a car that probably cost as much as four years' college tuition.

I shower and put on swim trunks—wishful thinking,

considering I really doubt Mom will let me swim today. Plus, we're making ravioli this afternoon. Maybe she'll at least let me go on a morning walk? But maybe not. She's going to know I want to walk straight to the Outpost and continue the search for Leland.

Downstairs in the kitchen, Dad reads the *Longboat Key Observer* and sips coffee. He lifts his mug when he sees me but doesn't speak only because Mom is on the phone speaking fast-paced Italian to one of our New York relatives. I don't exactly speak Italian, but I understand a lot more than my mother realizes, which is why I lurch to a stop when I hear my name and recognize the word "ragazzo."

Boyfriend.

"Mom!" I squeak. "We haven't even had our first date!"

She tries to shoo me away with a flapping hand in the air, but I remain.

"What about my coffee?"

She makes entirely too much noise reaching for a coffee mug. Hot liquid almost sloshes over the top when she hands me my usual breakfast of caffeine and more caffeine.

Hand upright, I put all my fingers together and shake them toward the sky in homage to the Italian gesture I've witnessed all my life. Dad laughs quietly and shakes his head before returning to his morning java, and I go in search of some damn peace. Unlikely I'm going to find it, though, when I step outside and Liz is in the midst of a sun salutation.

"Morning, lover boy," she says as I slump into an Adirondack chair. "What did I tell you about coffee and your adrenals? This is a big day; you need to stay calm."

"I am calm."

"Liar."

I'm not lying. I don't know why I'm calm, but I am.

"What are you wearing for your date?"

Liz practices yoga with her eyes shut, so to be annoying, I shrug and sip coffee.

"I said, what are you wearing for your date!"

"I have no idea!" I shout back.

She lands on her stomach. I'm 98 percent sure "belly flop" is not a yoga posture. "How can you have no idea?"

"Dude. I just woke up."

She leaps to her feet, ponytail flying, and curls her spine to loom over me. "Emory Jones, this is the most important day of your life!"

"Mm, I'm pretty sure the day I got a full ride scholarship to NYU was the most important day of my life."

Under normal circumstances, she would whack me upside the head, but since I sustained a head injury yesterday, I assume she changes tactics. She grabs a handful of my shower-damp curls and yanks.

"Ow! Why?"

When she reaches out to touch my hair again, I curl my arms over my head and cower—but she doesn't pull. She finger-brushes. "Wonder if we have time to do a conditioning treatment."

"No. What's the matter with you today?"

"Everything needs to be perfect!" she roars and quickly covers her mouth with her hands.

My sister thrives on drama. She is the drama equivalent of an ambulance chaser. In the past, she always loved hearing about my botched dates, every gory detail. She never once worried about what I was wearing on said dates or if my hair was properly conditioned—so what the hell is this?

"Liz?"

She sits on her yoga mat, half covered with sand because everything in Florida is half covered in sand. "You like him so much, and I don't want you to get hurt."

I join her on the ground, shower fresh skin be damned. "I know."

"He likes you a lot too." She plucks at the spandex on her calf.

"Yeah?"

"That doesn't mean it's going to work, though."

"Uh, thanks?"

She lifts her lip in a sneer. "No, listen. You guys are fine as friends, but, like, romance changes things."

"You don't believe in romance." She really doesn't. A guy once bought her flowers, and she gave them to me.

"Okay, fine, well, I guess sex changes things."

"I am not having sex with him tonight."

"But you might someday."

I take a big, deep breath to keep from screaming. "Liz, it's a first date! If you could pass that information on to our parents, too, that would be great. Everyone's acting like I'm getting married!"

"Princess!" She grabs my hands in both of hers. "I'm sorry. Just... protect your heart, okay? Promise."

I open my mouth to speak but take pause. "I don't think I can promise that."

She clicks her tongue. "You're such a fucking softie."

"I know. I stole all your emotions in the womb."

She shoves me in the shoulder, and although the metaphorical storm has momentarily passed, I fear my sister is only going to get more psycho as the day progresses, inching ever closer to 7:00 p.m.

———

For a little while, Mom does actually allow me on the beach —but I'm forbidden from going near the water, which means I'm a stinky monster. I read *Salem's Lot*, but the book is half destroyed by the time I go up for lunch, aged paper soaking wet with my sweat. Mom is so disturbed she makes me rinse off in the shower again before getting ready for ravioli.

Like her great-grandmother before her, Mom doesn't use a pasta machine but rolls out her dough. She's in charge of the rolling because, so far, no one else in our foursome family has mastered the trick. While she does that, I'm in charge of the filling: spinach, ricotta, and garlic—vegetarian to make Liz happy, although I love it too. Anything with garlic is a masterpiece.

Halfway through our preparations, Dad comes back from an afternoon stroll. He takes off his aged Cleveland Indians baseball cap and gives Mom a smooch. "I walked down to the Outpost."

"Oh?" she asks.

"Oh?" I repeat. "Did you see Leland?"

He shakes his head no.

I whine, "Dad."

"Why don't I call the sheriff?"

"Yeah?"

He pats me on the shoulder. "It is strange that he hasn't been around lately. And his shopping cart looks terrible in the Nichols's garage."

I smile. "Thanks, Dad."

"It's nice of you to keep an eye on the old guy, even if he gets you drunk."

I start whistling and turn away. Back to work. Nothing to see here.

Before dinner, I have to sneak out to see Roberta because my mother keeps trying to make me nap as if I'm five years old. I find Roberta in a purple muumuu today, brushing at her seashell sculpture. She explains that yesterday's storm really did a number on it. Speaking of...

"Woo, boy, that was one handsome young gentleman who came by yesterday."

She's talking about Connor helping my injured ass by walking Ella.

"Friend of yours?" she asks.

I shrug one shoulder and press my lips together. Like most people on the key, Roberta doesn't know I'm gay. Christian as she is, I'm not sure how she'd react. There was a small contingent of kids at Perrysburg High School that used the phrase "pray the gay away," and I've been hesitant around God people ever since. Not that I think Roberta would start hurling holy water and speaking in tongues—but I'd rather not find out.

She walks with me some as I walk Ella. She grabs my whole head in her big, soft hands so she can glare at my butterfly bandages. "You need to be more careful, child."

I nod, although there is a certain amount of pride in knowing my current injury was not actually the fault of my clumsiness but a botched kiss. I almost trip over my own feet when I realize I might have a successful kiss within the next few hours.

Back home, because the Angelli ravioli recipe is awesome, dinner is awesome.

By 6:30 p.m., I've showered for the third time in one day at Liz's insistence, because apparently I can no longer be trusted to run my own life. I'm wearing a towel, and my bed is covered in clothes.

Standing at the closet, Liz shouts, "Nope," and throws another shirt onto the pile, almost completely burying me. "What about the black one?" Liz sips. She snuck a beer from downstairs, and we've been passing it back and forth. So much for never drinking again.

"I like the black one."

She puts her hands on her hips. "Will Connor like the

black one?"

"I don't know, Liz, but I need to get dressed."

Apparently in a fit of indignation, she spits beer on the floor. "How are you calm right now?"

I frown at the tiny puddle. "It feels good." I look up at her. "Going on a date with Connor feels... right. Does that make sense?"

"No. You're usually a wreck when you go on dates."

"I know." I feel all dopey and soft inside.

"Oh, God, this isn't one of those *Invasion of the Body Snatchers* things, is it?"

"Maybe for Connor. The fact that he actually wants to go on a date with *me*."

She almost bounces me off the bed when she sits. "I told you, that's a huge duh. You're hot, and he's bisexual. Put on the stupid black shirt."

"I thought you liked the black shirt."

She chews the inside of her lip and aggressively twirls her hair.

In the bathroom, I put on the aforementioned slim-fit, black button-down from Express over dark skinny jeans. My hair's doing that Shirley Temple thing Liz gets so bitter about, and I'm tan, so I don't look quite as hollow and gaunt as usual. When I dressed up as Edgar Allan Poe for Halloween one year, people thought he'd actually been reincarnated—minus the mustache.

Liz does a slow clap when I exit and give her a twirl. I grab the now lukewarm beer from her hand and finish it.

"Did you brush your teeth after dinner?"

I crush the empty can and hide it in my closet for now. "You've asked me that eighteen times."

She stands and gives me a hug. She still smells like tanning oil and the beach. "Okay, big brother, this is it. Go be you. Only, you know, cooler."

"Screw you." I laugh and pinch that ticklish spot on her side until she screams like a B-horror film actress.

———

I get a little jittery when I hear his voice in my family's kitchen, so I pause on the steps and give my hands a little shake. It's not bad jittery. It's the jittery I get during the opening credits of a horror movie I've never seen before. Like I can't wait to start screaming.

I rein in the fangirl when I see him; otherwise, I *will* start screaming. It should be illegal how good he looks in a navy-blue polo. It should be illegal the way his slim jeans cup his ass and amplify exactly how his thighs resemble tree trunks. He's even got product in his hair. Looks freshly shaved too. I pause to make sure my knees are still supporting me before taking a step forward.

I hear my mom say, "And he fell out of a chair in front of the whole school."

I freeze and press my fingers to my forehead. "Christ, Mom."

"We were telling him about your award," Dad says. They both look so preppy-suburban-parents right now. I don't remember them in all pastel earlier. Oh my God, did my parents dress up to meet my date?

Connor turns to greet me, and his blond eyelashes shimmer when he blinks. He opens his mouth and closes it, gaze landing somewhere near my collarbone before gifting me with the most covert eye fuck of my life. He says, "You look—"

"We should go," I say suddenly. Whatever he's about to say, I'd rather he not say it in front of my parents—and Liz, who's probably eavesdropping from the top of the steps.

"Yeah." Connor nods and pulls car keys from his pocket.

He smiles at my parents. "I'll have him back before he turns into a pumpkin."

"Oh." Mom pats his shoulder. "Get home when you get home."

"Enjoy the carnival, boys," Dad says, and I get the hell out of there before they can tell any other embarrassing stories about me. There are so many.

The Nichols's SUV is parked outside, and Connor actually rushes ahead of me so he can open the passenger side door.

I lift an eyebrow. "Seriously?"

"This is a date, Emory."

"Hmm." I climb in but not before I notice he smells like cologne. It's a clean sort of spicy scent, and he's never smelled that way before. Did he buy cologne in the city today—for our date? I try to get a quick glimpse of myself in the rearview mirror before he gets in the car because I suddenly wonder if I look good enough. Maybe I should have gone for that conditioning treatment?

As soon as he leaps up into the driver's seat, he looks at me.

I look at him.

We look away.

I look back at him as he says, "You look amazing," but I say, "You smell good," at the same time, so it's a mishmash mess of words followed by silence.

I hear Connor struggle to swallow. "Shit, I'm terrified right now. Why am I terrified?"

I pop my lips. "It's like in *What Lies Beneath*. All your life, Harrison Ford was a hero character, and all of a sudden he's murdering people."

More silence, but this time, it's a silence waiting to be filled, so I don't ruin the anticipation. Eventually, Connor says, "You're saying your character changed."

"No. Your *perception* of my character changed."

His smile is wide, face golden in the dwindling sun from the beach. "So instead of being something I could only touch with my camera, now——" He reaches ever so slowly across the center console and pokes me in the back of the hand. He bumps his fingertip over the backs of my knuckles.

I shiver and sneak my hand back, tucking both beneath my armpits, but no matter how much I try to hide my grin, I can't quite bite my lips enough.

"You know, when you do that, it makes your lips all puffy." The way he says it? Not an insult, nope. More like a prayer.

I cover my mouth with my hand and look out the window.

Previously, when guys picked me up for dates, the drive mostly consisted of awkward getting to know you chitchat, not *this*, whatever *this* is—verbal foreplay with my parents watching from the window.

"If we don't leave, I'm afraid I might do something stupid." *Like kiss you all over.*

"You never do anything stupid," he says.

"Watch me." I focus resolutely on outside and hope he'll start the car and drive before I latch onto his neck like a leech.

He mutters, "Interesting," but does start the car. Tepid air-conditioning shoots from the vents but starts to cool as he pulls out of our driveway and onto Gulf of Mexico Drive.

"How was family day?" I ask.

He groans.

"That good?"

"Well, Mom and I had fun. There's this shop in St. Armand's that sells fancy shoes. They had this pair of crystal-encrusted stilettos, and the sales guys were, like, salivating because I guess nobody ever tries on those shoes."

"Except your mom."

He nods. "Except my mom. Dad wouldn't let her buy them, though, because they were two grand."

"Holy shit."

"Yeah. He said nothing that expensive should go on her feet. He bought her ice cream instead, but twenty bucks says she'll own those shoes by summer solstice."

I run my finger across the windowsill and sink comfortably into the slick leather seat. "Your dad doesn't seem like a pushover."

Connor peeks away from the road long enough to smile at me. "He'd give my mom anything—anything to make her smile."

I don't see it, not in the way Connor's parents shout at each other—or the way Mr. Nichols treats his son. Or me, for that matter. But I guess we never really know what love looks like for other people. My parents make love look easy, but maybe some people like it hard.

Damn it, that wasn't a sex reference. Connor has got me so far in the gutter, I might as well be hanging with Pennywise.

"Hey, so tell me about the award you won."

"Oh, uh. Nothing." I tug at my shirtsleeves. "It was no big deal."

"Your mom said it was statewide. I think that's kind of a big deal."

I roll up my shirtsleeves and realize I'm fidgeting the way I always do when I want to deflect and disappear. I spent my childhood being picked on; it's still surreal to think someone actually now cares about what I do and who I am. "It was the perfect writing prompt for me. I swear it was a setup, like one of my counselors was behind it. I don't know. English students Ohio-wide had to do a rewrite of an Edgar Allan Poe story."

"You're kidding." We start crossing the first bridge closer

to Bradenton Beach, and Connor squints in the sun. "Hey, watch for dolphins."

Despite the clear water and white sand, I don't see any dark shapes. "Maybe it's their happy hour."

"So which story did you pick?"

"'Black Cat.'"

"Classic."

I turn one of the air vents away from me and toward Connor who's more in the sun. "Yeah, I wrote 'the cat,'" air quotes, "as a model for a nude art class. The teacher ends up bumping him off. It was really messed up, honestly. I can't believe I won. Then, I fell out of my chair at the award ceremony. It was very me."

There's some traffic up ahead, a mix of families leaving the beach and tourists hitting the bars. As we pass the main strip—a three-block segment of shops, restaurants, and one (apparently) epic dive bar called The Drift Inn—Connor says, "I don't think you're klutzy. Are you klutzy?"

"I wasn't. Then, I got all gangly."

"You're not gangly. You're gorgeous." He doesn't look at me when he says it, but I think he's blushing.

I spot the Ferris wheel first as the sun's setting and roll down my window. Back on Longboat, I bet the piper is playing "Amazing Grace." Here, on an open stretch of beach between Bradenton and Anna Maria Island, there are cars, blinking carnival rides, and the overpowering scent of popcorn and cinnamon almonds.

I grin with glee and hope I don't look deranged, but I probably do because Connor says, "You really like carnivals, don't you?"

I spin around to face him as he parks in the middle of sea grass. "Dude, have you ever read *Something Wicked This Way Comes*? Or, *The Night Circus*? Carnivals are creepy as shit! The lights are all blinking, and there are animatronics. And discordant music that makes your ears bleed! One time, I met this carnie guy who'd lost both his eyes, but he had glass eyes that were all crooked. All... *woooooo*." I dangle my fingers in front of my face and make them dance like worms.

"You are so twisted. Now, come on, the haunted house beckons. I want to hear you scream like a girl."

I scoff. "Will not!"

I'm so distracted looking around, Connor has to hold my hand like I'm a child, to keep me from running into people. I lean up on my toes to talk over the sound of a multicolored vintage calliope spewing music to our left.

I ask, "How's your stomach?"

He leans down, and his lips tickle my ear when he talks. "What do you mean?"

"Do you puke on rides?"

"Yes."

"So no Tilt-a-Whirl?"

He waggles his eyebrows. "You make me dizzy enough."

"Oh my God, that was sick."

"Come on." He slings his arm around my shoulders and draws me forward.

It's insanely packed with people everywhere. There's not a lot to do around Longboat except burn on the beach all day and pass out after too much seafood at dinner, so the carnival is a welcome distraction. Parents are here with their kids, and high schoolers are here with would-be dates. There is so much noise, what with the screaming voices and music, that it soon becomes a buzzing hive of ambient sound, cut only by Connor's voice.

"Those girls just checked you out."

I glance over my shoulder, and a dozen high school chicks with bleached blonde hair stare back.

"No," I say. "They just checked *you* out. They probably want to claw my eyes out for being with you."

"Oh, so you're *with me* now?"

I turn my face away, probably glowing like a lightning bug, but Connor squeezes me tighter. When we're forced to pass through a human bottleneck, he pushes me in front.

A dude who looks like Vincent Price sips frozen lemonade and watches us pass. Despite his dour expression, he's dressed like Leland: beach bum couture. I apologize when I bump into a short lady with a screaming kid, and by the time I look back, the Vincent clone is gone. Maybe I imagined him, what with the head wound and Vincent being a childhood icon of mine.

Away from all the food vendors and games, the crowd thins enough for Connor and me to walk side by side. "Can I ask you something?"

Shrug. "It'd be a really short date if you didn't."

He puts his hands in his pockets. "At all the parties at the Outpost, why haven't I ever caught you kissing anyone? I mean, I've seen Liz—"

"Oh, God, no, please. Desist."

His laugh is a flash of white. "Seriously, haven't you ever liked anyone down here?"

Shrugging is now my defense mechanism. "Maybe."

"Wait, wait." He puts a hand on my shoulder to get me to stop moving—and shrugging. "Liz said you're attracted to me. How long have you been attracted to me?"

I bark out a laugh and keep walking. "Oh, no. Hell no."

He takes running steps to keep up. "Emory!"

"Haunted house, up ahead. Let's go." I spin on my heel and walk backwards. "And I bet you scream like a girl before I do."

He shakes his head. "No way."

We pretty much race to get tickets and get in line, both bouncing on our toes like excited toddlers. There are only ten people in front of us leading up to the red-painted open maw of a mouth that indicates the entrance. I hear wonky carnival music from inside, ghost howls, and human screams. I must be high on proximity to fear because I say, "You smell amazing."

He swoops forward and lands a quick kiss behind my ear. "So do you."

Bang, I'm a just-rung gong.

The dude manning the door looks like every stereotypical fortuneteller I've ever seen in every movie ever. With long, greasy hair and a drooping mustache, he might as well have a grinder monkey on his shoulder while he plays a tiny accordion. Wait, he would need a clove cigarette, too, and plaid pants. He has none of those things—just the hair, but my imagination often runs away with me.

In my vision, the character would also give us some kind of wise warning before entering the haunted house—something like, "Beware a yellow strawberry" (insert French accent)—but this guy yawns, takes our tickets, and waits twenty seconds before letting us in.

I go in first because I always go in first at haunted houses. I don't like receiving secondary surprises.

The darkness smells like a fog machine. It takes my eyes some time to adjust to the flickering black light after the brightness of all the carnival rides outside. I run my hands over a sticky wall, and Connor puts his on my shoulders to use me as a guide.

Even though our walkway is slim, I know there have got to be hidden doors everywhere. Okay, there's a perfect hiding place up ahead. Paint glows in fluorescent strips made hazy by fake smog, but it's an optical illusion. There's a trap door right—

A girl covered in fake blood shrieks and grabs for us. I stumble back into Connor, who catches me, laughing. My heart *thump thumps* with a mixture of fear and *him*.

Five steps forward, and an animatronic clown swings down from the ceiling. Its bottled cackle is way scarier than the real thing. I clench my fists in front of me and giggle. I'm living for this.

Girls scream up ahead. Distracted by the sound, I almost knock Connor over when I take a lurching step backwards only to realize the fluffy-haired skeleton that scared me is actually— me, in a fun-house mirror.

"Shit," I mutter, clinging to Connor's shirt.

"Oh, is the little baby scared?"

Coming from anyone else, I would hate that tone of voice, so reminiscent of the boys who made my life a living hell growing up. Coming from Connor, it's sweet as candy corn, especially when he runs his thumb across my cheek. His breath smells like mint as he leans closer, closer—

Vincent Price's head pokes up behind him, and I shove Connor sideways.

The dude from earlier, the dude with the frozen lemonade, he was there—just there, by the trap door. I would swear on it, but he's already gone. Connor is back in my face, tucking curls behind my ear, and I see—

Red eyes.

Not here but, shit, after I hit my head in the basement at the Outpost, hadn't there been red eyes? Rats scattered, and those red eyes watched as I bled.

"Em, you okay?"

"Huh?"

"Are you all right?"

"Yeah." I run hands through my hair, feeling frankly nuts. "I thought—"

A chainsaw revs behind us, and big, tough Connor Nichols screams like a girl.

———

They set up picnic tables overlooking the beach, so here I sit, the stuffy smell of fog machine still in my nose, now mixed with the salty sea. Above black water, the half-moon hardly competes with the carnival's gaudy glow. Over the sound of someone's radio, I hear footsteps in the sand behind me and turn to find a smiling Connor with two plastic cups of beer. He hands me one and sits, our thighs touching.

"How'd you manage this?" I ask.

"I have a fake."

"Of course you do." I sip. "Nobody would believe me if I had a fake. They'd be like, 'Nice try, twelve-year-old.'"

Connor shakes his head. "Not anymore, dude."

"Before this goes any further, I think you should know I'm losing my mind."

"Sweet." He swallows a big gulp and licks his top lip.

"I'm serious. I saw Vincent Price in the haunted house. He was following us."

"Vincent Price?" For some reason, he runs his palm down my shin and squeezes my ankle. I get goose bumps. Everywhere. "Of Michael Jackson's 'Thriller' fame. The best voice in horror movie history?"

"It is so hot that you know that."

He smirks. "Price died in '93."

I whimper and dig my teeth into my bottom lip.

"Wait."

Shit, he noticed.

"Is horror movie banter like pillow talk for you?"

By the time he comes to his embarrassing conclusion, it's been silent for way too long.

"Oh my God!" He wears an openmouthed grin that makes me want to run off down the beach, hands flailing like a wacky waving tube man. Connor's hand on my knee grounds me as if he knows I'm prepped to flee.

Beer wedged between my knees, I tug my hair. "Why do

you do this to me?"

"What?"

"I feel like such an awkward idiot around you all the time! It is so frustrating."

He squeezes my knee. Jesus, his palm practically covers the entire width of my thigh. "Hey, I'm not attracted to you because you're cool."

"Gee, thanks."

"Emory"—he sighs and gazes out at the sea—"Because of football, I have been the cool kid my whole life. I've dated the cool kids. But it was never real. They all liked me because I was the football star, not because of my secret fascination with geeky horror films. You know nothing about football, but you like me anyway."

"I have a crush on Tom Brady. Who looks kind of like you, now that I think about it."

He pauses to take a sip of beer. "Don't worry about being cool, Em. Just be you. You're the one I like."

I blow hair out of my face on a strong exhale. "Even though I'm going insane?"

"It'll keep things interesting."

"I think I saw red, glowing eyes when I fell through that hole at the Outpost."

"Mm-hmm. Right, okay." His straight face only lasts three seconds.

"In my defense, there were rats, and I had sustained a blow to the head."

He concedes, "In your defense."

"But there would be red, glowing eyes at the Outpost, right?" I ask. "There's something spooky about that place."

Connor rests his elbows on his knees and drinks his beer. "Sounds like you want to move in."

"How do you know me so well?"

He smiles and nudges his elbow against mine, so I nudge

back.

For the record, I have never had banter like this on a first date. No one has ever caught all my movie references or answered in kind. No one has ever set me up for jokes; adversely, the jokes have never come so easily. Liz always says I'm funny, but I may not have believed her until now. Maybe I am funny. Maybe I am attractive. What else might I be?

I swirl a bit of beer in my mouth, considering, until it's warm and flat, which is obviously when Connor tries to kiss me (again), and I spit beer all over his face and my jeans.

He sits there with my beer-spit dripping down his chin while I squawk like a duck. Pretty sure I'm muttering some as-yet-unidentified version of the English language known as "Vowels for Dummies." I apologize and apologize some more.

"We are never going to kiss," he says as he uses his Polo to wipe his face.

I'm sitting on a Florida beach on a cloudless night with the boy I like who actually likes me back, so I figure, why not? I might be funny. I might be attractive. I might even be brave, so I lean forward and kiss *him*.

It's not hugely gratifying, more like a tease than anything else, with his upper lip between both of mine and his bottom lip dangling before I pull back. For a beat, his eyes remain closed, mouth half open. Then, blue eyes blink back at me before Connor surges forward, holds my head in his hands, and does a swan dive against my mouth.

Good thing I was prepared or someone would have busted a lip—and wouldn't that have been so *us?* When his tongue gets involved, I hike one of my legs up and over until I'm straddling him on the picnic table. Based on the place-ment of his hands on my ass, Connor is pleased with this development. As he kisses down my neck, I look heavenward and thank whatever deity gifted Connor Nichols with such a magical mouth.

SARA DOBIE BAUER

———

I gasp when Connor shoves me against the garage door of his family's beach house. Luckily, he's there to swallow the sound before any of our parents are the wiser. Crushed between the wall and *him*, my hands go up his shirt, fingertips digging into hard muscle. Connor kisses every inch of my skin he can reach, and I can only imagine the whisker burn I'll have in the morning. He tugs on my hair—again. It's got to be clown-wig size by now, and I don't care. I want him to wreck me.

This, dear friends, is the longest first kiss in history.

True, we had to take a slight breather on the drive back from Bradenton Beach, but I'm pretty sure Connor destroyed the speed limit to make it here, in the soft red glow of sea turtle lights, where we have a modicum of privacy.

He moves his mouth away, and I lean forward to make chase, but Connor just smiles and shakes his head before pressing our hips together. My eyes roll back in my head as he cusses against my ear. "You are so sexy," he says. "Please come upstairs?"

What did he say? Damn, it's hard to think with the taste of his tongue in my mouth.

"Can you be quiet?" he whispers.

Wait, what? Is he suggesting—? Oh, shit, he's *suggesting*. I do my best to blink away the lust haze, but the world is still tinted red, thanks to the patio lights, and his thumbs are teasing into my hips.

I like Connor. I do. Frankly, I'm obsessed with him, but I'm also a fan of being wooed. I lean the top of my head against his chest. "Too soon," I mutter, but I'm so out of breath, I'm not sure he hears anything.

"Hmm?"

I lift my head, and he's as far gone as me. His expression

is an indecent exposure charge waiting to happen. "Too soon," I repeat.

He closes his eyes, winces. "Shit, you're right. I'm sorry."

"Don't apologize." I rub my face against the side of his neck. "Silly thing to apologize for." I sound drunk, and I didn't even finish my beer back on the beach.

He lifts my chin and stares me in the face. "Kissing you is — You make me feel like my insides are melting."

In response, I wrap my arms around his head and start kissing him again until he pushes me away with his hands on my chest. He has to push a couple times before I get the message.

"If we don't stop—" He chews on his tongue. "Emory, we need to stop."

"Mm." I don't kiss him again—because I *can* be a good boy—but I do lift onto my toes and hug him. He hugs back, his face against mine, and doesn't even hide that he's sniffing me this time. "Do I really smell that good?"

When he speaks, his breath is hot and sticky against my throat. "Yeah, dude, like sunshine and rainbows."

"Fuck off."

He chuckles and revisits our earlier conversation in the car. "I'm still sort of terrified about this," he says. "Maybe more so now that I've discovered what an excellent kisser you are. Don't let me fuck up."

"I make no guarantees," I whisper. "Historically, I'm terrible at relationships."

"Well, let's do our best to keep each other in line, huh?" He pulls back first but not before kissing the tip of my nose. "For starters, you need to get out of here before I ravage you in the bushes."

"*You* get out of here."

"This is *my* side of the driveway."

"Blah, blah." I scoop handfuls of curls out of my face as I

adjust my jeans and stumble away, totally bowlegged.

"Emory?"

I spin back around, prepared for a friendly tackle.

"That 'Black Cat' story of yours," he says. "Can I read it?"

"Oh, uh..." No one I've dated has ever read my work. I'm always afraid they're going to hate it and then, poof, there goes the relationship. Hell, no one I've dated has even *asked* to read my work, so I've never had to deal with this situation. Would it be bad to say no? Am I supposed to say yes? "Um."

"I don't have to," he says quickly. "I thought writing is a big part of you, so..." Half his face is lit red, the other in shadow. "Emory?"

Christ, again, I've zoned out. Kisses make me dumb. "Sure, yes, you can read it. Sorry."

"Are you sure? It's not—"

"Yes, no, it's... No one's ever asked to see my work before."

He seems shocked, his chin scooping back toward his neck. "Oh. Really? That seems rude."

Now that I think about it, he's right; it is rude. All the guys I've dated knew I was a writer, yet none of them wanted to read my stuff. Rude, indeed. How am I just realizing this?

"Well," Connor says, "I want to read your work." He smirks like he's proud of himself, and I grin in response. "Now, get out of here before I kiss you again."

"That doesn't sound like a threat."

"It does to my self-control."

I give a dramatic bow before spinning around and opening the unlocked door to my family's house. It's silent inside. I have no idea what time it is, but all's quiet and dark. I lean back against the closed door and close my eyes.

Might as well have left a glass slipper in the drive. I am Cinderella without the dress. Someday my prince will come? Fuck that. He's here.

CHAPTER 11

Screamin' Jay Hawkins sings "I Put a Spell On You," so I flail around my bed sheets until I find my cell. I shove it to my face. "'M, hullo?"

"Mr. Jones?"

"Tom Selleck?"

"I'm sorry?"

I rub my eyes. "Oh, uh, sheriff?"

"Sorry to wake you, son. Thought you'd want to know that, along with your father's, we've had additional calls about Leland."

I sit up in bed, still woozy from the sudden wakeup call.

"The citizens of Longboat are indeed a bit worried about the lack of his presence around town, so I'll be looking into it." I hear the creak of his chair—a sound so ominous days earlier but now just a chair. "You mentioned you found blood at the Outpost?"

I sigh. "Well, we did, but when we went back, it was gone."

"Come again?"

I poke angrily at my pillow. "We did find blood in room

306, which was when we came to see you, but when we went back—"

"I told you it's trespassing."

It is too early for this, and the princess has not had his coffee. "It was nothing," I lie. "Leland liked to stay in room 306 when he crashed at the Outpost. That's all I know. Oh, and we have his grocery cart. I didn't want anyone messing with it."

"Fine, son. Why don't you hang onto it for now?"

"Yes, sir." Good thing he can't hear my eyes roll through the phone.

"I'll find Leland, don't you worry. Have a fine day, now."

Despite the fact that I don't entirely believe in Tom Selleck (well, I believe in his hairy forearms), I do feel a sense of relief knowing Connor and I aren't the only two people looking for Leland. I miss our afternoon chats, his stories and unassuming blips of wisdom. The man survived Vietnam, damn it; no way a hotel monster is going to spell his end.

Monster. Where'd that come from? *Salem's Lot*, most likely. But if we're going literary, it could be the ghost of a past tenant like in *The Haunting of Hill House*. Or maybe a demon like in *The Exorcist*. These are obviously the most sensible choices.

The witch cackles. I stick my head out the window in time to watch Connor sprint by, although he grins up at me as he slows and eventually walks in a circle before stopping beneath my window.

"I'm tempted to start spouting Shakespeare."

"Does that make you Juliet?" he asks.

"Ha."

"Sleep okay?"

"Like the dead. Tom Selleck just called."

"What?" He wipes sweat off his face with his arm, and I don't want to lick it. I don't.

"The sheriff. He's looking for Leland too."

"'Too' would insinuate we're still looking for him."

I blow hair out of my face. "Duh. Got something better to do?"

He eyes my bare chest. "I have a couple ideas."

I curl my shoulders forward and hug myself.

"You are so cute when you're embarrassed."

"Gah!" I duck beneath the windowpane so all he can probably see is the tangled top of my head. "Go do whatever it is you do in the morning!"

"Fine, fine. See you later?"

I wave my hand in the air but still cower out of view—as if he doesn't see me every day on the Florida beach with my shirt off.

I'm hesitant to shower. Occasionally, I still get a whiff of Connor's cologne, hidden somewhere between my ear and shoulder—maybe in my hair. But, no, I need to shower because I shower every day, and if I don't *today*, Liz will only give me more hell. I wash up and smack a new Band-Aid on my head wound. I'm already mentally preparing for my sister's verbal attack when I hop down the stairs and into the kitchen.

Dad is gone golfing, but Mom stands there with a steaming mug in her hand, one eyebrow raised. I immediately grin—nice poker face—and say, "Bless you," before taking my java to the patio. Liz is, I don't know, in Pissing Dog pose (trademark) when I speed past her and onto the beach, sand cold from the night air.

Behind me, I hear a *thump*, followed by, "Emory Marcello Santino Jones!"

Oh, boy, all four names.

Yes, I have four. Since my first and last names are so very Dad's side of the family, my New York uncles insisted Mom memorialize both Italian great-grandfathers through me. The bane of my kindergarten existence was learning to write my full name. That and Kitty Matthews licking my face. She would grow up to be prom queen, but she licked my face long before they gave her a crown.

If it's possible to stomp through sand, Liz stomps through sand. She reaches me as my toes touch the breaking waves and smacks me hard between the shoulder blades.

"Damn it, Liz!"

She whips her ponytail around like a horse fighting flies. "Tell me everything!"

I giggle. "No. Gross."

Her jaw drops open so far, I see her wisdom teeth. We Jones twins have big mouths. "You didn't have sex, did you?"

"No! And why would you even want to know?"

"I don't want to know." She grabs my arm and shakes, almost spilling coffee. "But I do want to know!" She grins, and there it is: the resemblance that lets the world know we're twins. We have the same smile that shows off all our teeth, the same nose crinkle, and the same smooshed up green eyes. She links her hand through mine and starts walking down the beach. "Seriously, how was it? Was it everything you've dreamed? Did he open doors for you and buy you a milkshake and did you share a straw? Or like in *Lady and the Tramp*, was it spaghetti?"

"Liz, we were at the carnival."

"So, no spaghetti. Did you kiss? Oh my God! Did you kiss?"

I shush her because her voice is louder than an entire ocean—and the Gulf looks wild today. Waves break strong and steady, and foamy residue tickles my toes.

"Did you?" she asks.

"Yes, we kissed." I gesture to my mouth. "Have you not looked at my face?" I put lotion on after my shower, but anyone paying attention will be able to tell I'm whisker chapped.

She leans up on her toes to gawk at me. "Holy shit, bro! You totally kissed!" She sighs and leans her head against my shoulder. "Was it perfect?"

I watch the breaking waves up ahead and take a breath to speak—but stop when I see something that does not belong on a Longboat beach.

There's suddenly too much spit in my mouth, a good indication that I'm going to vomit, but I need to get Liz out of there first. I drop my coffee mug and spin her around to face me. "Liz. Go back to the house."

"What?"

"Go back to the house, okay?"

"What are you—?" She glances over her shoulder. I try to stop her, but it's too late. She backs into me and starts screaming because there's a butchered body on the beach ten feet in front of us. The water around the corpse bleeds red, and there are... parts. An arm floats freely near the torso, and I'm suddenly a vegetarian. I at least won't be eating ground beef for the rest of my life.

A new wave brings a head, and Liz now sounds like a train whistle. A dead body is bad enough, but I recognize that big, black earring gauge from a party at the Outpost. Yep, a dead body is bad enough, but Liz made out with this dead body.

His name was Duke.

Liz tilts forward and hurls enough for both of us.

———

They cordoned off a big area of the beach, so the gawkers can't see Duke's body at least. The red-blue light of cop cars splashes into my eyes. Liz is still freaking out with my parents inside while Roberta and I watch from beneath a copse of trees. A couple coast guard boats whizz by as she mumbles the Lord's Prayer.

"Heavens, oh, heavens," she whispers. A big, white hat protects her face from the sun, and her huge sundress expands like a parachute in the breeze. "Deadly business like this hasn't happened in eight long years." She tugs on the sleeve of my T-shirt. "You promise me you won't go swimming today, Emory Jones."

"Hmm?" I keep seeing Duke's one remaining eyeball staring back at me. Fish probably got the other.

"You won't go near that water."

"Oh. No, not today."

Roberta presses her big, red lips together. "Mm-hmm. And maybe not tomorrow either, you being such a little snack. You hear me?"

"Hmm? Yes." I nod at her but keep staring at the beach where authorities run like ants under a magnifying glass and onlookers hope for a hint of the macabre.

"Good. Now, I'm going to go hug my dog." She waddles away in the imperious fashion only a real tough cookie can manage.

I'm pretty sure I leap a foot in the air when someone grabs me from the left. I crouch, ready to swing, but huff out a breath when I recognize Connor standing there with his hands in front of him.

"Sorry, sorry."

"Shit," I mutter.

"Are you okay?"

"Yeah." I violently push hair off my face and over the top of my head. Because hair is stupid, it falls right back into my face, and I consider scissors—but my hair. Everyone just *loves my hair*. God, I feel like tearing it out. Or punching something. Bet I could punch Connor, and he wouldn't even notice. He'd think I was a six-foot mosquito.

He crosses his arms, and we face the blinking lights together. "I've never heard of a shark attack around here. Have you?"

"Doesn't mean it didn't happen," I reply. Why is Connor being so obtuse? Sharks eat things. Why is he questioning Mother Freaking Nature? Is he a fool? I can't date a fool. Why am I—? Connor is not a fool. Why am I thinking...?

God, my brain is so loud, and I can't get the image of red water out of my head. I pinch the inside of my arm to try and calm down.

"It just"—he shrugs—"seems unlikely."

"Well, unless he got into a fight with a meat grinder—" A sob makes my whole chest heave, and Connor is there whether I want him or not. He shields me in a hug, my snotty face shoved against his chest. I grip the back of his shirt but not before I do smack my palm against his upper back once. A baffling mix of grief and fear fuels me. I swim at night sometimes. That could have been me. I even joke about the horrific opening scene of *Jaws*, and now, some guy is dead. Jesus, I'm terrible.

"Hey," he whispers. "Talk to me."

I'm only snuffling now, calming down. "I was in such a good mood this morning."

"Me, too." He presses his cheek against the top of my head. I want to melt into him, disappear, and forget about bloody stumps and ear piercings. "Why don't we go inside? We can watch *The Golden Girls*."

"*The Golden Girls*?"

"When I was a kid and got scared, my mom made me watch *The Golden Girls*. It worked wonders." He squeezes me and lets go, putting some space between us. "Maybe I can even sneak us some famous sangria."

I shake my head. "Nothing red."

"Right. Sorry."

I wipe half-dried tears from my face. They already feel sticky, but that might be the humidity.

Connor takes my hand and pulls me toward his house, but I take one last look back and spot the sheriff looking stressed out and sweaty. Something tells me the official search for Leland will be put on hold.

CHAPTER 12

Well, today has been one big bummer. Even watching *Golden Girls* didn't help, possibly because Maud played helicopter parent the whole time and kept bopping me on the head while force-feeding me sweet tea. I could have gone for a cuddle, but it felt weird climbing all over Connor with his mom flitting in and out like an overdressed gnat.

Instead of cuddling, Connor tried to guess which Golden Girl I would be. He concluded pretty easily that I'm Dorothy, but I say a mix between Dorothy and Sophia due to my tendency to slip into a New York accent when my Italian family is around. Connor didn't fit any of them, although I could see him growing into Blanche one day. He'd be that hot middle-aged dad in the suburbs with his wife and kids and teenage girls drooling all over him.

When I explained this, he made a funny face and said, "Who says I want any of that?"

I said that was just one of many possible storylines. I could as easily see him on an Oscar's red carpet or para-chuting out of a plane to fight terrorists.

I now sit on our sandy patio and watch the waves. With their frothy, white caps, they look innocent yet purr with menace. The biggest shark I've ever seen on Longboat was the size of my forearm, caught and thrashing on some kid's fishing pole. The only dark shapes you'll spot are dolphins. None of this makes sense.

All the cop cars are gone, and the beach is empty. I could run around naked, and no one would notice. Well, Liz would since she's creeping up on me like she has something to hide.

"What?" I bark. I'm not in the mood for loitering.

She changed out of her yoga gear right after we found Duke. I think I heard her muttering something about "smelling blood" on her clothes. Now, she's in a yellow sundress that floats around in the wind. "Where were you earlier?"

"Watching *Golden Girls* with Connor."

"*Golden Girls*?" When I don't say anything, she sits in a chair next to mine.

I'm far into my own head, but I need to surface—at least long enough to check on my twin. "How are you feeling?"

She shrugs. "I was just on the phone with some people."

I lean over and poke at my toes. "*National Enquirer*? 'The love of my life, killed by a man-eating monster.'"

"That's not funny."

"Sorry."

She hugs her freckled knees against her chest. "Promise you won't go all Fox Mulder on me."

An *X-Files* reference? That gets my attention.

She pushes her long, dark hair behind her ears before pulling it into a ponytail over her shoulder and whirling it around her fingers. "I thought it was weird, Duke getting attacked by a shark. Because Duke doesn't know how to swim. Didn't." She clears her throat, and I prepare for projectile vomit. "I found that out when we played Never Have I

Ever the night we met. He didn't know how to swim, Emory. He never went near the water. Then, I was talking to some people who were with him last night at the Outpost." She pauses and looks over at me.

"What, Liz?"

Whatever it is, she doesn't want to tell me. She has her lips pressed together like I always do, but I do it because I think my lips are too pink. When she does it, I know she's deciding between the truth and a lie. "He was drunk last night, but he didn't want to go home because his parents would know, so he— His friends said he went to sleep it off in one of the abandoned rooms. Duke didn't go in the ocean last night."

Then how did he end up there?

I'm on my feet before Liz can grab me, but she yells my name.

Then, like a banshee from hell, she screeches: *"Connor!"*

Three seconds later, he stumbles out the door of his family's patio, rubbing his eyes, all sleep-soft and confused. I have no clue why my sister is bringing him into this, so we all freeze for a beat, staring at each other before Liz points at me.

"Stop him!"

Connor looks back and forth between us. "What?"

She flails at me. "Make him stop moving!"

"Shit," I mutter. Liz knows she can't prevent me from going to the Outpost, but Connor can. I dart right, as if it's going to make a bit of difference. I hear scuffling behind me. Next thing I know, I'm suspended over six feet above the ground, folded over Connor's shoulder. His arms wrap tightly around my thighs as his shoulder digs into my stomach. I hang my upper body limply down his back because, frankly, this is embarrassing.

Nobody speaks.

Connor eventually breaks the silence. "Not that I mind, but why am I impeding forward progress?"

"Because if there is a serial killer hiding at the Outpost, I don't want my brother rushing off to meet him!"

Way to be dramatic, sis.

"A serial killer?" He puts me down but keeps fingers wrapped around my upper arm. "I think we should go inside."

———

In Connor's bedroom, Liz slouches at the end of his bed. I'm too wired to sit, so I stand with my back against the wall, arms crossed, and try not to bounce on my toes.

He sits in his desk chair and swivels around to face us. "So. Serial killer?" He lifts his eyebrows at me as if this serial killer thing is all my idea, but I gesture to Liz.

"Go ahead. Tell him."

Liz starts explaining, and as any annoying big brother would, I interrupt when she says, "We played Never Have I Ever."

"You mean you made out with him."

"Shut up, you whore!" she screams.

"Make me!"

"Guys, cut it out!" Connor shouts.

We behave immediately.

"So you were playing Never Have I Ever..." he leads.

"Yes, and someone said, 'Never have I ever gone swimming in the ocean,' and Duke was the only person who didn't drink because he's scared of water." She lifts her hands, palms up, as if that should be enough explanation for her serial killer conclusion.

Connor taps his finger on his chin, mulling this over. "Hmm, so not a shark attack then? Although a serial killer seems unlikely, you two."

I shake my head. "I didn't say I thought it was a serial killer."

Liz slaps the tops of her thighs. "Then what the fuck do you think, boy genius?"

"I think your antagonism is uncalled for."

Connor literally growls at me. It's a tie between sexy and scary. "Emory."

"Cannibals," I say. "Demons, maybe? Not sure yet. Need further investigation."

Now, Connor leans forward in his chair and covers his face with his hands.

"I was considering vampires at first since, you know, bad shit seems to happen at night. But that's doubtful since a vampire wouldn't throw a perfectly good corpse into the ocean. Then, I was thinking Outpost ghost, but I've never heard of a ghost dismembering someone before. I guess it could be a wendigo, but—"

"Em." Connor pulls his hair until it stands up straight. "No. None of those things are real."

I sound like a squeaking dog toy. "Hey, you're supposed to be on my side!"

"Just because I want to get into your pants?"

I choke on some spit, and Liz makes a retching noise. "I did *not* sign up for this shit," she says.

"Okay, look." Connor bows his head in apology to my sister, and the room goes silent. I imagine he'd be a great kindergarten teacher. If you can tame the Jones twins, you can tame anybody. "Let's be sensible."

Liz and I share a panicked looked because sensible, we are not.

He stands and paces. "The coroner will be able to tell if it really was a shark attack, right?"

I shrug. With all my horror movie expertise, you'd think this would be something I would know. I mean, as previously

SARA DOBIE BAUER

discussed, I've seen *Jaws* more times than I've seen the sunrise.

"Not necessarily," Liz says. "If there was a strong undertow, the body could be compromised due to sand, rocks, or small fish." She pauses. "Why do I know that?" And frowns at me. "God, I need to stop hanging out with you."

"So it could be a shark attack." He crouches down in front of Liz. "I heard what you said, but maybe if Duke was drunk enough, he went in the wrong direction and fell asleep on the beach. Tide took him out, and—"

I cut off this stupid sensible talk. "Roberta said there hasn't been a fatal shark attack on Longboat Key in eight years."

Connor stands. "Maybe it was just time. Like Vesuvius."

"Don't distract me with your knowledge of Roman history."

"Wait." Liz twirls hair between her fingers. "Eight years ago. Isn't that when the Outpost closed down?"

"Yeah." Connor nods.

"Why did the Outpost close down?"

Connor and I look at each other and shrug.

We do a search on the *Observer* website and come across an archived article, headline: "Financial Trouble Ends Outpost Beach Resort." Liz sits at Connor's desk and reads, but I fixate on the article's header image: a fuzzy, old photo of a thin, handsome, smiling man in a suit. God, he looks familiar. Where have I see him before? Something about the eyes...

"Gerald Krauss," Liz says. "Original owner of the Outpost. Once a successful businessman in the area." Her eyes skim across the glowing screen. "Then, all of a sudden, he declared bankruptcy eight years ago, lost everything, and disappeared. Huh."

I put my hands on her shoulders. "Why are we huh-ing?"

"It seems weird that nobody swooped in and bought it. The place was still in good shape when it closed down. Prime location. Growing tourist market."

"You really are going to be a business major, aren't you?"

She leans her head back and looks at me. "We weren't all born to be artists, princess."

I stare at the picture of Gerald Krauss and feel a little tickle along my spine. "We need the real story. Newspapers are all a conspiracy."

Liz sighs. "I told you not to go Fox Mulder on me. What did you have in mind?"

I press my lips together before speaking. "We need Roberta."

———

Ella Fitzgerald plays from an actual turntable. I didn't know people still owned turntables. The house smells like meat and potatoes. I blame the cheerful, white Crock-Pot on Roberta's kitchen counter for Liz's nauseous face. I'm not sure the last time she consumed meat, but after this morning's ground-up human, I'm sure she'll be a vegetarian for life. Even I'm having trouble swallowing all the spit in my mouth. Definitely taking my own minivacation from meat for a while.

Roberta shuffles in from her kitchen, humming along to the music. She carries a tray full of iced tea and vanilla wafers and sets it in front of the couch where Liz and I sit crammed together with Ella hogging most of the space. Connor has made himself comfortable leaning against the nearest doorframe.

Before sitting, Roberta adjusts her floor-length, zebra-striped muumuu and lands with a relieved huff into her favorite chair: a tattered green thing circa 1852. "Well." Metal bracelets jangle together on her thick wrists as she leans forward and grabs a sweating glass of tea. "I do love having guests. What can I do for you children this tragic day?"

I ignore the offered refreshments and lean my elbows on my knees. "We wanted to ask about the Outpost. It closed down eight years ago, right?"

"Mm-hmm. Quite the scandal when it happened. People lost jobs, and morale was very low. Folks thought it was the beginning of the end for Longboat. Of course, that was hog poop. Not a one resort has closed since." She slurps her tea as Connor steps up and lifts a handful of wafers.

He says, "There was a shark attack eight years ago too?"

"Oh, yes. Poor soul was one of the guests at the Outpost, baby." She raises a palm to the heavens. "God as my witness, that place has a veil of darkness over it, and do you know why?"

"Why?" I can't wait to hear, but I'm not expecting—

"Sasquatch, although some folks call him the skunk ape around here."

As slowly as possible, I turn to look at Connor, doing my best to keep a satisfied smirk off my face and failing miserably. He won't even look at me, just shakes his head with a similar smirk—although I'm sure his is one of disbelief.

Liz holds a vanilla wafer halfway to her mouth but, I assume, has no intention of actually eating it. "Why do you think it's Sasquatch, Roberta?"

She snaps her fingers. "It wasn't only me, girl. Guests at the Outpost, they started seeing things, hearing noises. Blamed it on some huge critter with gray hair. That son of a bitter mother has been spotted all over these Florida swamps. It's no surprise he might want a beach vacation."

I successfully turn a laugh into a cough.

I hear a quiet thud that is probably Connor hitting his head against the wall. "So you're saying Sasquatch is the reason the Outpost closed?"

"Mm-hmm. What else would it be?" She takes a sip that looks a lot like victory.

Liz stands and starts making excuses about how we need to be anywhere but there and Connor does the same, but Roberta gives me a look that's the ocular equivalent of "Sit your ass down." Not that Roberta would ever cuss.

"The young Mr. Emory Jones will be with you in time," she tells Liz and Connor, and the take-no-shit tone of her voice makes them both scurry. Roberta sets her glass down and folds her hands in her lap before tilting her chin down and gazing at me from below her wrinkled forehead. "I am no fool, Emory."

"I know."

"You send that tall drink of water down here the other day to walk Ella? Fine. But do not think I don't see the way he looks at you, boy."

My eyes have got to be as big as the moon. I check my exits. There's a possibility Roberta is about to bust out the holy water and start a gay exorcism, but I think I can make it outside before my skin burns. I need to hop the coffee table and—

"Do you need condoms?" she asks.

"*What?*" My tonsils leap up and squeeze my uvula.

Roberta sighs and comes to sit by me. It takes some maneuvering considering Roberta is a big woman and the room is small, but she makes it eventually and takes one of my hands in hers. "I know you are too young to remember, but we lost many a young man to that horrible eighties illness, and I need to make sure my Emory is healthy and safe."

I try to open my mouth and console her, but I drop my head instead. "You knew I was gay."

"Not until I saw the way Blondie was looking at you today.

Like he wanted to gobble you up—and you giving it right back."

I run fingers through my hair, mostly to mess it up so I can hide my face. "I thought you'd be... I don't know, grossed out or something."

She laughs. "Why, honey?"

"There were these kids at my high school who used to say they could 'pray my gay away.' I thought Christians—"

She pulls her hands from me and squeezes them into fists. "Oh, for the love of Otis Redding!"

I swear her cuss words get weirder every year.

"Don't you go lumping me in with those crazy Christians! *Pray the gay away*. That's like—" She gives me jazz hands. "—praying the Black away. Help me, Jesus. Now, listen. You are who you are, and you be who you are with who you love. You hear me?"

There were a lot of whos in that sentence, but yeah.

"When I lost my dear Harold, God rest him, twenty years ago, I was left with nothing but the love I felt for him. I've never lost that love. Love is all we have, child. So if you want to love that big, blond boy, you love him. He certainly can't take his eyes off you."

I disappear deeper into my hair to hide my blush.

She puts a warm hand on my arm. "But, honest now, do you have condoms?"

CHAPTER 13

We walk Ella down the beach. Waves tickle my bare toes, and Connor's hand occasionally tickles my arm as we saunter side by side.

"I guess it's sweet that she worries about you?"

I wince. "*Condoms*. A word I never thought I'd hear from Roberta's mouth." The leash gives a tug, and I jerk forward when Ella tries diving into a wave.

Connor grabs me by the hips to keep me steady. He doesn't let go. "How much do you weigh?"

"Huh?"

"You're really easy to pick up."

Ella keeps walking, so we do too.

"I *let* you pick me up," I mutter. "Wouldn't have been so easy if I'd unleashed the full power of my gangly limbs." I wave one arm and leg in the air like a coked-out marionette.

"Don't make it a contest, man. I'll win."

A warm sea breeze blows a bunch of hair into my face. Taming the wayward curls is a struggle.

"When did your parents do the birds and the bees talk?" Connor asks.

I glance over at him. In the near dark of twilight, his golden tan is even more impressive. "Well, pretty early, considering I kissed a boy in sixth grade."

"What? Really?"

When Ella again threatens to make me tumble, I give her leash a little tug until she slows to walk at my side. "Really, really. Matt... something. I can't remember his last name. Gave him a big old smooch under the bleachers on the soccer field. It was almost summer, so I remember my palms being all sweaty. And they'd just mowed the lawn, so my first kiss smelled like grass clippings."

"Ironic, considering your dad owns a landscaping business."

"I indeed have a longstanding, intimate relationship with the smell of grass clippings."

He chuckles as his hand bumps against the back of mine. "What did Matt do when you kissed him?"

I shrug. "Nothing much. Kissed back for a second. Then, we ran off to climb the jungle gym. He moved away that summer."

"The one that got away."

I kick at an ambitious wave. "Yeah, sure. I told my mom about it, and next thing I knew, there were all these books about sex nonchalantly scattered around our house. As if I might pick one up and start reading? The most passive aggressive birds and bees talk ever. When I didn't take the bait, Mom and Dad sat me down and asked if I wanted to kiss girls too. I assume I made a horrified face, because they actually looked relieved, like, 'Well, our son has a healthy libido, but at least he won't get anyone pregnant,' right?"

Connor laughs and puts his arm around my shoulder. "I love listening to you talk."

"Cut it out." I try sneaking out from under his arm, but

he holds tighter. "I can't even picture your dad giving a birds and bees talk."

"My birds and bees talk was actually sort of late," Connor says. "And it was because of *Rocky Horror Picture Show*."

"No shit?"

Ella hops and barks back at me.

"All right, all right." I pick up the pace. With the sun now securely beneath the ocean's edge, the light around us is faded red from nearby house lights. There is no moon.

"So you've seen *Rocky Horror*?" he asks.

"I'm an eighteen-year-old gay male. Growing up, I was never sure who I wanted to be more: Janet or Brad."

We look at each other and say, "Janet" at the same time.

He continues. "In eighth and ninth grade, I used to sneak out to the midnight showing in Saratoga Springs. I was already heavy into football, so I was pretty buff. One night, the guy who played The Creature got sick, so they asked me to stand in." He shrugs as if he hasn't just given me spank-bank material for the next fifteen years. "My dad found the gold speedo in my room. I had to come clean, so I took him to see the show."

I stop walking and do a twirl to duck out from under his arm. "Hold this." I hand him the leash in order to give a full, dramatic, hands-to-the-sky "What" pose and then scream the word.

Connor bends over, silently laughing, and my ego swells.

"Your father went to the midnight showing of *Rocky Horror Picture Show*?"

"Seriously, yes." He wipes the sides of his eyes.

"Holy shit, what did he think?"

"Tim Curry singing 'I'm Going Home' is, to this day, one of his favorite songs."

"Shut the front door!"

"Dude, the opposite. The door was blown off its hinges.

On the drive home, I told him I was bi."

I put my hand to my forehead. "I just can't. Your dad? When you first got here, he said I looked like a drag queen, and I remember thinking, 'How does Mr. Nichols even know about drag queens?'"

"Him and mom go to drag shows."

I shake my head, curls bouncing around. "Nope. Desist. If you keep talking, you'll alter my entire worldview, and I'll have to be committed."

He hums. "Emory in a straightjacket? That would make you way less wiggly."

I look at my hands like they have answers. "I'm wiggly?"

"Energetic maybe. Untamable?" He grabs my hand and pulls me closer. "But very fun to chase."

"I didn't know I was being pursued." I feel my mouth saying the words, but my voice sounds funny. I'm all breathless, like I ran a mile uphill in the snow in six-inch heels. My mouth falls open when our noses touch, and Connor talks into my mouth.

"My photo collection should be proof of that. Will you let me take pictures of you tomorrow on the beach? With you actually aware I'm taking pictures this time?"

I groan and lean my head back. "I look dumb in pictures."

He scoffs as Ella circles us. Her leash presses into the back of my knees, forcing me closer to Connor and his pissed off face. "Are you kidding? Em, you look amazing in photos. You're so photogenic, it's insane."

"Lies. Dirty lies." I'm not fishing; I'm really not. Even my own mother—who has pretty much worshipped everything I've done since I was a fetus—used to put my class pictures on the *side* of the fridge. From kindergarten to senior year, I could never get my face right. Like my face was allergic to the snap of a camera and would swell into embarrassing expressions as soon as the photographer said, "Smile."

"Come on, would I lie to you?"

"To get what you wanted? Probably."

His jaw drops open in mock offense.

I want to grab his chiseled chin and squeeze, because he's just too cute, but Ella chooses that moment to dart forward. Still tethered to her leash, which is wrapped behind my knees, she doesn't get far, but she does manage to make my knees buckle. I fall backwards, hands grabbing at air, before landing on my back in a breaking wave. I sputter at the salt water on my tongue and smack at the sopping wet hair in my face.

"Damn it, Ella!"

Oh, she loves this. She hops over and around me as my hands press fruitlessly at ever-shifting sand.

Connor extends his arm, but I can tell he's trying not to laugh. "Shit, are you okay?"

I use his grip to help myself up and am glad I have on nothing but board shorts and a tee. Sand-filled jeans would have probably weighed me down and dragged me out to sea. I lean down and rinse my hands. "I'm sort of nervous there's an evil spirit that shows up every time we almost kiss to muck things up."

"Shh, don't say that about Ella." He gestures to the wet, prancing Lassie dog that's having the time of her life. "Do you want to go back?"

"Not yet." I squeeze excess water from my hair. "Liz is picking the family movie tonight, and she'll probably want to watch some documentary about how chicken farms are evil."

He shrugs. "But they are evil."

"Please don't."

With a smirk, he starts walking again with Ella's leash in his hand. "Do you ever think about death?"

"Jesus," I hiss.

"Sure, he might be involved," Connor says.

143

SARA DOBIE BAUER

"No, I don't ever think about death—which is strange considering how much time I spend reading scary books and watching horror movies. You?"

"No, not really."

"Then, why'd you ask?"

He pauses to pick up a white shell that glows pink in the red night light. "I was thinking about that kid from today, I guess."

"Duke."

"Yeah. I'd like it if you didn't swim at night anymore. Is that weird?"

I put my hands in my pockets and try to shake some of the sand from my shorts. "I'm telling you, it wasn't a shark attack."

"No, it was Bigfoot obviously, but still. Would you not?"

"You worried about me, Connor Nichols?"

"No, you little punk. I just don't want Longboat's tourism to suffer because of your pretty, mangled corpse."

I kick at the back of his calf before shoving him in the shoulder. I duck and prep for retaliation—most likely a head-lock—but Connor stops abruptly and stares.

I didn't realize how close we were to the Outpost. Walking with Connor makes me lose all sense of time and space. I'm basically floating through a happy, horny void at all times when he's nearby.

I look where he's looking. Based on his wrinkled brow and scowl, I'm expecting a ghost or alien. Head on a spear? Nothing.

"What is it?" I ask.

He gulps. "What do you really think is going on?"

Ella chooses that moment to start barking her furry face off. It sounds like the dog equivalent of road rage, and it's all directed at the busted fence and overgrown palm trees of our favorite abandoned—possibly haunted—Florida resort.

144

I say her name, but she keeps barking. She howls once like a wolf when something moves ahead of us in the bushes.

"What the—"

Connor grabs tightly to my wrist when I move to investigate. "Emory, let's go."

"But—"

"No. You're not a superhero. Home. Let's go." He turns and drags a still-barking Ella and me behind.

I mumble incoherently and walk backwards, eyes on the gargantuan shadow of the Outpost.

"I can't believe you were about to investigate a strange noise. *And* you're not a virgin." He makes a slashing gesture across his neck. "Immediate death. Plus, dogs sense evil. After the day we've had, did you really want to go meet Evil?"

"Don't be so dramatic. It was probably rats having sex."

He puffs up his cheeks and blows out a breath. "Promise you won't set foot in the Outpost without me. Ever."

I'd like to make a joke, lessen the deep furrow between his brows, but my mouth goes dry. A stiff breeze makes me shiver in my wet clothes as I dislodge my tongue from my soft palate. "Why do you care so much about what I do?"

He twists his hand in the front of my shirt and pulls until his lips press against my ear. "Because I'd like to keep you around." He kisses the side of my neck and rubs one day's worth of scruff against my cheek. "And to think, Liz says you're the smart one."

"Hey, I am the smart one!"

He pulls away and gives me a playful shove. "Yeah, then, promise me."

I lift my right hand. "I promise I will not set foot on Outpost property without the supervision of one Mr. Connor Nichols. Happy?"

"Yes. Now, let's get this dog back to Roberta and go make out."

CHAPTER 14

When the witch cackles in the morning, I make her snooze twice—which is very unlike me. I'm an early-to-rise sort of guy. I also enjoy watching Connor run past, but I never hear the telltale sound of his sneakers on pavement. Maybe he's snoozing too? It certainly would be understandable considering what we got up to last night. I shiver just remembering and rub my face against my pillow, which— *ow*. Damn, my face hurts. What the—?

I groan my feet out of bed and force the rest of my exhausted body to stand. *Thwack-thwack* go my bare feet over the tile floor before I turn on the bathroom light and—

"Oh, shit."

The skin around my mouth looks burnt, and it's not from too much sun. It's from Connor's five o'clock shadow.

So, as it turns out, "making out" for Connor and me is a gateway activity. This may not come as a surprise. Last night, we did take Ella back to Roberta. We smiled and chatted for a bit, all manners. Near our houses, Connor went stealth mode to steal a blanket from his lanai without being noticed.

He grabbed my hand and dragged me to a semiprivate area with long beach grass and soft sand, and we made out. And we made out. And we made out. And we— I really need to work on my self-control.

Sensible Emory put the brakes on at the end of our first date, but Sensible Emory was apparently on vacation last night. Maybe it was the whole realization of our mortality, thanks to Duke's dismembered corpse? Well, maybe that explained Connor's enthusiasm, but years of fantasies and blue balls wrought my need to jump his bones.

Don't look at me like that! We didn't have sex, okay? Well, not like *sex*, sex.

God, I wonder where else I have whisker burn.

Although I had a little bit of whisker burn after our first date, there is no hiding my ruby-red face from my parents this time—not without Liz's help. I take a cool shower, hoping the angry blush will fade. It doesn't. I throw on swim trunks and a T-shirt and call my sister. She answers via Face-Time, upside down in a yoga pose. "Are you seriously calling me from upstairs?"

I cover my face. "I need your help."

She roars like a small dinosaur.

"Liz, seriously. Meet me in your room."

She hangs up without answering, but I know she's coming. When a Jones twin needs help, the other one always shows.

I check the hallway for parental presence. Finding none, I scurry to Liz's room at the back of the house and hide behind her door.

For someone who's so graceful when she does yoga, Liz stomps like an elephant up the steps and into her room. I put my hand over my mouth, whisper "Boo," and she shrieks.

"Goddamn it, Emory!"

I shut the door.

"What's the matter with you?"

I drop my hand.

Her mouth falls open. "Oh my God, your face! Are you okay? Are you allergic to something?"

I tilt my head and lower my eyebrows.

She lifts hers in reply and stares at me until realization dawns like caffeine hitting the blood. She wheezes on one huge guffaw. "Holy shit, is that whisker burn?" Her laughter shifts to a high-pitched hyena squeak. "Princess, you are in so much trouble."

"Liz, I need makeup." I put my hands in prayer position. "Please."

"I should make you walk around like this—your penance for being a slut." Her chin tips forward and back. If I were in a position to make fun, I'd say she looks like a chicken. "Where else do you have whisker burn?"

"Oh." I stick my fingers in my ears before singing, "La-la-la."

She latches onto my elbow and pulls. "Fine. I'll help you." She points to the end of her bed. "Sit."

I do what she says immediately. No need to poke the bear when the bear is saving your life. Not that I think my parents would literally kill me for being a horny teenager, but let's not find out.

In a white shirt and holographic turquoise yoga pants, Liz comes hopping with her makeup bag like a deranged bunny and almost knocks me off the bed when she lands at my side.

"Did you have caffeine today?" I ask.

"No. Remember? I respect my adrenals."

I have to squint my eyes to keep them from rolling.

I hear the click of compacts and makeup brushes as she digs around in her massive bag of stuff. My sister might be into organic food, but she's a makeup whore. She's always impeccable because she's watched every YouTube makeup tutorial ever made and is certifiably an artist. I even let her do me up once when we were younger in exchange for free movie tickets she won at a school dance. A man does what a man does.

"I'll use a bit of green concealer to—"

"Green? I'm not going for Wicked Witch."

"Are you doubting my abilities?"

I press my lips together and frown.

"That's what I thought. Green is opposite of red on the fucking color wheel, so it neutralizes redness." She sticks her tongue out at me like we're five and starts rubbing something alarmingly green onto my face. "Are you going too fast with Connor?"

"Too fast? This is our fourth summer together."

"Stop moving your mouth."

"Then, don't ask me questions!"

She groans. "Fine, then, I'll talk at you. I'm aware that this is our fourth summer spent next door to Connor and his family, but this is the first summer of you being your fabulous gay self and the first summer of Connor wanting, as stated yesterday, 'to get into your pants.'"

"Ugh, I can't believe he said that in front of you," I murmur through barely parted lips.

"You and me both." At least the next layer of foundation she pokes onto my face is flesh tone. "I'm just saying that sex is special, and you are special, so you shouldn't—"

"Besmirch the specialness?"

"Mm, yes. Exactly."

"Says the girl who lost her virginity to some frat boy at Bowling Green State."

She pokes my face with additional fervor. "Well, we can't all have Thom from Maumee."

"Mm, Thom from Maumee..."

I used to attend high school sporting events to check out guys from other schools. I'm not embarrassed to admit this.

Sure, it was sort of shady stalker of me to go to games just to cruise, but I wasn't interested in any of the guys at my own school, and my hormones were out of control. What the hell was I supposed to do? Hump trees?

Thom was a soccer player on the team of Perrysburg's most hated enemy, the dreaded Maumee Panthers. Located across the river from us, the rivalry mostly consisted of toilet papering public buildings and aggressively painting pillars in the middle of the Maumee River (long story). I had no stake in any of it, so when I spotted Thom in his bright purple and gold uniform—with purple socks even—I *wanted*.

I can't say for sure, but I assume he felt me watching from my post by the bleachers, surrounded by Liz and her friends, who I'd gotten good at ignoring over the years. Whatever the reason, Thom braved the Perrysburg sideline to invite me to a party. At sixteen, I'd dated a couple guys, all older and buff, and messed around some. I think boys liked how little I was back then, pretty—like a Christmas elf without the fun shoes.

Liz was gobsmacked that I would even consider going to a Maumee High School party, but she let me steal the car anyway. She offered to join, but twin sister cockblock is never a good look.

In hindsight, it could have easily been a setup. I was Perrysburg; Thom was Maumee. I was a sixteen-year-old gawky bird person; Thom was a senior star athlete. I could have shown up to a thorough beating. Instead, Thom kissed my cheek when I walked in. I remember he was freshly showered and smelled like cedar as he handed me a tepid beer that was half foam. I wasn't planning to lose my virginity that night; maybe people never do? It just happened.

Thom's house was huge—well, his parents' house, both of who were out of town on vacation in Mexico. After a couple beers and a ton of dancing, he took my hand and led me upstairs to a master bedroom with a mirror on the ceiling. *A mirror.* Apparently, things got kinky in Maumee?

I could have told him I was a virgin, but I didn't. I didn't know the etiquette. I also didn't want him to stop what he was doing, via some moral crisis, so I kept my mouth shut and let things happen.

I've heard people talk about how bad their first times were, how awkward and bumbling, how it hurt. Yeah, I had none of that. My first time was phenomenal, really, and despite my inexperience, Thom seemed to agree. We dated for a couple months before an amicable breakup. We were both mature enough to admit the only thing we had in common was excellent sex. I never saw him again.

Liz switches from liquid foundation to a powder and sighs. "Okay, I mean, it looks better. Connor is going to have to start shaving, like, twice a day to keep this from happening." She snaps the compact shut. "And I really do think you two should slow down."

I put my lips together and blow a fart noise. "I know, it's just— He's really—"

"Mm-mm." She shakes her head no.

"Good—"

"Mm-mm. Nope, I hate when you're in the sex haze. Maybe I'll talk to him."

"You will *not.*"

She zips her makeup bag closed. "Then, stop thinking with your dick. Use your heart a little. And maybe your brain. You know, that huge piece of gray matter that got you into college for free?"

I lift my hands in defeat.

"By the way, I got a text message this morning from that Tiffany girl. A bunch of the beach kids are having a memorial party at the Outpost for Duke tonight. I assume we're all attending in order to search for Leland's bloated body?"

"Wow, terribly not funny."

She squeezes her makeup bag in her hands. "I'm making jokes as a defense mechanism, because if I see another corpse, I'll either go blind or have to be committed."

"Leland's not dead."

"Well, Duke is." She chews the inside of her lip. "If something bad really is going on at the Outpost, we should start telling people not to go there."

I stand up and stretch. "On what grounds? Serial killer or Bigfoot?"

"I thought your conclusion was demon."

"Or cannibals."

"Right."

"It's not outside the realm of possibility."

She tilts her head. "Isn't it?"

"Amityville Horror was real."

"I thought that was a hoax."

"Oh." I poke at one of my chapped lips. "Shit, you're right."

"Mom's going to think *you're* dead if you don't go downstairs soon."

I hide a yawn behind my hand. "Thanks for doing my makeup."

"You owe me."

"Always."

We tromp downstairs together, and as soon as I'm in the kitchen, Mom has my coffee ready and waiting. Dad sits at the kitchen table reading the *Observer*—which I artfully steal before sitting across from him.

"Hey, I was reading that."

"Oh, were you?" I grin and skim for anything shark-related.

It's page one because of course it is. There's the usual media fear mongering: *vicious attack, bloodthirsty beast, terrible tragedy.* The coroner's report is unclear. Hungry fish dismantled so much of the body that parts were missing.

God, that's a thought—there might still be a severed leg waiting to wash up on the beach. Some little kid'll find it and use it to beat her brother.

Apparently, there was also a strong undertow night before last. Evidence was destroyed. We might never know what really happened—but authorities express caution. The coast guard will still be on alert, and Longboat Key will be covered in lifeguards for the first time since we've been coming here. Swim at your own risk, et cetera.

Sadly, there is no mention of satanic symbols or fang marks.

CHAPTER 15

I sit on a towel in the sand by my favorite hammock and read *Salem's Lot* for practical life advice: what to do when a monster takes over your town. Although King's massive tome is chock full of funky small-town characters, I relate most to a kid: Mark Petrie. When threatened early on by a bully, he kicks the bully's ass. Now, I've never done that. Despite years spent being bullied, I never learned how to actually fight. It felt futile since everyone was always bigger. Me fighting would closely resemble a skinny tree branch whirling in the wind. I mean, not now. Now, I'm like buff and stuff.

Ha. Kidding. I have "filled out," though, okay, which makes me feel like I've been a half-limp balloon my whole life waiting for air.

So, in *Salem's Lot*, Mark kicks the shit out of the school bully and, because it's fiction, gets away with it. From what I've seen, this is not how real life works. If I'd ever punched a bully in high school, I imagine I would now have a permanent fist print for a face. Like me, Mark loves scary stuff. He's a self-sufficient kid. He eventually keeps his wits about him even after being captured and strung up as a midnight snack. He escapes to fight another day.

If a vampire was trying to eat me, I hope I'd be like Mark. I hope I'd keep my cool. I've seen enough horror movies to know the rules. To stay alive, you have to keep your cool. Okay, so I'm not a virgin. That is admittedly a huge strike against me, but Sidney survived *Scream*, so there's hope.

Leaves rustle to my left, behind a thick grove of trees outside the Outpost. I glance over my shoulder once, expecting nothing less than a grinning rat. Wouldn't be a bit surprised. I'm beginning to think the rodents are sentient, like they smell fear—and probably sex, what with all the fornication that goes on at the abandoned resort.

Sex.

Let's face it: I'm thinking about sex way too much when I should be focused on possible monsters and worrying about Leland. The intellectual side of me—which, Liz is right, is a big part of me—knows Connor and I need to slow things down. Despite doing a running dive into losing my virginity, I'm not actually a slut.

Well, jeez, okay, I'm sort of a slut, but that's only because my opportunities for actual hookups back in Ohio are few and far between. So when an opportunity presents itself, I'm Clark Kent in a phone booth. Only, you know, naked.

But Connor is— Jesus, am I really going to say this? *Special.* I think he likes me, really likes me, so much so that he's already looking toward a future with me in New York. We have time; we can wait. Shame I don't want to.

I yelp and twitch at the sound of a shutter click. *Salem's Lot* flips in the air and beats its pages like wings. Connor laughs and snaps another picture.

"No." I hold my hands up and toward him, hiding my face from his viewfinder.

"I told you I wanted to take your picture today." He kneels in front of me, and blue-green waves mimic his eyes.

"But I didn't say yes!"

He takes another picture. Sun lights his hair gold as he grins, teeth white as sea foam. "I'm pretty sure you said 'yes' a lot last night."

"Arggguhh." I reach for my book and press my nose into the open binding. It smells like mildew and the dead skin cells of a dozen strangers. "You're a menace." My bottom lip catches on dry paper because I can't bring myself to show my beet-red face.

He really, really is nothing but trouble and proves my point when he straddles my upper thighs. With his thumb and pointer finger, he removes the big book from my face and places it gently on the hammock above us. I can't imagine his camera focuses this close up, but he takes another picture anyway, and another, until my only option of escape is to try and crab walk away.

I don't get far because Connor is a giant with hands like catcher's mitts. The bastard uses a single big mitt to pin both my wrists above my head in the sand. He slings his camera around on its strap so it's behind his back and hovers over me.

It's hot. It's, frankly, real damn hot.

I roll my hips up once, sort of trying to escape but not really.

He puts his free hand on my waist. "Mm, tempting, but probably shouldn't in broad daylight."

I scoff. "I'm just trying to get out from under your caveman body."

"You've never complained before." He swoops down and starts kissing the side of my neck. He definitely shaved this morning, not that it matters. We need a time machine to fix my face today, made all the more apparent when he kisses my mouth and I wince. He leans back, forehead in cute creases. "You okay?" Before I can answer, he squints down at me. "Are you wearing makeup?"

"Your whiskers destroyed my face."

He laughs and swings his camera back around at me. He takes one picture, two, while I wiggle in the sand beneath him.

"New regimen!" I shout. "You have to shave every three hours."

"If it means I still get to kiss you, fine."

I turn my face to the side and press my lips together.

"That nervous tic is adorable," he says, "but I really want to see your mouth."

"I hate my mouth."

He freezes before dropping his camera. It bounces on its strap like a tiny person on a bungee cord and nearly whacks him in the face. "Wait. What?"

"My lips are too pink. Like I'm a Barbie or some shit. It's the worst."

He makes a funny sound—a mix between a cough, laugh, and wheeze. "Em. Dude. Watching your mouth is better than watching porn."

My face wrinkles like a raisin. "What kind of porn? Amateur porn or—?"

He shakes his head and sits his weight on my thighs. "Can I get romantic for a second?"

"Are we still talking about porn?"

"No." He waves his hand between us like he's wiping clean a chalkboard. "Your lips are the perfect shade of pink and always wet, probably because you're always messing with them."

Case in point, I suck my bottom lip into my mouth and chew.

"But when you talk, you don't open your mouth all the

way. Your lips pout out and shape each word like you're tasting them. I've wanted to taste your words for years—and see if they taste as sweet as you make them look."

A hot breath is expunged from the base of my diaphragm when I sit up. Then, Connor goes all fuzzy because, of course, I'm crying.

Liz gets really bad PMS. I once watched her cuss out a harmless DVD wrapper, then start sobbing on the floor. She later apologized to the DVD wrapper. A mishmash of emotion, to be sure, but I'm starting to understand how she feels, because I've never been happier yet more in need of hiding in a closet. The feelings in my chest are too big, like my ribs are going to explode outward and poke Connor because, of course, he leans closer when he sees my tears and wipes them from my face. As if that isn't the cutest thing ever.

"Why are you crying?" he whispers.

I shrug. "Maybe I'm freaking out?"

"Okay." He tips to the side and sits next to me. "Why?"

"I guess I don't want you to go."

"Where would I go?"

I dig a little hole in the sand with my fingertip. "I don't know. Back to someone your own age. Or to some girl so you can have a bunch of athletic babies."

He lifts his chin and looks out at the sun-soaked sea. "Where is this coming from?"

"My habitual self-loathing."

"This isn't a summer fling for me, Emory. I told you I'm done with that shit." He sighs. "Look, I get it. I think. At least for me, I'm—" He clicks his tongue. "—a little scared of how much I like you. I'm in the thralls of some crazy infatua-tion-friendship-sex thing with you. And I read your short story this morning."

I shove hair out of my face, tears forgotten. "You did?"

"Yeah. And it was fantastic."

I'm pretty sure sunlight shines from my eyes.

Connor folds his arms over his bent knees and turns his head to face me. He says, "I love your writing." His gaze doesn't falter and neither does mine. I hold that stare for almost a whole minute, then grin and eye the ocean. He ruffles my hair before pulling me close by my shoulders, and I tuck my head under his chin.

We both know he isn't talking about my writing.

CHAPTER 16

My mom isn't Catholic per se, but when you're half-Italian, owning a rosary is a requirement. Apparently. She owns, like, seven, all in different colors as if she plans to match them to her outfits. I've never seen my mother actually wear one of her seven rosaries, but I am glad she has one with her in Florida. She keeps it hanging on her bedpost. I lift it before we leave for Duke's slapdash memorial at the Outpost.

What? I've been reading a book about a vampire, okay? I know, I know, it's probably not a vampire who abducted Leland. (Still holding out that he's alive.) And a vampire would never leave Duke's body so full of blood. Not a good vampire, anyway. So maybe I'm paranoid. It's just... two people I care about are freely entering a possible/probable murder site with me tonight, and one can never be too careful.

I hide the rosary under my polo shirt before Connor arrives. Once he does, he gives me a soft kiss on the cheek because my mouth skin is still mangled. I giggle because he's wearing a wildly inappropriate Hawaiian shirt with yellow flowers but, in his defense, a black background.

He must realize why I'm cracking up. "Who brings black clothes to Florida?"

"Me apparently." I gesture to my black polo and dark jeans.

"Well, you should. You look hot in black."

"You'd say I look hot in anything."

"Or nothing." He waggles his eyebrows as my cheeks give off steam.

"Gross!" Liz shrieks. "Let's go!"

Even though, according to local authorities, we're not supposed to hang at the Outpost, no one's being very covert. From the beach, I see the orange, dancing glow of tiki torches from behind the busted fence and hear the murmuring of many voices. Liz—in a black sundress she bought this afternoon—ducks under the overgrown foliage and fence and disappears. I'm quick to follow. After shimmying through some dead, crunchy palm fronds, I stand up straight and look around.

There are about twenty kids—more than the first party I attended, which means summer solstice rapidly approaches: the biggest Outpost bash of vacation season. The torches make the light dance over tan skin, and someone brought a stereo. Not even kidding: it plays organ music like we're either in church or at Dracula's castle. See? Glad I brought Mom's rosary.

Connor grabs my hand and makes me walk ever closer to the socially adept people I tend to avoid. Tiffany (possibly with a double E) steps right in front of us and crosses her arms. She was all over Connor at the first party of the summer. Now, she glares at our clasped hands. I rush to thumb through my mental file cabinet of snarky retorts because I know she's going to say something awful.

Instead, she pokes me in the chest. "All the gorgeous ones are gay." She lifts a perfectly plucked eyebrow at Connor, pulls out her phone, and starts texting. A minute later, I hear at least sixteen beeps. Several kids check their phones—and look right at us. Tiffany makes a clicking sound with her tongue, spins, and saunters away.

"Guess the news is out," I mutter.

Connor chuckles, and I run my fingers through my hair, ruffle it, so I can hide behind the curls. Realizing people find me attractive is still taking some getting used to.

Liz and Connor nod greetings to half the crowd, but I don't know anyone. I grab a beer and wander to my usual lonely edge of the empty Outpost pool. A filthy puddle of water reflects the golden torchlight, interrupted by a dusting of dead leaves on its surface. Further down, the rusted drain stares up at the sky like an all-seeing eye.

Connor comes to stand next to me, smelling like cheap beer and manly cologne with notes of leather and smoke. I refrain from shoving my face against his neck and sucking air —but only just. I assume he notices the way my body swerves toward him and back, because he smirks in triumph.

A girl in a frankly fantastic, flowing maxi dress starts talking halfway down the pool and lifts her arms up like she's summoning a spirit. "I'd like to thank everyone for coming," she says. "It would have meant so much to Duke for y'all to be here."

Duke's ghost doesn't care that I'm there. We never said a word to each other because, apparently, he was too busy making out with my twin sister. Speaking of... Maxi Dress puts her arm around Liz's shoulders, and my sister freezes, eyes wide in what I recognize as panic.

"I thought we could all say a few words," Maxi says, "but I really think Liz knew Duke best. Liz, would you share your memories of Duke? His spirit is listening."

If there were water in the damn pool, my sister would dive in, because let's face it, the thing Liz knew best about Duke was the taste of his spit.

"Um." She puts her hand to her chest. "Well, uh, Duke... He... was an excellent kisser."

"Jesus," I whisper in horror.

Connor puts his arm around my shoulders and squeezes to shut me up. I shake my head and cover my face, hoping everyone thinks I'm super grossed out by the thought of my sister kissing anyone.

"He had, um..." Liz clears her throat. "Really nice abs."

Every girl at the pool nods.

As a distraction from my twin's mortification—which I can feel rolling off her like waves—I crack open my beer and catch my finger on the metal edge. I hiss at the little cut and put my finger in my mouth, tasting blood.

I wonder if I can sneak away to do some investigating. Connor loosens his grip on me as if knowing it's time to skedaddle. He told me earlier he wanted to take some video of the Outpost, which I was thoroughly against.

"It feels very *Blair Witch*."

"So?" he asked.

I stared at him like my answer should be self-evident. When he just stared back, I shouted, "*Blair Witch* didn't end well, man!"

Although he agreed to leave his camera at home, he brought his phone to take video anyway.

I check my finger—it's only a little cut—and am about to do the slow back away when I hear someone whisper my name. I look toward the direction of the sound, away from the crowd, and assume one of the rats has finally learned to speak—but the rats are, oddly, missing. The rats love our parties because they lap up spilled beer, so where are the rats?

"Emory."

There it is: my name again.

Connor is sipping his beer, listening to Liz ramble on about Duke's, I don't know, nose freckles. He has not noticed the disembodied voice calling to me.

"Emory?"

It's coming from the pool. It's coming from beneath the rusty grate at the bottom of the pool. It wants me to come closer; I know it does. It wants me down there with it.

"Emory."

I take a step toward the edge. I want to go down there. It'll be dark and quiet down there. I'll have time to be alone and think. I like being alone. In the quiet and the dark. It would be so easy. All I need to do is step to the end and jump, headfirst. The rusty grate will open, and I'll slide right through. The voice and I will be together. I like the voice. I need it even.

Yes, if I jump right in, everything will be nice and quiet, and all these stupid kids won't bother me anymore. The edge of my flip-flop teeters between concrete and open air.

"Emory."

Just a quick dive into the grate, and it'll all be over.

"Emory!"

Arms like iron wrap around me from behind and pull me backwards. I struggle for a second, because I need to get into that grate—but then, it's like I'm waking from a dream. Connor has one arm around my chest, the other around my waist. We're six inches from the edge of the pool, and the grate watches, as do all the kids at Duke's memorial because I almost just nose-dived ten feet down into concrete.

"What the hell were you thinking?" Connor asks, but he doesn't let go.

"Didn't you hear it?" I whisper.

"Hear what?"

"Something was calling my name."

"No," he says. "I'm taking you home." He releases the vice-hold around my torso but grips my arm.

"We need to look for Leland."

"No." He drags me forward as I try to drag him back. By now, Duke's memorial is a wash. Everyone's too busy staring at the crazy kid.

"But Connor—"

"Em." He spins around and pulls me close so all the gawkers don't hear. "You scared the shit out of me. Please, let's go home." It's not just a figure of speech; I think I did almost scare the shit out of him. His glowing, golden face is two shades too pale. Deep frown lines circle his mouth like parentheses, and his broad shoulders are up by his ears. He keeps clenching and unclenching his jaw, and it's all my fault.

But I heard it. I did. Something called my name, I swear. Something wanted me to hurt myself. Something wanted me to bleed.

I'll argue later. Right now, Connor needs... Well, I'm not sure exactly. He needs to get me away from the Outpost, I guess, so I let him. Silently, I let him drag me back through the fence and across Longboat Key sand.

He storms into his family's house and stomps past his mom and dad, who are drinking sangria and watching some true crime show featuring a scary-voiced narrator.

Connor doesn't answer when his mom asks if everything is okay, but I smile and wave at her with my free hand. I can't feel the other one, since Connor's grip cut off my circulation five minutes ago.

Once in his room, he closes the door. I'm expecting an argument, expecting him to call me reckless. Instead, he hugs me—hard. Breath whooshes out from my parted lips as he crushes me between his body and the door. I gulp some air, enough to say his name and tack on a question mark.

"Wow," he mutters, his mouth in my hair.

"Connor…" I wheeze. "Can't… breathe."

"Sorry." He lets go and takes a step back before running both his hands through his hair. Blond locks stick up for a second before falling back perfectly into place. "I thought you were going to fall, and…" He stares at his hands. "My palms are tingling. Why are my palms tingling?"

Oh, boy. "Okay, come here, you need to sit down." I guide him gently to the edge of his bed. We sit side by side, and I run my hand up and down his spine. "You're having a panic attack. It's okay."

"Panic attack? I don't get panic attacks."

"How's your vision?"

He blinks at the closed door. "Spotty."

"Does it feel like your ribs are trying to crush all your internal organs?"

"Yeah." He nods.

"Tell me five things you can see."

"What?"

I nudge the side of his face with my nose. "Tell me five things you can see."

"Um…" He looks around, eyes wide. "Door. Dirty sock. *Sandman* graphic novel. Blue chair. Emory."

"Good. Now, four things you can touch."

He looks like he's breathing water, not air, but one of his hands squeezes the crumpled sheets beneath us. "Blanket." He squeezes my knee. "Emory."

"Four things."

"Emory's knee." His hand moves. "Emory's elbow. Emory's chin."

I nod. "Three things you can hear."

He closes his eyes for this one. Some of the tension has left his shoulders. "Ocean. The rumble of bad TV. Emory breathing."

"Two things you can smell," I whisper.

"Saltwater." He leans over and sticks his nose behind my ear, which makes me giggle and twitch. I'm ticklish back there. "Emory's shampoo," he says. He doesn't move his face away, just keeps it pressed to my neck.

"Almost done," I say. "Tell me one thing you can taste."

He lifts his head and kisses me once before tucking his hand in the back of my hair and kissing me some more. His lips are wet when he pulls away. "I taste Emory."

"Feel better?"

"Yeah," he says. "What was all that?"

"A mindfulness thing I used to do when I got panic attacks at school. Frozen in panic is not a good look when bullies are coming at you."

"No, I would think not. Lie down with me?"

I nod, and we both shift around on the bed. We, strangely, have never done this before. We've made out for hours and mapped pretty much every naked inch of each other's bodies—but we have never just lain in bed together, cuddling.

I'm quite content to be the little spoon. As soon as I lie on my side, Connor's front is against my back, his arm snuggly around my hips and pulling me closer. Two pairs of very long legs first wrestle and then tangle together like huge noodles. He squeezes me even closer.

"Just so you know: I don't think I can actually fit inside your body cavity."

He blows a raspberry against the side of my neck. "Stay the night?"

"My parents would murder me."

He harrumphs. "Stay until I fall asleep?"

"What if I fall asleep?"

He removes his hand from my waist long enough to pull his cell phone from his pants pocket. Using one of his long, quarterback arms, he holds the phone out in front of me. As

I realize what he's doing, his camera clicks. I groan and cover my face way too late.

He fiddles one-handed with his phone, setting the alarm for midnight. "You realize you're going to have to get used to me taking your picture. You're sort of my muse."

I grumble.

He returns to his place wrapped around me and kisses the side of my neck. I feel the rosary move as he pulls back, beads stuck momentarily to his lip. "Are you wearing a necklace?"

I turn my face toward the pillow. "It's a rosary."

"Worried about vampires?"

"Worried about something, but now I'm not so sure if this will do any good."

He drapes an arm around my waist and squeezes. "Well. Sleep for now."

I shimmy against him, getting comfy. When Connor's hands start to wander, I sure as hell don't stop them, and by the time his alarm goes off, we haven't slept a wink.

CHAPTER 17

I drink coffee on the patio, watching languid waves creep in and out. We kids are alone today. The four parents decided to do touristy things like visit the nearby art museum and botanical gardens—but not before Mr. Nichols got in one of his digs.

Earlier in the driveway, he nudged my dad, pointed at me, and said, "He's the pretty one, so you're paying for the wedding."

I never saw my dad turn quite that shade of tomato before.

With that, they were off to do... couple things, I guess. I know the men only do day trips for the women, since I can't imagine Mr. Nichols, in particular, gives two shits about exotic orchids. This is probably something I will eventually learn—how to make concessions for the guy I love. I haven't had to make any changes for Connor yet, possibly because we have all the same interests. Oh, except football.

Oh my God, he's going to want to watch football.

Then again, maybe I'm getting ahead of myself. I have to

find a missing homeless war veteran and explain hearing voices from pool grates first.

Liz bounces out the back door. She's already fully dressed for a day at the beach in a bathing suit and red cover-up. Despite the shark scare, the brave tourists have returned to Longboat, but it's way less crowded than usual.

She smacks me in the back of the head. Well, she tries. I duck before her palm makes contact because I know my sister almost as well as I know myself. She sits at my side, posture perfect. "Someone slept in late today."

True, although I managed to blink an eye open long enough to wave at a running Connor as he passed. I blow a curl out of my face. "Yeah, what's it to you?"

She points her finger in my face. "Do not be a defensive bitch. *You* abandoned *me* at the memorial after interrupting my heartfelt eulogy."

A surprised laugh wiggles its way out my nose.

Liz sighs. "Seriously, are you okay? What the fuck happened last night?"

"I heard someone—" I shake my head. "This sounds so freaking crazy."

"Princess." She rests a hand on her chest. "It's me."

"I heard someone saying my name."

"Yeah, it was probably Connor. You know how I joked once that you looked like a praying mantis being eaten by its mate? Well, that's actually the way he looks at you now, like he's a cannibal who hasn't eaten in ten days. Or maybe ten years. It's disgustingly cute, and I hate you."

I nudge her knee. The coffee has gone cold in my hands. "It wasn't Connor, okay? It sounded like Lord Voldemort. In the pool grate."

"Not that I would ever watch *It*, but I thought that was more of a Pennywise thing."

I stand up and run my fingers through my hair. When I

catch a knot and end up just pulling—hard—it actually feels good because at least I know I'm here, alive, and not in some horror movie. Which is when my shoulders slump. "Liz, I think we have to stop brushing this off with pop culture references. I mean, Leland is missing. Duke is dead. And now I'm hearing voices. And not only that, but I think the voice wanted me to kill myself."

"What?"

"It wanted me to nose-dive into an empty cement pool, and I listened. If Connor hadn't—"

Liz grabs my shoulders and stares up at me. It's still novel that we aren't the same height anymore, like she's the female mini-me now. She's about to speak when we hear feet in sand, and there's Connor, looking as freaked as I feel.

"Hey," I mutter.

Liz doesn't let go of me, as though she can hold my sanity together by the force of her grip alone.

Connor says, "I."

We wait, but when he doesn't say anything else, I whisper, "You," like I'm talking to a nervous squirrel.

Connor doesn't look right. He's showered and dressed, but his T-shirt is backwards. He's in khaki shorts, barefoot, his MacBook closed and hugged against his side. His hair stands up on one side, and his face is twisted like he just smelled boiled garbage.

I put my hands on Liz's elbows in a silent entreaty to disengage and walk over to Connor. He looks at me; I look at him. He glances over my shoulder at Liz.

"Oh, God, is this a sex thing?" she says from behind me.

But it isn't, I can tell. Something is really wrong. "Connor?"

"I..." he starts again. "I am freaking out."

"What a relief. Me too. What's your reason?"

His Adam's apple bounces on what appears to be a boulder-sized gulp, and he lifts his laptop before walking toward the back door. Liz and I follow, although she tugs on the back of my polo like I'm hiding answers to unasked questions in my shirt.

In the kitchen, Connor puts his laptop down but doesn't open it. Instead, he turns to face us. The only thing that'd make him look more like a nervous motivational speaker would be a PowerPoint presentation. "Something you said on our first date."

Liz asks, "Is this a *Jeopardy* question?"

He shakes his head. "No. Emory, you mentioned seeing some guy who looked like Vincent Price at the carnival. Then, I was looking at the photos I took of you yesterday."

"Ew," Liz mutters.

"Not those kind of photos," I reply.

Connor creeps up on his MacBook like it's going to bite. He looks legitimately scared of the object he has, until now, treated like a newborn baby. He opens it, the screen glows, and there it is: a photo of me laughing on the beach.

I wince because I feel like my teeth and gums show too much when I laugh, but as I look closer, I realize I don't actually look that awful. I look kind of... *huh*. Handsome sort of. I definitely look happy, but that's because Connor was taking the photo.

"Aww, you look cute," Liz says.

"Obviously," Connor whispers, mostly to himself. "But look behind you in the photo."

Nope, I don't want to, because whatever is behind me is decidedly not good. Something has managed to scare the shit out of a six two, ex-football player who—I'm pretty sure—would jump in front of a moving car for me. I do not want to know what that something is. But, of course, I love a good horror story. I lean forward and squint.

I'm expecting a fanged beast with red, glowing eyes. Instead, I see...

"Vincent Price?"

It's the guy from the carnival, complete with mustache and maniac expression. He's hiding behind an overgrown tree outside the Outpost fence, and he's watching me.

I breathe a quick "What the fuck?"

Connor's voice is tight, squeaky. "Is he following you?"

Oh. *Oh,* that's why he's scared. My heart would melt if it weren't pounding like a dubstep bass beat.

His voice gets louder now, angry, but shaking with emotion. "I mean, you were alone out there reading. How long was he watching you before I got there? What if he'd hurt you? I don't think I could..." He clenches his jaw.

We boys need a moment, so I say Liz's name in an effort to get some privacy. When she doesn't move, I look at her, and she's got her hands curled under her chin, eyes in the shapes of emerald hearts, and she squeaks like a hungry pup.

I'm about to say, "Don't," but before I can, she shouts, "It's so cute how protective you are of my brother. Oh my God!" She rushes into Connor's arms, and he stumbles back a couple steps at the force of her embrace.

Connor pats her back, but his eyes never leave me.

"You think I have a stalker?" I ask.

"What other explanation is there?" he says as Liz wipes her snotty nose on his shoulder and steps away.

I try to think back over all the famous-people-stalker scenarios I've seen on true crime shows and realize having a stalker is really not cool, considering to make it on a true crime show, you're usually dead—as are your friends.

Friends.

"Leland!" I shout.

Connor whips his head around like my homeless pal is in the room.

"No, what if Vincent saw me with Leland and, I don't know, hurt him?" I hiccup on a gulp of dread. "What if Leland's missing because of me?"

"Em, he wouldn't be missing because of you; he'd be missing because of a psycho."

I shake my head and hurry for the mudroom where we keep random sports paraphernalia that I never use. I pick up an ancient tennis racket and swing it like a baseball bat, but before I take two steps for the sliding door, my wrist is trapped in the cage of Connor's Hulk hand.

With the calmness of a koala, he asks, "What are you doing?"

"Gonna go kick some stalker ass." I try to twist my wrist out of his grip but end up bent backwards at an awkward angle.

I hear Liz mutter from the doorway, "Yeah, that's going to work."

"You don't even know where he is."

I gawk at Connor from under my arm, which is now twisted like a tree limb up in the air as I continue flailing. "He's *my stalker.* He's got to be nearby!"

"Even stalkers take bathroom breaks!" Connor shouts.

"How do you know?" I shout back.

"Guys!" Liz shouts over both of us. We turn to look at her, and she points to the patio. "Um, look."

Vincent Price stands there in the sun, waving.

Connor and I both man scream, which is a nice way of saying we shriek like little girls.

By some miracle, I remember how to move my legs—and start moving them for the door—but Connor wraps his arms around my waist and picks me up from behind until my bare feet kick the air.

"Let me at him!" I twist and flail until Connor apparently loses his footing because we crash to the tile floor, his full weight on my back. I can barely muster a whimper as I try to breathe. "You're... so... heavy."

When I look up from my roadkill position, Vincent is even closer, still waving. His widow's peak comb-over is more prevalent than in Connor's photo, and his mustache is way less shapely up close. His fashion sense is still castaway chic— shorts and a shirt with stains and frayed edges. But those eyes...

Connor whines above me. I'm pretty sure his elbow took the brunt of our fall.

I slither a hand forward and shove at the sliding glass door.

"Emory, don't—" Liz starts as I say, "Gerald?"

Vincent drops his waving hand and announces, "You're the kid I've been waiting for." Sadly, his voice holds none of his namesake's gravitas.

———

When I suggest we let "Vincent" into our house, Liz cusses me out and smacks me in the forehead. Lucky for me my head wound from the Outpost is just about healed or the cut would have cracked open like the desert in an earthquake.

Connor is more sensible. He grabs Vincent by his dirty shirt and lifts him straight up off the ground. "Why are you following Emory?"

Hairy feet toe at open air. "Because I think he can save us. All of us!" He sounds like a TV evangelist.

"That's some creepy cult shit, man," Connor says.

"No! The Outpost *needs* him!"

"Connor." I put my hand on his shoulder.

It's hotter than a cast iron skillet in the direct sun of my patio, and the sea breeze is doing nothing to help. Flaring tempers feels like adding more fire to... well... fire.

"Connor, please let him down. I know who he is, but I'd like to know why he's here."

Connor doesn't put the guy down. Also, his sizeable muscles aren't even shaking—which, let me tell you, does not make it any cooler outside. "What do you mean, you know who he is?"

"It's Gerald Krauss." I do my best *ta-da* pose. "He owned the Outpost until eight years ago."

Liz steps up next to me and squints. "Holy shit, bro's right. It's in the eyes."

Connor lets go, and Gerald-not-Vincent tumbles to the sandy patio before standing and brushing himself off with more attention than his crappy attire requires.

"You lay one finger on Emory"—Connor growls—"and I will end you."

"I would never hurt him. I need him."

"Did you hurt Leland?" I ask.

Gerald's eyebrows squish together like kissing caterpillars. "I don't know the man."

Liz groans. "You could cook an egg on my forehead right now. I'm going inside, and the weirdo is coming too. Come on."

Once in the living area, Liz pours us all iced tea, except Gerald. She glares at him. I'm expecting an explanatory monologue like they do in the movies, but Gerald doesn't say a thing, just twiddles his thumbs and avoids eye contact. I think he's pouting.

"Oh my God," Liz says. "Have my damn iced tea."

He accepts her sweaty glass, sips, and smiles. "I need your help with the Outpost."

"Why?"

"Because I conjured a demon."

Connor stands and throws his hands in the air. "For Christ's sake!"

Even I'm less than thrilled. "A demon. Sure. I thought it was Bigfoot."

Gerald winces. "An unfortunate rumor I started to explain odd occurrences. That costume cost a fortune, although it was tax deductible."

I thwack my head against the back of the couch.

Liz sits next to me. "Hey, Emory loves a good ghost story. Do tell. Why'd you conjure a demon?"

"For success, obviously." He frowns; his mustache pokes up and out. "I now realize the decision was ill-advised, but business is business so"—he winks—"I offered the demon life on earth in exchange for"—he shrugs—"good things."

"Can you be a little more specific?" I ask.

"He could influence people, so I would have business meetings with investors, women for dinner, things like that, and the demon would... you know." He gazes at Connor for confirmation, but Connor grunts and stares out the window. "Hi-ho, the demon made me very rich, but I didn't expect his hunger."

"You keep saying 'he.' Does your demon have a name?"

His chin trembles left and right. "He's called Athsaia. Or her. Or it. You see, it's the resort." He slurps loudly at his iced tea. "The resort is a demon. For now."

"For now?" I cross my arms over my chest. "What does that mean?"

"He feeds on blood." This is such a nonchalant pronouncement, it's like he said cats like fish. "I used to give him a little of my own—drops down a bathroom drain, for instance. In order for the... *influencing*... to work, I'd have to offer the blood of my guests. Something simple as a paper cut would do. However, I didn't foresee the eventual consequences of his feeding. It soon became dangerous for guests to cut themselves shaving. Athsaia would grow fond of the taste of certain people, and well"—he wrinkles his nose

—"under Athsaia's influence, one gentleman might have slit his wrists." *Slurp, slurp*.

"I've heard enough." Liz stands and joins Connor by the window, but I'm all ears.

"You're saying this demon of yours made a guy kill himself?"

"I can neither confirm nor deny." Pause. "But yes. He can make a person do just about anything if his or her blood is in the air."

I lean my elbows on my knees, practically tipping forward off the sofa. "Does Athsaia talk? Does he have a voice?"

"Emory..." Connor starts.

I tilt my head to face him. "I heard a voice last night, a voice telling me to jump headfirst into an empty pool."

Gerald's voice loses some of its game-show-host appeal. "Wait, you're saying *you've* bled on the property? But what happened?"

"All right, that's it!" Connor moves really fast for such a big dude, probably accustomed to dodging... whatever quarterbacks dodge. In a blink, he lifts Gerald from the couch and shoves him toward the mudroom. "Show me."

"I beg your pardon!" Gerald clings tightly to his iced tea. Liquid sloshes onto the floor.

"Your demon. I want to see it."

I scramble to catch up. "Me too."

In an unexpected show of tenderness in the midst of anger, Connor lets go of Gerald and puts his hands on my face. "This is a futile request, but please stay on the couch?"

I make a sound like *pshh*.

Near the wonky broken fence on the Outpost's edge, I don't stop walking until Gerald grabs my shirt and pulls me backwards. "I won't go in," he says.

"We go in all the time," Liz replies as if daring him to start talking about bloodthirsty demons again. Well, one demon, I guess. Apparently they're solitary creatures.

I wave toward the fence. "How are we going to see this demon of yours if we can't go inside?"

"Blood will bring him to the edge of the property."

Connor nonchalantly uses his massive wingspan to push both Liz and me behind him.

Gerald pulls out a cheap imitation Swiss Army and pokes at his fingertip. He winces and looks back at us, chuckling as if to say, "What are you going to do?" He pushes harder.

Meanwhile, I stare into the rotting palm fronds and overgrowth beyond the rusty fence, searching for some red-faced dude with horns.

Gerald eventually howls in both success and pain because using a Swiss Army knife to cut skin is probably like Chinese water torture. Careful to not actually set foot inside the property line, he leans across the fence entrance and squeezes his finger, *squeezes* until a drop of blood falls silent in the sand.

"Watch," he says.

I don't know what I'm expecting, but it's not the ground opening in the shape of a tiny mouth with sharp teeth. The mouth opens, slurps, closes, and smiles before melting back to wherever it came from. The drop of blood is gone, and I don't even hear my sister faint.

CHAPTER 18

I manage to drag a semiconscious Liz a dozen feet away from the sucking, slurping sand mouth with teeth. Gerald follows while Connor still stands by the fence like a mannequin in a department store.

I take off my shirt and use it to fan Liz. "Why do people ever conjure demons?" I screech. "Haven't you watched one goddamn horror movie in your entire life? It's *never* a good idea!"

We're lucky it's so hot and that people are still a little nervous about the whole shark attack thing—although that's looking harder and harder to believe now that I've seen the ground swallow blood. Which explains exactly what happened to the bloodstain Connor and I found in Leland's favorite room: here one second, gone the next, swallowed by *apparently* a demon because unless I popped LSD today by accident, I don't know how else to explain what I just saw.

"Connor!" I yelp.

He jumps, trips over his own feet, and barely avoids a face-plant.

"Connor, will you please get away from the bloodsucking

sand? And you!" I point at Gerald, who lowers his chin like a kid about to be grounded. "Do you have any control over that thing?"

"I did!" He uses the game-show-host voice again, all fake enthusiasm to cover the fact that he's a damn fool. "He grew too strong, obviously."

"*Obviously!*" Okay, I'm screaming a lot, and I do love scary movies, but this—this—is why I love scary movies. Because they're not supposed to be real. I've always avoided Oscar-winning films because I don't want to watch some depressing true story about bullying or gay bashing because I've spent a lot of my life walking down those halls. Then, there are horror movies. I've never been chased by a guy with knife hands or haunted by a girl crawling out of a television screen. In horror movies, there aren't grand moral questions or inflated angst. There's just "Don't die." Simplicity is comforting, but this? I keep fanning Liz. "Oh my God, it's karma," I mutter. "I've been laughing at people in horror movies my whole life, and now, *I'm in one!*"

Connor, who's still wide-eyed and walking like he's made of wood, crumbles to my side and wraps his arms around my bare shoulders from behind. He mushes his face into my hair and says, "Calm down."

"Of all the times to be calm, this is not one of them!"

"I know, but you look like your head's going to explode like a fire cracker."

I'm covered in Connor as Liz mumbles with her eyes closed, hair matted with sand, but I do try to breathe—at least long enough to get more air for shouting. "Gerald, how did he become too strong? Explain."

He puts his hands on the natty fabric covering his hips and stands tall like a superhero on a cereal box. "As I said, Athsaia feeds on blood. At first, my blood. But imagine how much blood flows through a tourist resort. As I said, perhaps you cut yourself shaving." He extends his hands at me like I'm a fancy new car. "Not you, of course."

"What the f—"

"But men who actually shave might spill a drop here or there. Women shaving their legs, the same. A cook cuts his finger chopping vegetables. It is easy for us to forget, but blood is everywhere." He smiles like we're supposed to applaud or something. When nobody moves, he frowns and keeps talking. "I started seeing him—glimpses of a shadow, red eyes, even hearing his voice—so I bankrupted the resort. Removed his power source. Now, that real estate agency, Keebler and Crown—they plan to remodel and reopen. I have spent the past eight years destroying business deals, breaking into offices, hacking into computers to keep anyone from buying the Outpost." He must notice my lowered brows, because he wrinkles his nose. "I had no choice! It was for the good of humanity!" He again adjusts the front of his shirt like he's wearing a fancy suit and not week-old clothes that smell like cheese. "That *woman*, Tabitha, she found a way around all my tricks and has no idea what she's gotten herself into."

"Wait, but..." Connor's voice is muffled, face buried in my hair. "If they tear down the resort, isn't that a good thing?"

"He's more than the resort. He's the land. You saw! They're going to tear down and rebuild and give Athsaia everything he wants, bringing tourists back. Blood and more blood! Athsaia will become fully formed, walk around, and"— he tugs on his collar—"eat people."

I twist my shoulders back and forth so Connor will loosen his death grip on my torso. "You said you need me. Why do you need me?"

Gerald falls to his knees in the sand and holds his crusty hands up in prayer. "Athsaia has one weakness: virgins."

Connor snorts against the back of my neck, and Liz says, "Emory is a whore."

I glare down at her. "Nice of you to join us."

She sits up, opening and closing her eyes like a slow-moving strobe. "I think I have sand in my underwear. This day is terrible."

"Wait, but..." Gerald stutters. If I didn't know better, I'd think he was trying to beatbox. "You must be a virgin."

I nudge Connor off me. "Why do people assume I'm a virgin? Am I that ugly?"

Both Liz and Connor start arguing, but I tell them to zip it and wait on Gerald's response.

The business guy hubris is gone, replaced by disappointment and dread. "But you... you're so long-limbed and awkward. Like a baby horse learning to walk. You're just a kid, and yet, you never spend time with other kids. You're always alone *reading books*."

Which he obviously thinks is disgusting.

He winks, hutzpah returned. "Now, be serious. You can tell the truth. It's nothing to be embarrassed about."

"Dude, I'm not a virgin! I'm an accomplished lover, okay?"

"More than accomplished," Connor mutters.

Liz covers her ears and hums. The back of her hair is caked with sand.

"Why is your demon afraid of virgins anyway?" Connor asks.

"Their pure blood makes him sick, has the opposite effect of all other blood. Virgin blood lessens his power instead of increasing it." Beneath his mustache, his mouth trembles. "If you're not— If you—" He opens his mouth and sobs. "Oh, God, where am I going to find a vir-ir-ir-gin?"

"I wouldn't suggest walking up and down the beach asking people." Connor stands. "You give off a creepy enough vibe without adding pervert to the list."

Gerald snivels. "You were perfect. Intelligent, quick-witted. A bit gangly, yes, but a *Stephen King fan*."

I gracefully ignore the Stephen King dig. "I cut my finger on a beer can last night, and that thing tried to make me dive into an empty pool. Pretty sure it wouldn't want that if my blood was going to make him, like, demon hurl."

Gerald buries his face in his hands. "Now, I have nothing. We're doomed."

I scoot closer to Gerald. I don't feel bad about my lack of virginity, but I do feel bad that I was this guy's hope for taking down a demon. "Have you gone and talked to Tabitha? Explained the situation?"

"Of course, I have. You think *you* were my first option?" He hiccups and doesn't wipe his booger nose. "At first, she didn't believe it was me. Oh, how the mighty have fallen! Once she did, she said I wanted my resort back."

"Why don't you bring her here? Show her the creepy mouth thing?"

His shoulders droop so low, he looks hunchbacked. "I tried. It didn't work. It was as though Athsaia knew I needed to show her. The demon is no fool. Tabitha just laughed and walked away."

I shield my eyes from the sun and look up at Connor. "We should talk to her. She has a crush on me."

Connor scoffs. "Oh, really?"

I stand and brush sand from my shorts. "You're the one who looked like you wanted to claw her eyes out the first time we met, and we hadn't even kissed yet. Don't think I didn't notice."

He shakes his head but not in disagreement. Nice to see he's moving like a normal person again—and his skin is no longer the color of spilled milk. "Fine, we'll go see her."

Gerald hugs his knees against his chest. "She won't listen. She'll think I sent you."

"We have to try."

"I'm going home," Liz says. She sways a little when she stands, but I catch her arm and hold tight.

"Are you okay?"

Her mouth opens, and a huge wrinkle grows between her brows. "No, *princess*, I'm not okay." She jerks her hand away and walks down the beach toward home.

"This isn't my fault," I say to myself.

"Come on, let's go talk to our friendly neighborhood real estate lady."

Gerald doesn't look like he's going anywhere, rocking back and forth in the sand like a seesaw.

I tell Connor to wait before asking, "So you really haven't seen a middle-aged homeless guy anywhere? Penchant for Hawaiian shirts and a big straw hat?"

I think Gerald's in a trance until he says, "This Leland friend of yours?"

I nod.

"If he spends time at the Outpost, I wouldn't hold out much hope, kid."

I swallow the lump in my throat because I am not crying in front of this asshole. As I turn to walk away, his voice stops me.

"Emory."

"Yeah?"

"You've spilled blood at the Outpost?"

I glance at Connor. "Yeah. Twice."

"Then, Athsaia knows you. Don't go in there."

The backs of my hands tingle.

"As long as he doesn't go into the Outpost, he's safe, right?" Connor asks.

"Safe." Gerald snickers. "For now."

"What if we need to find you again? Do you have a phone?"

"No phone. I'm living in the Squid Shack." An old restaurant that closed down and no one thought to bulldoze. "But I don't know how I can help. If I could have gotten rid of Athsaia by now, I would have."

"You're a pathetic excuse for a demon conjurer," Connor says.

Gerald ignores him and looks at me instead. "Be careful."

————

Liz doesn't even ask what we're doing back at the house. She sits on the couch watching *Golden Girls*. Apparently, thanks to Connor, this is a thing now.

What *are* we doing home? Connor says we should probably dress like grown-ups to go have a meeting with one. Up in my room, he sits me on the edge of my bed and starts going through my closet. It's, oh so, Liz.

"We probably shouldn't open with demons," he says.

"I suppose not." I scratch the back of my head. "What are we opening with exactly?"

He blows air through his lips. "Uh."

"Right."

To my pleasant surprise, he chooses the slim-fit, black button-down and skinny jeans from our first date. He pulls both items off their hangers and extends them to me like gifts.

"I wore this to the carnival."

"Yeah, and you looked hot." He nods to the bathroom door as if he hasn't seen me naked and hopes to protect my chastity. "Go get dressed."

In the bathroom, I splash some water on my armpits and reapply deodorant before brushing all the dry sand off my shins and stepping into my jeans. Halfway through buttoning up my shirt, I notice my hair looks pretty much like a Brillo pad, and why the hell didn't anyone tell me?

Oh, right, demons and shit.

I do the finger-curl thing Liz taught me and try to get it back to its usual Shirley Temple glory, but Connor walks in midway through without knocking. He stands in the doorway staring.

"What the hell?" I ask. "I could have been picking my nose."

He doesn't seem to hear. In fact, I'm pretty sure all his senses have honed down to sight. His stare makes me feel so vulnerable, I cover my clothed crotch and take a step back toward the shower. There is the fleeting thought that maybe Connor is possessed by a demon that wants to eat me.

Then, he kisses me the way he does—the way I've already grown accustomed to—which means sort of messy with teasing tongue and quiet moans and hands like claws in the back of my hair and then down my back and latching onto my ass. I give as well as I get considering, contrary to popular opinion, I'm not actually a virgin.

When Connor's body weight pushes me backwards, I have to grab the shower curtain to keep my footing, but we still almost stumble into the tub.

Connor rights me with hands on my hips and shoves his face against my throat like he's a vampire.

"Are we—?" I bite his ear and try to remember what was happening before he kissed me. "Wait. What are we doing?"

His sigh is a warm, tickly wave across my throat. "We're going to talk to the real estate lady, but I would much rather pretend none of this homicidal demon shit is happening so I could spend the next few days wrecking you."

Only a few days.

Jesus, already, the summer solstice is tomorrow. Soon, I'll go back to Ohio; he'll go back to New York. We'll have two months away from each other before we're both college students in the Big Apple. What if he meets someone else before then? What if he realizes I'm just an awkward, skinny kid? What if—

Connor interrupts my thoughts. "If you meet some other guy in your hick Ohio town before we're officially boyfriends in New York, I'll kidnap you and keep you as a pet."

Dude always knows the right thing to say. I hug him tight. "You know I won't."

"Well, you should know *I* won't either, so stop thinking about it."

I tug his short blond hair. "Get out of my head. It's creepy."

He pulls back and points at himself. "I'm creepy? I'm creepy? I read your spooky short story, and your first words as a baby were probably 'Freddy Krueger,' but *I'm* creepy?"

"My first word was actually 'duck.'"

He purses his lips together like a duck.

"I had a rubber ducky I chewed on as a baby, okay? What was your first word, 'interception'?"

His blue eyes go wide. "Did you make a football joke?"

Trying to escape the incoming headlock is a futile effort, so I barely struggle as he wraps his arm around my shoulders and ruffles my hair.

I bat at his hand. "I just fixed that!"

"Your hair looks perfect every minute of every day. It's as sexy at midnight as it is at noon as it is at seven a.m. Seeing a pattern?"

"Your armpit smells good." Pheromones might make me semi-delusional, but in this case, I'm serious. Connor wears deodorant that smells like fresh, clean male—although, to be honest, I don't mind the smell of his sweat either.

He releases me from the headlock and shoves me in the shoulder. "I love how gross you are. Now, come on, I need to change, and we'll go."

I grab Mom's rosary before we leave and hide it under my shirt.

Downstairs, we pass a still catatonic Liz. Connor heads next door for some adult-ish clothes while I stand in front of the TV and do a bit of river dancing to get her attention.

"Move." She chews the straw of her iced tea.

"Just making sure you're not in a coma."

"Mom and Dad called. They'll be back for dinner. Getting takeout from Harry's. Now, go away. I hate you."

"What did I do?"

She flails the hand not holding her tea. "I don't know! But something. You—you're always reading scary books and watching scary movies. This was bound to happen."

I sit on the edge of the coffee table and pose like Rodin's Thinker. "A man-eating demon was *bound to happen* on Long-boat Key?"

"Yes, fuck-face, that's right. Weird shit begets weird shit." She shimmies down into the couch as though hoping it'll swallow her whole. "I'm never leaving the house again. I'm going to die here and leave nothing but an ass imprint in the furniture."

"You sound like me before every high school dance ever."

"And isn't that terrifying—me sounding like you?" She spits out a piece of ice, and it almost hits me. "You know what? This is backwards world. Here I am alone watching TV while your dumb ass is running around the beach with a boyfriend. I should have known my life was over when you got hot. I'll no doubt end up living in your basement in the suburbs while you and Connor adopt twenty Asian babies."

"Twenty is a bit much," Connor says from the back doorway in khaki pants and a bright blue button-down. "Is she all right?"

"Existential crisis." I look at my wrist even though I don't wear a watch. "She was due for one."

Liz leans forward, grabs my hair, and pulls.

"Ow!" I bend closer, but the pulling continues with violent intent.

"You need to figure out this demon shit and not get killed, you hear me, big brother? Because you know I hate scary movies and creepy sand mouths and"—she hisses—"*Vincent Fucking Price.*"

"Liz, Liz, hey." Connor puts his hand on her hand in my hair and tries to uncurl her fist. I feel them having a mini finger war until the pulling pressure finally lessens. I reach up to rub my head, but Connor beats me to it and massages my scalp while holding Liz's hand in his. "We're going to figure this out. We need to talk to the real estate lady now, but will you be okay here alone?"

She tugs her hand away from his. "Don't try to sweet-talk me, Captain America."

"If she's exhibiting violence, she'll be fine." I stand and pull my phone out to search "Keebler and Crown" with Connor right behind me. There's no listing for an office address on Longboat, but there is one in New Mexico. Then, I remember that recent article in *The Observer* that talked about Keebler and Crown and Tabitha Crown and our greasy mayor, so I search that instead, and there, at the bottom of the article is a temporary office address for anyone with "inquiries." Not sure we fit that description, but Connor and I start walking anyway.

Luckily, there's some late afternoon cloud cover, thank Christ, because we're both in long pants, and I'm basically all in black and in danger of melting. Tabitha's office is only a couple blocks down Gulf of Mexico Drive, and Connor grabs my hand as we cross the street onto the shadier side, protected here and there by sprawling banyan trees with their aggressive-looking arms and spindly vines. I tilt my body away because if ever a tree were to pick me up and eat me, it would be a banyan. The Spanish moss creeps me out too; like, what lives in there, you know?

I'm eyeing one with such single-minded suspicion, I run into Connor. Our ankles tangle, and his arm around my waist is the only thing keeping me upright. He chuckles. "There's my Grace."

"Shut up. I don't trust the trees."

Three golf carts race by on the road—a bunch of rich, white dudes with no clue there's a literal demon hoping to eat humanity. A breeze that smells like buttery fish and hot pavement assaults us as we pass the Lazy Lobster restaurant. Laughing tourists and screaming kids eat overpriced seafood, and it starts to sink in: there is *a literal demon hoping to eat humanity*.

"What do we tell Tabitha?"

"You're the creative genius, Em. You'll think of something."

I hide a blush behind my hair. "I'm serious. I have no idea what to say, and I also have no idea how to be charming."

There's a hiccup in Connor's step before he shoves his hands in his pockets. "That's true, actually."

I press my lips together before speaking. "I'm pretty sure you were supposed to disagree with me there?"

"No, Em, you're not charming. That's one of the reasons I fell for you. You're awkward and say ridiculous things and are super easy to embarrass. It's adorable, but you're no Tom Cruise in *Top Gun*."

A bicycle whizzes by on our left. "That's your definition of charming?"

"That's every man's definition of charming."

"Shit. So teach me how to be charming."

He lifts one eyebrow, lowers the other. "Right now? We're going to be at the office in two minutes."

I step over a crack in the sidewalk because being superstitious seems like a good idea.

"Besides, if memory serves, I think Tabitha Crown liked you nervous and stuttering—like a lamb primed for slaughter."

"Might want to lay off the slaughter jokes when there's a demon nearby with a taste for my blood."

He grabs my hand and squeezes but doesn't say anything.

The temporary offices for Keebler and Crown are in a rundown strip mall filled with tourist shops selling seashells—probably imported from China—plus a liquor store where all the beach bums hang out. And tan twentysomething guys with puka shell necklaces apparently.

Used to being attacked, I try to pull my hand away from Connor's, but he clings with the strength of rigor mortis. I glare up at him, silently begging him to let go, but he stares straight ahead as we pass the guys sipping a fresh bottle of Fireball by their fancy crotch rockets. I wince, prepped and ready for the gay slurs, but no one says a word. One guy looks at us and looks away just as fast but doesn't say anything. I'm not sure if it's because Connor is huge or because, for once, I'm not alone.

Ten feet past, I don't dare glance back, but my shoulders drop a little. I hadn't noticed they were up by my ears.

"You need to stop doing that," Connor says. "Being scared. You don't need to be scared. Look at you. You're not a scrawny kid anymore. Shit, you're almost as big as me."

"Hardly."

He lifts my hand and kisses the inside of my wrist. "Well. I want you to be proud of who you are."

I frown at my flip-flops. "I'm working on it."

"I know." He stops walking and kisses me once on the lips. "Now, let's go save the world."

"Jesus, when you put it that way—" I glance at my reflection in the window of a parked car. "Does my hair—?"

"Stop messing with your hair. It's one of your best features. Why do you think I'm always pulling on it in bed?"

"We actually rarely make it to a bed."

He closes his eyes. "No sexy banter right now. Focus."

"Focus, sure." I sigh and push through the door with a paper sign marked "Keebler and Crown" but not before I notice Connor adjust his pants.

If possible, and despite the big glass windows, it's actually dark inside. Like, shadowy. Cloud cover but not. I'm suddenly cold, but no air-conditioning wheezes from the overhead vents. I wrap my hands around opposite elbows and stand there waiting for my goose bumps to go away, but they don't.

There's a tall desk where a receptionist might stand, but there is no receptionist. The walls are boring beige, no artwork, although somebody left some nails behind and hanging wire. The recessed lighting paints everything in dim, off-white, but half of them are burnt out, which would explain the dark.

"I don't think I want to be here," Connor whispers.

"Noted," I reply before raising my voice. "Hello?"

We're greeted by a cheerful female voice: "Hello?" I hear those Louboutins click down the black linoleum hall, and Tabitha Crown appears with her frankly fabulous red hair. She removes a pair of navy-blue wire rims when she sees me, and there it is: eye fucking. The woman is eye fucking the hell out of me, from head to toe, and her famished grin reveals bright white teeth. "Emory." No one says my name like that except Connor in the midst of, well… She *click-clicks* ever closer and places her fingertip in the center of my chin. "How nice to see you again. And your friend," she says, although she never looks at Connor, just me. "What can I *do* for you?"

My skin doesn't exactly crawl. True, I'm a Kinsey Six, but

as a film buff, I appreciate aesthetics. I realize Tabitha is what straight men consider extremely attractive, so I'm not vomiting in my mouth over the veiled innuendo. But her effort at seduction is still off-putting, possibly because we're there to talk about a demon or possibly because I've never felt objectified or, most likely, because Connor's hand is twisted in a fist at the back of my shirt. If he were a pit bull, he'd be growling.

"We need to talk to you about the Outpost," I say before the big dog at my back lunges for the sex kitten at my front.

"Oh, well." Her eyebrows do a little dance. They're plucked perfectly and match her hair—a real redhead. "Come have a seat." She stands to the side to give us room to pass as I do my best to bat Connor's hand away.

Tabitha's office is as sparse as the rest of the place. There are no family photos or trinkets, just a computer and some varied paperwork. Connor and I stand inside the door and wait for Tabitha to point to a circle of chairs before sitting. Of course, Connor sits to my left and Tabitha to my right. She even scoots her chair forward a couple inches until our knees almost touch before leaning forward and looking interested while also giving me a shot right down the front of her blouse.

"So. What about the Outpost?"

I take a slow deep breath and dig my fingers into the worn arms of the circa-seventies office chair. "I think it'll lose money for your company."

She rests her chin in the palm of her hand and nonchalantly runs a fingertip up the side stitching of my jeans. "Really?"

"The land isn't good, and honestly, bad things happen there."

"Like a curse?" she asks in a musical voice.

"No, just—" I scoot my ass back and my chest forward,

closer up top but far enough for her to stop playing with my pants. "Do you ever get the feeling that a place is evil?"

She chuckles. "Longboat Key doesn't strike me as evil, hon."

"Not Longboat but the Outpost. Doesn't it feel weird to you, like something's wrong?"

She leans back in her chair and crosses her legs within the bounds of a skintight pencil skirt. "How old are you?"

I assume she's wondering if I'm just a dumb kid, so I don't hesitate to say, "Eighteen," with a bit of pride.

I realize I totally misread her intentions when she says, "Let me take you to dinner, the two of us."

Oh. Oh, shit. Whoops, I'm legal.

"He's not available." I've never heard Connor sound literally homicidal before.

Now, it's Tabitha's turn to "Oh". Her mouth makes the letter's shape as she looks from Connor to me and back to Connor. "Pity." She's disappointed, sure, but her jaw clenches like she's angry too. I'd be damn chuffed about their tug-of-war if I didn't find the woman so terrifying. But she's not finished. "Something so"—she glances at me—"*sweet* really deserves a lighter touch, and you look so brutish. Like Frankenstein's creature." She presses her lips together and both smiles and sneers at the same time.

Just another bully. Great.

Her attention is back on me. "In regards to your concerns over the Outpost, I appreciate you coming in to share your suspicions, but there's really nothing to worry about except the rats. And we're dealing with them." She starts to stand, so I put my hand over hers on its armrest. She stares at our stacked fingers and smirks up at me.

"Look, it's not the rats. There's a—"

"Emory," Connor starts.

"There's a demon, okay?"

"Sure there is," she says.

"Its name is Athsaia, and he drinks blood and basically kills people, and if you rebuild on the property, he'll become more powerful and maybe start walking around killing people all over the world."

The silence after my speech is reminiscent of the time a bunch of bullies held my head in the toilet in elementary school. I didn't scream, just tried not to swallow the sick ass water until they let me up and kicked me in the ribs. But it was so quiet under that water—a suffocating quiet like this.

I don't look at Connor, but out of my peripheral vision, I can see his hands are on his cheeks. Tabitha, for her part, is nothing but amused, painted lips pressed together in that freaky pantomime smile. She slinks forward in her seat and puts both hands on the arms of my chair, caging me in. I try to lean back as she leans forward, but there's nowhere for me to go. I'm hoping Connor is against hitting women as she speaks right against my ear. I get a whiff of her perfume, spicy, as she says, "You might as well learn early: just because you're gorgeous doesn't mean people will listen to you. In fact, they're less likely to listen to you because they'll assume you have nothing to say. Find a way to *make* them listen." She presses a quick kiss to the skin in front of my ear and stands. "But in this case, stay away from Gerald Krauss. Crazy people are often dangerous."

I'm pretty sure we've been dismissed, but then, she pokes a finger under my collar and drags Mom's rosary into view.

Her top teeth dig into her bottom lips as she stares at the tiny cross. "Religious?"

I tug on the beaded string, trying to escape. "Can't be too careful."

She drops the jewelry—"God is dead."—and smiles. "Have a nice day."

Connor lifts me by my arm and pushes me out the door of

her office in front of him. We keep walking until we're down the sidewalk, past the liquor store and tourist shops, and under the Spanish moss veil of a banyan. The trees are not scary anymore because, right now, nothing is scarier than Tabitha Crown.

"Holy shit." I bend over, hands on my knees like I'm going to be sick.

Connor sits his ass in the grass. "If anyone's a demon." He points in the direction of her office.

"I'm glad you didn't knock her out."

He holds up his thumb and forefinger in a "this close" gesture.

"I thought real estate agents were supposed to be, like, chipper and shit."

"I don't know what she is, but that did not go well. Did you really think the demon thing was going to convince her?"

I pull my hair. "I panicked!"

"Dude. Remind me to never take you to a poker game."

"Me?" I wave my hand in his face. "You looked like Jack Nicholson in *The Shining* the whole time."

"She was touching you."

"If you ever meet my New York family, they smother me in touches. You can't punch all of them, mostly because my uncles will put a hit on you."

"Em, she wasn't touching you like family!" He tugs up a fistful of grass. "Jesus, I thought she was going to climb into your lap."

"Yeah, and I would have turned to stone. Boom." I snap my fingers. "Gay guy statue. Now what? Talk to Tom Selleck?"

"Tell the sheriff there's a demon? Yeah right."

I pace back and forth as traffic passes languidly on Gulf of Mexico Drive. "You know the shittiest thing? I'll probably be dead before I get a chance to tell all these rational adults 'I told you so.'"

"*That's* the shittiest thing?" He stands and brushes grass from his pants before wrapping me in a hug.

I bop my head against his chest. "I wish we would find Leland, because I could really use a drink."

"I do love a good *drunk Emory*." He slides his whole palm up the back of my neck and massages the base of my skull with his fingers. "Been a long day. Let's go home."

I can barely speak, the massage feels so good, but I manage a few words. "I need to walk Ella."

"I'll come with."

"No."

"Hmm?"

Understandably, he can't hear me what with my open mouth pressed against his left pec. "Nooooo," I repeat. "I need time to think. Your hotness fuzzes up my brain."

"I think that's actually true. Last time we were in bed, you said 'more better.'"

I draw back like I've been burnt. "I did not."

"Yeah. You did."

"Oh my God, we have to break up."

He ruffles my hair.

"You know I feel about five when you do that," I say behind a veil of curls.

"Tough shit. I like touching your hair. Get over it."

By the time we get home, the dads are already on the Nichols's screened-in lanai smoking cigars. The smell reminds me of graduation when a bunch of the cool kids bought cigars and smoked after the ceremony in their caps and gowns. Mom made Liz and me pose for pictures, my chest painted in an ironic rainbow of honor cords. I expected some despised jock to bark one more slur, but nobody picked on me. One of the popular girls actually went out of her way to grab my cords and tug before saying, "Smart is so sexy," exhaling cigar smoke in my face, and

THIS IS NOT A HORROR MOVIE

sauntering away as if all of Perrysburg didn't know I was gay.

For a beat, I think of telling my dad—just shout, "There's a demon at the Outpost," but Connor pinches my wrist and shakes his head before we get anywhere near our parents.

Although Connor is immediately captured, escaping the dreaded how-was-your-day conversation is easy for me because I really do need to walk Ella. Before leaving, I wave into the living room at Liz who's still watching *Golden Girls*. She flicks me off, which means she must be feeling better.

When I arrive, Roberta is dusting sand from her shell exhibit, which is an ongoing, futile struggle for anyone who chooses to build a statue at the beach. She straightens up as I approach, hand to her lower back, and waves her little cleaning brush in my direction.

She says, "Boy, your clothes are nice, but you look like cow poop," which is the closest to a cuss word she's ever been.

Again, I have the fleeting thought: *Tell her. Tell someone.* Roberta believes in Bigfoot, so is a demon really a stretch? Plus, she's religious. Maybe she'll know some demon-banishing quiche recipe, a church lady secret? Instead, I chicken out and talk to Ella as we walk.

The pup is in high spirits as she drags me along the beach, and I tell her all about my nightmare day. She barks a couple times, so I assume she's exhibiting either sympathy or concern. I will accept either. When she starts barking, like really barking, I look up and realize where I am—right at the wonky, broken Outpost fence.

I shush her and pull on her leash, but she keeps barking. She's practically howling by the time I get her to calm down by wrapping her in a big hug and whispering against her fur. Then, I hear voices.

"The young man was seen here before he went swimming."

"I'm not sure what a shark attack has to do with the property, Sheriff."

It's Tabitha and Tom Selleck.

I practically army crawl with Ella closer to the secret illegal entrance.

"What with all the underage drinking that goes on here, I'm not sure the area is safe, ma'am."

"Kids these days. They don't care about safety. They just want to have a good time." I see a flash of her red hair between tumbled palm fronds. I make out the khaki of the sheriff's uniform, too, as they walk away from me.

"I only suggest we secure the exterior. Make sure the young'uns don't get in anymore."

Yes! An excellent idea. Tabitha has to understand that, right?

She laughs, but the sound is far away. I'm losing them. I hazard a glance at Ella, who's pawing at a dried up, dead crab. I study the ground that opened up earlier today in the shape of a tiny mouth and know I shouldn't go into the Outpost, but damn it, this is recon. Know your enemy.

I tie Ella's leash to a tree, as she is perfectly content with her crab corpse, and duck beneath the familiar fencing. The earth doesn't shake as I set foot on Outpost property. No wolves howl, and a sudden breeze doesn't knock me backwards. I've walked from one bit of sand to another, nothing more, so I pick up the pace and follow the sound of Tabitha's voice.

"Kids will be kids, Sheriff. They party, they drink. They have sex. Drinking a few beers at an abandoned Longboat resort is better than having them drive down to Bradenton and getting in a car wreck."

"Well, I suppose, ma'am, but—"

"There's nothing to worry about," she says, her voice close and clear.

I hide behind the corner of a dilapidated gardeners' shack and picture the sheriff's mustache when he sighs. "Kids grow up too fast these days. Have any of your own, Mrs. Crown?"

She giggles like an out-of-tune piano. "No, definitely not. And it's *Ms.* Crown."

I glance around the corner and spot them, standing closer than professionally necessary. Hand in the air, Tabitha looks like she wants to reach up and play with his mustache.

"Pretty lady like you ought to have a husband," the sheriff says.

Tabitha pulls her hand back, and her upper lip twitches. "A woman should be strong enough to stand on her own."

He ducks his head, chastised. "Oh, I don't disagree. Only saying there's a lot of young bucks around these parts that'll be knocking on your door."

She curls one of her pointy, manicured nails into the fabric of his shirt. "What about you, Sheriff? A little missus at home?"

He laughs nervously as I whisper, "No, no, no," and then, she kisses him—a quick, soft peck on his hairy mouth.

Tabitha pulls back and smiles. "No need to worry about kids coming in. The more the merrier. Right?"

"Right." He nods and seems hypnotized. I wouldn't be a bit surprised if he crowed like a rooster. Under any normal circumstance, the sheriff would never agree to this, but apparently, I'm witnessing what some of the dirty straight guys at my high school used to call "pussy magic."

I sense it's time for me to retreat, especially when Tabitha smooches the sheriff again. I turn, but because I'm cursed to be a klutz, trip over a fallen vine and scrape my arm.

I land flat on my chest, the air whooshing out of me like a vacuum set on reverse. I missed whacking my head against a tree by three inches, and the scrape is nothing much—but a sheen of blood creeps out.

Gerald's words come back to me: *He can make a person do just about anything if his or her blood is in the air.*

"Shit."

Fingers digging in sand, I push off the ground and hear my name. I know that voice. I heard it last night from the bottom of the Outpost pool.

It's Athsaia.

Blood pulses in my ears.

"Emory."

I rise to my knees and try to scurry, but it's like the fallen vine has a grip on my ankle. I look back, expecting to see an actual demon—horns, red skin, and all—but it's just a vine. I cuss again, tear the vine off my leg, and push to standing with the help of the tree that almost knocked me unconscious.

"Emory."

Closer this time. I have to get out of here.

"Emory."

So close that— Shit!

I leap backwards, away from the tree that now smiles at me. Aged, brown bark crinkles and creases until opening to reveal a black maw with sharp teeth. Inches above, the bark dances and blinks to reveal two glowing, red eyes.

"Fuck," I squeal and fall right on my ass.

There's no way Tom Selleck didn't hear my manly squeal. A tongue pokes out from the tree face, and I cover my mouth to keep from screaming as the sheriff's voice gets closer. "I think someone's here."

I run on all fours until I'm close enough to leap through the fence, rolling like a log in sun-warmed sand. Ella barks at me, and I shush her, untying her leash fast as I can. Then, we flee.

Old as she is, Ella irritably nips at my ankles as I make her sprint down the beach, back to Roberta's. When Roberta sees what I assume is pure horror on my face, she grabs me by the shoulders and shakes. "You look like you've seen the ghost of Abe Lincoln."

I make her promise to go inside her house and stay there.

Back at the Nichols-Jones complex, I spot Liz and Connor talking on our back patio and practically fall to my knees when I reach them.

Liz glares at me. "Since when do you run?"

I swallow big gulps of air and flap my hands.

Connor crouches down. "Ella work you hard today?"

I shake my head. "The mouth and the teeth!"

Liz asks, "Are you high?"

"Tabitha, sh-she had the sheriff at the Outpost. Then, they were kissing, bu-but m-my name. And the tree was talking to me. It said my name with its teeth and tongue, and oh my God!"

"You. Were at the Outpost?"

Oh, boy. I've never heard Connor use *that* tone of voice before. He might have been pissed with Tabitha earlier, but now, it's like he's got fire in his throat. I am in deep, deep new relationship shit, but I'm more concerned about talking trees that want to eat me.

I look away from Connor's eyes, because I'm pretty sure they've got to be beacons of rage, and beg Liz instead. "We have to tell the cops. We have to do something!"

Liz crosses her arms. "There's nothing to do! We're three dumb kids!"

I scream, "With the fate of the universe in our hands!"

The sound of shouting gets my mom's attention. I assume Dad is still next door with cigars and scotch, but she rushes out the sliding door with a big bowl of fruit salad in her arms. "What's going on out here?"

"Mom. Something bad is happening at the Outpost."

She adjusts the big bowl in her hands to point at me. "You

know I don't like you going there, especially not on your own."

"Me neither," Connor growls. He hasn't moved, a frozen statue of fury.

"Look, fine, I know, but I'm serious right now. We have to call the sheriff's station." I buzz past all of them, back into the house, because if you want to get a job done— I dial the number for the sheriff's office and am fully prepared to sound semi-calm. Who am I kidding? I probably sound like a dog's squeaky toy when a guy picks up, and I shout, "There's a demon at the Outpost!"

A strong hand grabs my cell phone and hangs up.

I spin on Connor. "What the—"

"You promised," he says.

I'm not sure I recognize the guy standing in my parents' living room right now. Maybe I do. I caught a glimpse of this Connor the summer he spent angry—the summer he hated the world—although right now, he looks like he hates a certain Emory Jones.

"You promised you wouldn't go there without me."

Liz walks in and stands off to the side, sort of between us. When Mom, still hugging that damn salad, pokes her face in, Liz shakes her head. Mom presses her lips together, lowers her dark eyebrows at me, and disappears back into the kitchen.

"Look." I hold my hands in front of me. "We need answers, and it was the perfect opportunity. I didn't expect the demon to show up, but I learned something. I think Tabitha has some weird sex powers, and she wants people at the Outpost." I use both hands to shove hair out of my face. "I think she knows exactly what's going on. Gerald was wrong. I can't believe she's just some real estate mogul. I think she knows about Athsaia."

"I don't give a shit right now, Emory."

"Well, you should!"

"Princess," Liz tries to interrupt.

"Maybe the way to the demon is through Tabitha. If I—"

"No. Stop." Connor's voice echoes off the ceiling and bounces back off the floor until we're standing in a ricochet of his rage. "You keep doing this, Emory! You think you can handle things that are just going to get you hurt." The way he over enunciates makes it look like he's actually in pain. "I was a wreck two summers ago, okay?"

I remember, although I'm wary to know where this is going.

"I was angry at the world, at my parents, at stupid community college. But not at you. You were this sweet, beautiful kid— who stepped in the middle of a fist fight?"

I duck my head. "I didn't want you to get hurt."

"We were all twice your size, Em! This is what I'm talking about. You can't keep fighting these battles that are so much bigger than you on your own, or you're going to get hurt."

Liz gazes down at the floor, but subconsciously or not, she's moved closer to Connor like we're playing Red Rover and I'm on the losing side.

Connor runs a hand across his face. He's sweating. "I don't give a shit right now about a demon or the sheriff or Tabitha Crown. You promised you wouldn't go into the Outpost without me, especially now that we know what we're dealing with, but you did. You broke your promise and put yourself in danger. You might think you were trying to help, but you were being reckless. You're not a lonely loner anymore, this isn't some slasher flick, and you are not Neve Campbell, so cut it the fuck out." His eyes go wet and red before he can leave, and although it's near impossible to slam a sliding door, he tries.

I could really use a hug, but Liz shakes her head. "I'm on

his side." She disappears into the kitchen where I hear her talking quietly to Mom.

Since everyone I love has spontaneously gone asshole, I stomp up to my room and flail around on top of my bed sheets until I stop wanting to cry. Then, I pull out my phone and start searching things like "kill a demon" and "demon capture." Unsurprisingly, my search proves fruitless unless you count all the *Supernatural* GIFs.

When Mom calls me down to dinner, I opt for the very mature "I'm not hungry" routine even though I'm starving. I haven't had anything to eat since breakfast. I hide in my room a little longer until the approach of dusk and think "Amazing Grace" might be just the ticket. I shrug off my family's offers to join me and walk down the beach by myself, feet bare in the warm, evening sand. It'll be an excellent sunset tonight, as wispy clouds already decorate the horizon. They'll soon be painted in vivid rainbows as bagpipe music coats the shore.

Of course, after the day I've had, peace is not an option.

Connor stands in my usual spot, close enough to hear the music but far enough away to avoid mingling. I think about turning right around and hiding under my bed until the apocalypse—which could be really soon—but he sees me before I can cut and run.

Ten feet away, we stare at each other. His face isn't wrinkled in wrath anymore. Instead, he looks like he might melt, shoulders slumped and face in a frown. He ambles closer, hands in his pants pockets, and I think I'd like him to punch me. It's better than bearing the brunt of disappointment.

Over the sound of breaking surf, he says, "I'm sorry I yelled at you. I never want to be 'that guy.'"

I shrug, so he sighs.

"Em, do you understand why I got angry?"

I squish sand between my toes. "Because you love me?"

"I never said that."

"Fine. Then, you like me a lot."

He chuckles. "I don't know when I fell for you. Two years ago? Last summer? Yesterday? It's all really—" He steals my awkward move and runs a hand through his hair. "I don't remember not being crazy about you. Even when you were a scrawny kid with a torn Stephen King book, you were fascinating. You're in my head all the time. Shit, every December twenty-third back home, I think about what new books you might be getting."

"You know my birthday?"

He nods. "Liz bitches about how it's too close to Christmas."

"Yeah, our birthday sucks."

"So do you understand why I'm angry?"

The tears I squashed earlier are coming up like vomit. "I'm sorry."

"Me, too," he says.

"You already said that."

"I'm saying it again. Promise you won't do any more stupid heroic shit."

I wipe my booger nose on the dark sleeve of my shirt. "What if you're with me?"

When I try to wipe my whole face, he takes hold of my wrist. "Don't ruin your shirt. I like that shirt." He licks a tear from my face, which makes me giggle. Makes us both giggle. "Fine, you can be heroic when you're with me, but only to a point. I'm not giving you permission to be a moron."

I sniff and nod agreement as "Amazing Grace" sings down the beach, a far-off echo that sounds ominous when the sea breeze swallows certain notes.

Connor moves to sit and pulls me down with him. Once in the sand, his arm around my shoulders, he says, "Now. Tell me exactly what happened at the Outpost today."

CHAPTER 19

I knew he was coming over once all the "grown-ups" went to sleep, but I still manage to zonk out and startle awake when someone whispers my name. The night is a black mass behind him, half his face lit red by the sea turtle safe lights. I still know it's Connor. Pretty sure I would recognize him in the dark. He hangs from the drainpipe on the side of my house and says my name again before I step into the pool of light from outside.

"Hey," I mutter, wiping drool from my lip and wild hair from my face. Disoriented, I struggle with the screen before sliding it up and open.

Just like last time—seems like ten years ago—Connor ninja rolls inside without making a sound. He pops to his feet, and I squint.

"Are those *Evil Dead* pajama pants?"

He plucks the fabric at his thighs, decorated in skulls and chainsaws. "Jealous?"

"No. Maybe."

He sticks a finger in the elastic of my boxer briefs and

pulls before releasing. The fabric snaps against my hip with a bite.

After I explained everything earlier at the beach, Connor did the opposite of panic. He first calmly stated he would be sleeping in my bed for the foreseeable future in case Tom Selleck—or Tabitha, for that matter—decided to come knocking. Although his paranoia is unfounded—I'm pretty sure neither see me as a threat—I'm not going to say no to having Connor climb my drainpipe every night.

Not a euphemism.

He further stated he wanted to look up this Athsaia character, along with any other records of demon sightings. I, of course, explained the futility—but did share some lovely *Supernatural* GIFs. (I've always had a thing for Dean.) Connor claimed he would do "better research," whatever that means. Seriously, I'm a writer. I'm the king of researching creepy shit. I'm probably on a government watch list by now. Again, though, I conceded to his age and hotness.

Finally, he said he wants to confront the sheriff, which I said was utter madness. The last thing we need is to end up behind the bars of a sex-hypnotized behemoth.

Connor must notice I'm standing there in my underwear distracted because he attaches his mouth to the side of my neck. His fingers dig into my hips as he walks me backward toward the bed.

Connor supports most of my weight as we fall, so we land on top of tangled sheets with little more than a quiet "oomph." He's not being careful to be gentle; he's trying to keep my parents from walking in.

Truth? When Tabitha called Connor brutish earlier, I almost nodded in enthusiastic agreement before realizing it was intended to be a put-down. Connor is not a gentle lover, partially due to his own predilections, but probably mostly due to how much I like being roughhoused. See, before I hit second puberty and grew a million inches senior year, I was pretty and little. I'm sure there were guys around who got off on dominating someone small, but I never slept with any of them. All my ex-conquests treated me like a porcelain doll. For my first time, with Thom, gentle was appreciated. It didn't take long, though, even with Thom, to figure out that hair pulling was one of my things, as was biting and clawing and...

You know what? TMI.

Suffice to say the fact that Connor pins me down and tosses me around feels like starting a fire with lighter fluid.

He sinks his fingers into the back of my hair and pulls, slow but hard, until my mouth opens on a gasp—the perfect place for his tongue. I clutch to his shoulders as we grind, and I silently curse those damn *Evil Dead* pajamas. He covers my mouth with his hand before twisting one of my nipples, catching the sound I make in his palm so my family doesn't hear. He dives down and sucks on my neck again until I have to shove at him and hiss, "No hickies!" It's practically my mantra when I'm in bed with Connor.

He smiles down at me, ever amused by my aversion to hickies when my parents are around. Even though he's out of breath, he calms enough to finger-brush the front of my hair —and stare.

"What?" I ask.

He licks his top lip and runs his thumb over mine. "That thing we've been talking about— Did you want to?"

Gulp.

With Connor, I've wanted to do "that thing" for years— probably before I even fully understood what "that thing" was. I wrap my legs around his waist and grin, even though I've got bad news. "I don't have anything," I whisper.

He shifts one of my thighs so he can reach into his pocket

and pulls out a couple necessary items. I take it back—God bless those damn *Evil Dead* pajamas.

I rub my face against his neck and lick behind his ear. "Please," I beg.

I've never seen a man smile so hard—and then get right to work.

Although I'm not sure why, I cry a little once we're finished. Everything Connor did was perfect. Obviously, there were first time logistical issues, especially with two six-foot men trying to have silent sex in a small bed. It has also been a while for me, and Connor is stacked like an African fertility statue. Despite all this, everything felt right and good, but I'm still crying when we're done as Connor scoops me up and hugs me to his chest.

I hear him sniffle, so I ask, "Wait, why are *you* crying?"

"Dunno, why are you?"

"Because I'm a moron," I reply.

"Did I hurt you?"

"No."

"Didn't think so."

"*No.*"

"I guess I'm overwhelmed," he says. "You're so beautiful."

"Shut up." I pull his chest hair in retaliation. "Don't be gross."

"Are you ever going to start accepting compliments?"

"Not when they're gross." My breath hitches on a sigh. "You're beautiful too."

We say "thank you" at the same time.

Don't know if he's thanking me for the compliment, but I'm thanking him for everything we just did and everything he is.

CHAPTER 20

Not sure if my overwhelming stickiness this morning is due to Connor or the out-of-control Florida-in-late-June humidity, but when my alarm cackles at 8:27 a.m., my sheets are glued to my body, and I roll like a warm cannoli from the bed and onto the sand-laden throw rug. I cuss and kick at cotton so I can get to the window in time.

Connor left my bed before sunrise. Although we're consenting adults, I don't think our parents are ready to know we're now officially "doing it." I hear his sneakers on pavement as I stick my head out the window, but instead of looking up and giving me a movie star grin, he glares at me and silently points from me to the first story of my house.

I open my mouth to speak, but he presses a finger to his lips, so I mouth, "What?"

He holds his hand in the air, pointer finger to the sky, and moves his hand in a circle as if this should mean something to me. It's too early for charades.

When I shake my head in confusion, he points again to the ground floor of my home before galloping into his. The entry door by the garage slams shut, and I'm left wondering if sex made him stupid.

Whatever. I need to get downstairs apparently. I take the fastest shower in human history and do a diving leap into navy-blue swim trunks and a white polo. In the hallway, I already hear voices: my parents and— Oh, shit, what's *he* doing here?

I land heavily at the bottom of the steps, so they all turn to look at me: Mom, Dad, Liz in her yoga gear, and Tom Selleck in all his butch, hairy-armed glory. He holds a coffee mug, which he sips from when he sees me. Is that a twinkle in his eye, or adversely, is the whole world a big twinkle now that I've had sex with Connor Nichols?

"Sweetie," Mom says. She comes close and puts her arm around my shoulders. "Coffee?"

"No, I'm all right." I catch Liz's eye for a second, long enough for her to transmit her feeling of panic but not so long that we look like creepy *Shining* twins.

Dad has his hands in his pockets. He rolls back on his heels and onto his toes. "Emory, Sheriff Willick wanted to have a word."

Odd that I never knew his name until now—now, when I don't trust him.

I put on my best sweet face, the one that teachers and middle-aged women can never resist. "Oh?"

Willick shoots the dregs of his coffee like whiskey and hands the mug to my dad. "We know you made that phone call to the station last night, son."

Connor comes crashing into our house from the mudroom. His hair is still dripping from the shower. "Oops, sorry to interrupt," he says. Man, he's a bad liar—which should be a comfort but just comes off as suspicious right now.

Dad puts a hand on his shoulder and tries turning him around, but Connor doesn't budge.

Mom says, "Connor, honey, it's not a good time."

"No, it's fine." I need reliable backup, because Liz looks like she's going to hurl. "Yeah, I made a phone call last night."

"A demon at the Outpost?" Willick shakes his head. I can smell the Old Spice from here. "Prank calling the police is a criminal offense."

"It wasn't a prank." Connor stands ramrod straight as if his height will make him more believable. I'm about to tell him to shut up when he says, "There is a demon at the Outpost."

Liz stays perfectly still like if she goes full statue, this'll all go away. Mom stands with her mouth open, eying the two of us. Dad chuckles, but Willick's mustache turns down at the edges, pointing straight to hell.

"Is this about finding Leland, guys?" Dad asks. "I know you're worried about him, but making up an insane story isn't going to help anything."

"I saw it too," Liz whispers.

"We can show you!" Connor gestures to the back door. "Remember, Em? The blood thing on the ground."

Right, the way the earth opens up in a toothy grin whenever human blood is served.

Dad looks at Mom. "Are they too old to ground?"

"Dad." I walk toward him and then past him. "Come outside for a minute?"

Because my father is cool and has always treated me like an adult, he listens and does indeed follow me onto the back patio where the morning sun could already burn skin. There is no breeze, none. Drops of sweat materialize on the back of my neck, and soon, a drop tumbles between my shoulder blades.

"Emory. What's going on?"

THIS IS NOT A HORROR MOVIE

Liz's girlfriends have always considered my father a DILF. It grossed me out for years, but now, I'm thankful for his buff bod and big green eyes like mine. He looks like an aging action star about to make a comeback—white-haired, American Liam Neeson. Of all the adults, he's the one in which I place the most hope right now because he's the one who should, in theory, understand.

"Dad." I puff up my chest and exhale. "Okay, look, you know in *Nightmare on Elm Street* when all the kids know Freddy Krueger is real but the parents ignore it until basically all their kids are dead?"

"Um." The wrinkles around his eyes deepen. "Okay?"

"So what if there is a demon at the Outpost? And we've seen it? But nobody else believes us." I pause. "Would you believe us?"

"Emory." He closes his eyes and presses his lips together the way I do.

"And what if the demon was kind of after me?"

"Well." He scoffs. "Emory, of course the villain would be after you. You're the smart kid who doesn't drink—much— and knows all the scary movie rules. You're any bad guy's persona non grata. Come on, you act like I've never seen a horror movie in my life. I taught you everything you know about horror movies."

I grab him by the shoulders and shake. "Dad, I know! Do you want to be one of those horror movie parents with dead kids?"

"Oh, for fuck's sake."

My hands drop, and my eyes go wide because my dad never cusses.

He points right in my face. "You know, you were the easy twin. You never got into trouble, and you never dated. But now, this summer, I feel like I missed so many things—the bullying, the fights. And how many guys snuck in your window like Connor does?"

"You know Connor sneaks in my window?"

He gives me the "you're-a-goof" face that is patented Liz.

I wince.

"Look, if you say there's a monster—"

"Demon."

"Whatever. Fine. But I'm not the one you need to convince. You need to convince Tom Selleck."

"God, he does look like Tom Selleck, right?"

Dad nods. "Give him a Hawaiian shirt, and he'd be Magnum PI."

I give my dad a quick hug, but before I can go back inside to plead my case, he hangs on a little longer.

"The football star in there," he says. "He makes you happy, right?"

"Yeah."

"And I hear he'll be in New York with you and Thing 2 in the fall—although Nichols isn't very happy his son is going to be a 'filthy artist,' I think was the phrase."

I snicker and pull away because it's too hot for long-term hugs. "New York is kind of why Connor made his move. He wanted this to be more than just a summer thing, me and him."

Dad squeezes my shoulder, thumb right on the tendon. "It was always headed for more than just a summer thing, you and him. For years. You were too busy hiding in books to notice."

My jaw drops. "If you knew, why didn't you say anything?"

His eyes follow a seagull and then land on blue sky. "Maybe I wanted you to be a kid a little bit longer."

I was in such a rush to get the hell away from my stupid high school and go to college, but maybe I understand Dad's sentiment because if being an adult means fighting battles way bigger than I am, give me childhood forever.

"Now." He puts his hand on my back, and it doesn't feel as big as it used to. "Show me this demon."

———

We walk down the beach together: Sheriff Willick, my parents, Connor, and Liz bringing up the rear. I imagine this is what walking to the gallows feels like, although maybe I'll get a stay of execution. Maybe this will actually work.

As we near the busted fence at the back of the Outpost, Willick makes to walk right through, but Connor holds me back, and I grab onto my mom and dad.

Dad uses his facial muscles to ask, "Seriously?" His dubious expression melts when he sees how hard Connor is hanging onto my wrist.

"Sheriff, just—" I beckon him back through the fence and wonder if he's bled at the Outpost. Maybe Tabitha bit his lip during their kiss? It would be wholly inappropriate to ask, but he does get the message. He does step back through the broken fence and onto neutral sand—sand not owned by a freaking demon.

I shake my hand out of Connor's vicelike grip and pull the kitchen knife out of my pocket.

"Em." Somehow, his voice is both irritated and concerned.

Mom uses her soft mom voice. "Sweetie, why do you have a knife?"

"We need a little of my blood."

Connor tries to pull me back toward him, but I hold my ground. "We'll use mine," he says.

"What? No!" I point at the Outpost's earth. "It already knows me. I don't want it to know you too."

"*Know* you?" Willick asks, but I ignore him.

"Look." I walk right up to the secret entrance but don't cross the plain. "Everyone, come here."

"I'm fine." Liz hugs herself. "I've seen it, thank you very much."

They curl around me like I'm a magician about to make a rabbit disappear—or a rat, more likely, at the Outpost. Come to think of it, I haven't seen rats at the Outpost lately.

I've never actually cut myself on purpose before. I don't realize how much the thought makes my skin crawl until I'm standing there with an audience and a pointy knife pressed to my finger. But okay. Don't look like a wuss, Emory. I can practically hear a bunch of Stephen King characters cheering me on.

I wince when the knife's tip breaks skin. A small, red bead blooms.

I hand the knife to Connor and extend my arm across the divide. It honestly feels that way to me now. I am here; evil is there. I half expect the ground to sigh in expectation. I squeeze my fingertip. A drop of my blood quivers and jumps free like an itty-bitty skydiver. I watch it tumble and land in the sand on Outpost property.

"Watch," I whisper.

My fresh drop of blood shivers before being sucked down into the sand like any normal drop of blood would.

"Anytime now," Connor says.

They're all leaning over me, staring beyond my shoulder at my bloody contribution. I even hear Liz shuffle closer.

Any minute now, the ground will open in the shape of a toothy grin and gobble up my yummy blood. Any minute...

"What are we looking at exactly?" Dad asks.

Then, I remember: the trick didn't work for Gerald when he brought Tabitha. Athsaia only shows up when he wants to.

We are totally screwed.

Willick kicks at sand. "Son, I'm not sure what you hoped

to accomplish this morning, but I ain't buying it. I appreciate your concern for Leland, and I'll let this little infraction slide, but no more prank calls to my station, you hear?"

Connor, bless him, is still watching my drop of blood, but I turn around and nod to our very hairy sheriff. Dad puts a hand on my shoulder, and Mom chews her lips the way she does when Dad makes her watch scary movies even though she hates them.

Willick starts walking away. "Y'all have a good day, now." If he had a hat, he would have tipped it like some classic film cowboy. Instead, his mustache dances in a sea breeze as he retreats in the direction of my house where his cruiser is probably parked. I assume that's how Connor knew there was a freaking cop at my house at eight in the morning.

Mom sighs. Here we go. "Sweetheart, are you feeling okay?"

"He's fine," Liz says. She twists our arms together and drags me toward water. "Come on, princess. Connor!"

He jumps when she yells his name but turns to follow.

Mom's voice is gentle behind us. "Let's have lunch together, okay?"

I wave, but Liz ignores her, just tugs me along with Connor, a lovesick puppy at my heels.

We sit in the sand with our feet in the water, waves breaking below our butts. Connor does that thing—I think it's subconscious—where he wraps me in his arms, until I feel mildly suffocated but safe, and leans his chin on top of my head. He circles me with his legs, too, either protecting me from a cruel world or making sure I can't escape. Not sure.

Liz kicks a wave, which attacks her in retribution, splashing warm salt water all over her expensive yoga gear. "I think I want a burger," she says.

The only response I have for my strictly vegetarian sister is, "Huh?"

"If the world is ending, I deserve a burger."

"Why didn't it work?" Connor's voice vibrates against my back. "Why didn't it want your blood?"

"Gerald said it doesn't always work. Remember? Athsaia can choose to hide if it's in his best interest."

"I definitely want a burger," Liz says as some girls in bikinis approach.

One of them yells, "Y'all coming to the summer solstice party tonight?"

Her friend pushes her. "You're crazy. That place is cursed this summer. Nobody's gonna show."

Liz puts on her fake smile. I've seen it a million times, and although other people believe it's real, I think she looks like a ventriloquist dummy. "Yeah, um, we'll see. Thanks."

The teenyboppers flounce away as I shift in the embrace of my human straightjacket. "I want to go see Gerald."

If possible, Connor hugs me tighter. "Why?"

"Because he had an intimate relationship with that thing back there, so he deserves harassment."

Liz catches a wave in the back of the knees but doesn't seem to notice or care. "Where did he say he was squatting?"

"The abandoned Squid Shack." I try to ignore all the sweat gushing down my back, but my boyfriend is like a space heater. "Connor, I'm going to need you to let me go."

He smells my hair. "Is your finger okay?"

I stare at the little cut on the tip of my finger. There's a dried smudge of red but nothing else, so I show Connor. He sucks my finger into his mouth, and Liz makes a retching noise.

The Squid Shack isn't far from our house, so the walk only takes about twenty minutes. Walking on sand always takes longer, although Liz's pace helps. She's stomping, cussing, and kicking at sand as though it attacked her fashion sense. After the past couple days, she should really get her blood pressure checked.

"Liz? Wait."

I see the ramshackle building up ahead, hidden by overgrown palm trees and sea grass between two fenced-in mansions. No way am I letting her go in first. She looks like a shipwrecked trophy wife; in other words, an easy target. Gerald did conjure a demon, so what else is he capable of?

We're a clumsy train as we near the back entrance. I grab Liz's arm and pull her behind me and Connor grabs mine to push me behind him until we're all banging shoulders and hips like fat penguins crossing Antarctica.

When Liz stumbles over the back of one of my flip-flops, she screams "Goddamn it" in frustration.

Something crashes behind the closed door, wood worn with too much sea breeze and not enough lacquer. Despite my protests, my sister shoves the door open and steps inside.

It's dark and smells of dead fish. A bit of sunshine streaks in through broken, boarded up windows. Old tables remain, some even with salt and pepper shakers. Dust hovers like snow in the air, and two bare feet point at the ceiling.

"He's dead," Liz says just as Gerald groans.

"Gerald?" I step over a knocked down chair, which I assume he'd been standing on, watching the beach, when my sister's shriek scared him shitless. I extend a hand, which he takes, but Connor has to take his other to actually get him standing.

I expect Gerald to do that thing he does where he brushes at his clothes and tugs on them as though he's wearing Armani and not "lunatic chic," but he doesn't. He whispers, "Did *he* send you?" The whiskers around his mouth are stained yellow, and I question the last time he bathed.

"Who?" I ask.

"Athsaia. He's getting stronger. Can't you feel it?"

Frankly? I might. Even though the sun shines on Long-boat Key, it feels darker. Even though the sand mouth didn't open when I shed blood, my stomach ached. Even though I had the best sex of my life last night, the expected euphoria isn't there. It's almost like the feeling I got at the carnival haunted house: You know someone is going to jump out at you with a chainsaw. You're just not sure when.

Gerald backs further into the now empty restaurant, and Connor follows. "How could he be getting stronger?"

"Someone is feeding him." He reaches over the edge of a decrepit wooden bar and pulls out a dusty bottle. He pops the cork free with his teeth and spits it on the ground before gulping.

My stomach drops to the bowels of Hades and back. "A finger. I saw a rat with a human finger, first party at the Outpost."

Liz swats me upside the head. "That wasn't something you thought to mention?"

I swat back at her. "I wasn't sure it was a finger at the time, because I don't usually *realistically* think 'Hey, look, a human finger.' I thought it was like a piece of bread with marmalade, okay?"

Gerald slams the bottle against the bar, but it doesn't break. "One body wouldn't be enough. He needs several!"

Connor looks down at the dirty floor, covered in dust and some fabric—remnants of a makeshift bed. When he looks at me, his forehead is wrinkled in the middle.

"What?"

"Leland," he says.

"No. Oh, fuck, no." I lean down and put my head between my knees. Connor's hand rubs between my shoulder blades.

"A full grown man would make an excellent meal, along with that shark attack—" Gerald cackles and downs more booze. "—so-called shark attack."

Liz touches my shoulder but addresses Gerald. "You're saying Duke died at the Outpost."

"Obviously. Then, someone chopped up the remaining evidence and threw him in the ocean. It only makes sense."

I press my hands against my knees and force myself to stand, even though I'm still dizzy at the thought of some demon tearing Leland to shreds. "What do you mean, it makes sense?"

"Well." When Gerald shrugs, his beady eyes bulge out. "That's what I did when it happened eight years ago."

Liz, who'd been standing a bit in front of me, now does a slow retreat to behind my left shoulder. She curls her fingers around mine, and thanks to our creepy twin thing, I feel the fear coming off her like punches to the ribs.

Connor seems less horrified and more curious. He rubs his chin. "I'm sorry, you chopped up a body and threw it in the ocean to make it look like a shark attack when, in fact, your demon killed someone?"

"No." He laughs. "No, I told you! At Athsaia's bidding, the gentleman committed suicide, Athsaia consumed his blood, and I disposed of the body. It's what any successful businessman would do in that economy."

Liz tugs my arm. "I want to go."

I squeeze her hand. "But then who chopped up Duke?"

"Someone who knows about the demon—" *Glug, glug, glug.* Rum drips down his chin, so he wipes his mouth with the back of his hand. "Someone who is trying to bring Athsaia to his full demonic form. He'll come for me first. I know he will." He stares at the three of us, hopeful, like maybe we have all the answers, even though there isn't a virgin in the room. The hope alters, changes, as his right eye twitches. "Unless... unless I offer the three of you as a sacrifice. I give you three to Athsaia, promise to serve him. Maybe then he'll spare me. Young blood; he loves young blood." He fingers his mustache. "And the summer solstice party tonight. The perfect night for a bloodbath."

I keep my eyes on Gerald but tilt my face at Connor. "We have to warn people, make doubly sure that party doesn't happen."

"I don't think so," Gerald whispers. He digs in the pocket of his torn, stained khaki shorts. I'm hoping for a good luck talisman, but he pulls out his pathetic Swiss Army knife instead and frees the blade.

When Gerald takes a step closer, I don't think twice. I pull the kitchen knife from my pocket and nudge Connor behind me with my elbow before holding it out and taking up a defensive posture. After all the bullies I've faced, trust me, I know defensive posture.

Gerald snickers. "What are you going to do with that, pretty boy?"

I flick the tip of my knife at his Swiss Army. "Dude, if this is a dick-measuring contest, I win."

Calmly, Connor asks us both to lower our weapons, but I'm not moving a muscle until Gerald is freaking hog-tied.

Gerald sneers. "You don't have the guts."

"Really? Because a couple days ago, you wanted me to fight a demon. What makes you think I won't take *you* down?"

He drunkenly swings the mostly empty bottle around although his knife hand is steady. "Because you're too good. You don't know what evil is."

I think back on all the bullies who called me names and shoved me in lockers. I think of the guys who hated me because I was a "little twink," the boys who fractured my ribs because I threatened their world order. Don't know what evil is? Fuck yes, I do.

"Look, stop. Both of you," Connor says, but I barely hear him.

Even with Liz's nails digging into my back, this is tunnel vision, and just like in other fights where I've been the center, it's like I can see the hit coming. Intentional or not, Gerald shatters the bottle in his hand on the bar's edge. He now brandishes something that could actually be dangerous, so I tell Liz to run and try to push Connor away from the path of attack.

Connor and I scuffle in an effort to defend each other, but we separate and circle when Gerald erupts in a war cry and comes running. Luckily, he's got a weak swing. The busted bottle is easy to avoid, and he drops his Swiss Army when I hit his wrist. When he focuses all his mad attention on Connor—take down the strongest first?—I drop my knife and wrap my hands around the arm brandishing the busted bottle. I squeeze hard and feel tendons shifting beneath my palm. Gerald roars in pain. I catch his elbow in my sternum and lose my grip.

The last thing I want is to end up on my ass on this floor with Vincent Price's psychotic cousin hovering above me, so I backpedal.

Should have fallen.

Gerald swings the bottle. Liz screams, and I'm angry with her for a second because I told her to run. Connor tackles a kicking, screaming Gerald to the floor—as any self-respecting football player could—and pins his arms behind his back.

Then, wide, blue eyes look up at me. Connor's lip trembles when he says, "Em."

The white polo shirt must make the blood look worse, because the cut across my upper abdomen doesn't hurt. I put my hand over the wound and lift a red-painted palm in front of my face. "Shit." My knees disappear. When I hit the floor, there it is: the pain. Yep, this is bad.

Liz is there, kneeling in front of me, pushing hair out of my face. "Emory! Oh my God!"

"It's not that deep. It's not..." I rest my forehead on her shoulder.

"There you are." Christ, it's practically a purr.

I know that voice.

"Have you been hiding?"

My breath stalls. My whole body shivers. I hold tight to my sister's shoulders. "Liz, I can hear him."

"Come to me."

"What?" Her voice breaks. "Connor, what's he talking about?"

Gerald's says, "I told you! Athsaia is getting stronger. He senses his favorite blood even from here!"

"Emory."

I try to think, try to breathe, say *no, no, no*, but there's nothing but searing pain and the need to walk my ass to the Outpost and nosedive into a concrete pool.

I hear scrambling nearby, fighting bodies, followed by running feet.

The loud opening and quiet closing of a broken door.

Then, someone strong is lifting me, moving me, until I recognize the feel of Connor's lap beneath me, my face against his neck, and his arms around me like soft, warm ropes.

"Liz, get help!"

I reach out and grab onto her shirt. "I don't want you out there alone."

"I'll be right back."

"Take the kitchen knife."

I don't know if she does or not, but I hear her flip-flops moving farther and farther away. Now, it's just me, Connor, and Athsaia's voice in my head.

"Come back to me."

"Tell me five things you can see."

Connor is using my old panic attack trick. Sadly, the room

is fuzzy, whether from blood loss or shock or a demon in my head—who knows? "Sunlight. Uh, old table. Your shoulder." I wince and double over in pain.

"Emory!"

"I'm okay, uh... salt shaker. Knocked over chair."

"Four things you can touch."

I chuckle once, and it hurts. "I don't want to get blood on you."

"I don't care."

I touch him and list: "Bicep. Pec. Adam's apple. Chin."

He holds me tighter, my ear against his chest. "Three things you can hear."

"Connor's heartbeat—"

"Bring your friends. All your friends."

"Ocean. Ocean waves, um..." I squish my eyes shut. "Seagull."

"Two things you can smell."

"Blood and dead fish."

"You can do better than that," he whispers, so I stick my nose behind his ear.

"Stress sweat."

At least he sort of laughs. "One thing you can taste."

I lift my chin and lean my head back. "You?" I murmur as I open my eyes.

Connor still clings to me with one arm but uses the other to touch my face, cup my cheek, and kiss me. Athsaia doesn't make a sound.

CHAPTER 21

B y the time I'm coherent, I'm in a hospital room that smells like antiseptic and shitty cafeteria food. Fluorescent lights come in and out of focus above me because I'm on drugs. I feel zero pain, just a cheerful floating sensation that's interrupted when I remember I've been stabbed.

I lurch upward, and a familiar Hulk hand pushes me back down onto bright white sheets. "Fuck, no." Connor is here apparently.

I smack his hand. "You have to bust me out." I'm not sure he understands. Even in my own head, I sound like *wah-wah-wah*.

"No."

"Where's Liz? Is Liz okay?" I gawk around the room, but moving my head too much makes me feel like I'm flying again. I giggle weakly.

"She's in the hall with your parents talking to Sheriff Willick."

"Mm-mm, no, he kisses Tabitha and hates me. He thinks I'm crazy."

Connor sits on the edge of my bed. I put both my palms on his right thigh to stay grounded as his fingers trace my face. "Well, not now. Gerald Krauss tried to kill you, and all the cops are looking for him."

I try sitting up again, but Connor plants his hand on my shoulder and holds me down. "No, no, I don't want to be Matt Burke."

"Dude, I don't know what you're talking about."

"In *Salem's Lot*! He's the English teacher who was in the hospital, and it didn't end well for him, okay?" I claw at his arm until he grabs both my wrists and leans closer. I can now see his wind-mussed blond hair, all-American blue eyes, and stone-cut jaw. There's still a spot of my blood on his chin. "Oh, there you are," I mumble. "You were a handsome fuzz ball a minute ago. What drugs am I on, anyway? They're wonderful."

He kisses my forehead. "You looked so fucking small when they brought you in here, even though I know you're not. Maybe it was because you weren't awake, I don't know. You seem so much bigger when you're awake."

"Now, you sound like you're on drugs."

"I would *love* some drugs right now."

I slip one of my wrists out of his grasp and tug the back of his hair until he closes his eyes and smiles.

"You're stupidly brave."

My face wrinkles up. "I'm not stupid."

"You look like a pouting toddler right now."

"So should I call you daddy?"

"Wow, you're on *a lot* of drugs."

"Is he awake?"

Connor leans back at the sound of Liz's voice. Thanks to the cornucopia of pain meds in my body, she looks fuzzy, too, but I recognize that her yoga outfit didn't have red on it this morning. A lot of red. Add excessive blood loss to pain pills, and my giggly state makes sense.

Connor kisses the back of my hand and stands. "I'll give you two a moment."

"Wait, but where are you going?" I ask.

Connor snorts. "Nowhere, Em. I'm obviously staying here, okay?"

I nod. The thought of any of us being separated right now puts me in a damn panic. I've seen how monster movies work —divide and conquer. Not on my utterly incapacitated watch.

Liz nods to Connor as he leaves the room and fills his empty place on the edge of my bed. "I hate you," she says. "I can't believe you actually told me to run."

I flail my hand around and get momentarily distracted because it has tails. "Whoa. I was trying to protect you. I am your big brother."

"By five minutes."

"And half a foot."

She blows hair out of her face with an irritated puff. "Yeah, blah blah, Mom and Dad are totally freaked. Thank God, Connor managed to calm them down. He's like a huge, protective Teddy bear."

"What's evil Tom Selleck have to say?"

She adjusts the collar on what I assume is my hideous hospital gown, although I'm too drugged to look down. "All hands on deck to find Gerald. Stop him from feeding a bunch of innocent kids to a demon."

I think my brow furrows, but my forehead is numb. "You talked demons with Willick again? Why would you—"

"No, dumb-dumb. We need his help, not his skepticism. Shit, he's even stationing an officer outside your door in case Gerald makes a second attempt."

"I don't think Gerald was actually trying to kill me, Liz."

Her huff rattles the windows—or I'm hallucinating.

Probably hallucinating. "He wanted to sacrifice us to a man-eating demon to save his own ass! And let us not forget he chopped up a dead body eight years ago. That's fucking dedication!"

I cover my face. "Stop yelling. It's making my eyeballs feel funny."

"Look, you need to rest, and I'm going to a nice restaurant for a huge burger." She pats the hands covering my face. I feel her slight weight vacate the edge of my bed, but before she can leave—

"Hey."

In my druggie haze, she looks just like me.

"Connor and I had sex."

A momentary glimmer of white teeth. "Good, princess. Now, get some rest. I'll come back tonight."

———

In the dream, an octopus has its big sucker right on my mouth and won't let me breathe. I wake, but before I can even open my eyes, I realize something is in fact covering my lips. My eyes shoot open, blinded momentarily by orange sunlight through the hospital window. I flail against the apparent octopus until I recognize red hair and Tabitha Crown with a finger to her lips in a mime of "shush." Then, I recognize the pain. My chest is on fire; lava courses beneath my ribs. She must expect this, because she pushes her hand even harder against my mouth when I groan and squeeze my eyes shut.

"Shhh," she hisses. "No need to wake him up." She looks to her left, and so do I.

Connor naps, curled up on a hospital cot.

No, lady, I need to wake him up immediately because you're kneeling on my bed with your hand over my mouth looking like a *Harry Potter* Dementor. I need him awake *right now*, thank you.

I've never been good at controlling my face, especially while half dumb with pain, so she must read my expression. She leans back enough to open her suit coat with the hand not slowly suffocating me to show me a knife—like, a real one. Not a Swiss Army. Not a kitchen knife. Tabitha has a Bowie knife under her designer jacket.

My eyes dart toward the door, but the cop is gone. The stupid cop Willick left behind is up and gone.

"I told him to go get a coffee," she says. "Seeing that you and I are such good friends."

I breathe harshly through my nose, but the panicked up and down of my lungs does nothing to deter the line of fire across my chest.

"Oh, I know it hurts, but I turned off all your IVs. I need you coherent, Emory."

Don't cry. Don't you cry right now. I try to slow my breathing, focus on her face that isn't as pretty this close up. I see the way her makeup creeps into wrinkles, hiding the early signs of age. Her lips are dry under that red lipstick.

"I'm going to move my hand now, and you're going to be very quiet."

I nod, and she frees my lips. When one trembles, I bite it. *Don't show weakness.*

"Gerald came to visit the Outpost," she says. "Didn't come inside but ran the perimeter, promising his allegiance to a demon. I had to shut him up."

"Is he dead?"

"Not yet." She smiles. "You know about the demon." She runs her palm gently over top my bandages. I brace myself, waiting for her to dig in claws. "Athsaia likes you. He says your blood is strong."

"Oh my God, who are you?"

"Tabitha Crown. We've met." She cups my jaw and runs a thumb across my cheekbone. I shudder; it's like being touched by a spider. "I'm a Satanist, darling. The whole real estate firm is. We buy land with *history*, links to other worlds. I felt Athsaia floundering years ago, but nobody believed me because I'm only second in command. Keebler's eye candy. I bought the Outpost myself in secret. Then, I might have called some unfavorable men early on and told them to steal copper. Murdered them, fed them to Athsaia, strengthening him. I will prove to Keebler that a pretty woman can bring a demon to life. But no one was supposed to notice Leland."

I press my lips together, and come on, how long is that cop going to take a coffee break? If she tries to kill me, I doubt I'll be able to fight her off. My screams will wake Connor much too late.

She holds my chin between two fingers hard. "But you notice everything, don't you? Wouldn't shut your damn mouth." She leans close. I think she might bite my ear off and eat it. Instead, she whispers, "Most men are so easy to influence once you get in their pants, but you had to be *so* difficult. You and your buff boyfriend." She moves back but keeps a hand near my throat like a threat. "I didn't know you had a sister until today. Twins. She looks sweet."

I swallow the bit of spit I have left. "What do you want from me?"

"Any other year, tonight would be the biggest night at the Outpost: the summer solstice party. Did you know supernatural forces are stronger on solstice nights? Equinoxes too. Nights meant for revelry and spell-casting. The veil between us and them is thinnest, so a perfect night for a party. But this year, kids are scared." I flinch when she pokes her finger against my Adam's apple. "I need blood at the Outpost tonight, Emory. I need drugs and sex and death for my master. Thanks to Leland and that surfer boy, my master is almost fully formed, but I've been depending on the solstice party as the big finale—Athsaia's chance to finally walk the Earth, but due to rumors of a stupid curse, he might never get the chance." She touches my hair. It would be a caress if she weren't pulling so hard. "You will guarantee me a party."

I curl my fingers in the cheap, hospital blanket. "Why would I help feed a bunch of teenagers to a demon?"

"Oh, hadn't you guessed?" She grins. "I have your sister."

Before I can start screaming, she uses both her hands to cover my mouth and nose. I can't breathe, and the cut across my chest feels like a crack about to rip in two.

"Shh, calm, calm. Do you want to breathe?"

Yes, shit, please. I still and stop fighting.

She pulls her hands away, and I gasp for air. "Make tonight the party of their lives, considering it'll be their last, and maybe I'll have Athsaia spare you and the people you love. If you don't do what I ask, I'll kill your sister, then Connor, then your parents, and if I'm feeling particularly generous, maybe I'll even let you die too." Her tongue touches her top lip. "Or maybe you'll bow down and serve my master. He promises great power when you do his bidding."

Not in a million years, bitch. Although I think it, this is not the opportune time to say it.

"By midnight, I want the Outpost hopping with decadent, drunk young blood, or I will feed your sister to Athsaia, piece by piece. Is that clear? Nod your head, Emory."

I nod and wonder what the hell I'm going to do.

"And no cops. And no running to Mommy and Daddy, either, or I start cutting. I tend to do fingers first. Like fleshy appetizers."

I chew the insides of my cheeks.

"See you soon." She pats me on the head like I'm a cute little kid and tiptoes from the room in her red-soled Louboutins. The worthless cop still isn't back, and Connor still snores as I stare at the two IVs in my arm, no longer doing a bit of good. Breathing is a struggle without the pain meds, but Tabitha was right: I need my brain clear right now.

Okay, so a demon is about to take over the earth, and his evil minion is holding my sister captive. Great. First step: get out of the hospital. I look at the IVs again. This is going to hurt probably, but what's a little more pain, right? I slowly pull the first one out, mouth open on a silent scream because, yep, this feels a lot like being stabbed, only backwards. I press my lips together and take a few forceful breaths through my nose.

I know I'm trying to be the man right now, but I really don't want to take out my second IV. God, I really don't. "Come on, Emory," I whisper and tug.

Thankfully, the psycho lady is no longer staring me down, because I'm crying now—big, stupid, frustrating tears that blur my vision until I wipe them away with a sheet.

I shift sideways and put my bare feet on the cold tile. I don't want to wake Connor. I don't want him to have any part of this, whatever my plan might be. I don't want him hurt.

I stand. Okay, standing isn't so bad actually. Maybe I'm not as hurt as I thought, or maybe my whole body is just buzzing with pain to the point of numbness. Who knows? I won't question my luck.

I'm about to sneak past my sleeping boyfriend and shelter him from Tabitha's bestowed bloody fate when I stop and sigh. I mutter, "What the hell, man?"

This is what fictional heroes always do—try to go off on their own and spare the people they love—and how does that turn out, Emory Jones? Never good. This is so *Buffy*, season two, episode one, where she leaves her friends to fight her own battles, and they all end up kidnapped in a basement. Have I learned nothing? Sigh.

I grab Connor's knee and shake.

He flips his head back, probably whiplash, and gawks at me with red, puffy eyes. "What are you doing out of bed? Your hands!" He stands and scoops them up. Oops, I hadn't noticed there was blood dripping from my empty IV holes.

"We need to get out of here before that cop gets back from his coffee break."

"What? No." He takes a step forward, trying to shuffle me back into bed.

I push against him. "I'll explain once we get out of here, but this is really important. Tabitha has Liz."

"Wait, what?"

"Connor." I flip my bloody hands around and grab his wrists. "We have to go. Please, trust me."

And here's a situation where it's good my expression is an open book. He reads the lines on my face like lines of text before giving a curt nod. "Put your hands behind your back."

I give him a "huh?" face.

"Dude, you're dripping blood everywhere."

I put my hands behind my back, and Connor pokes his head into the hospital hall. He looks left and right, then gestures me forward. We start walking left. I'm totally dependent on Connor for direction, because I don't remember coming in here at all.

The hall is quiet but for a smattering of hushed voices. The smell—I hate that smell—of bland food and rubbing alcohol assails my senses as I dodge the bright light of overhead fluorescents. Although I'm confused, I don't speak up when Connor drags me into a closet.

Floor to ceiling, we're surrounded by medical supplies.

"Oh," I manage.

"Oh, he says." Connor fumbles around. "You shouldn't even be standing up right now. What the hell is going on? What do you mean Tabitha has Liz? What does Tabitha have to do with anything?"

"She's the one trying to fully conjure Athsaia, and if we don't get a bunch of teenagers to the Outpost tonight for a massacre, she's going to kill my sister."

He cusses as he rips open an alcohol swab and cleans the blood from my arms. "How the hell do you know that?" He reaches for gauze.

"Because Tabitha was just in my room."

Wrong thing to say. His jaw turns to stone and his eyes, ice.

"She threatened you. I couldn't wake you up."

He goes back to work, wiping the blood away before fumbling for big Band-Aids. "Wait, start over."

"I don't have time to start over, Connor! We have to get out of here."

He pushes Band-Aids over both my little cuts and gestures to my outfit. "Not like that!"

Oh, right. I'm in a hospital gown. No wonder my ass is freezing.

Man of action, Connor finds a thin pile of medical scrubs on a high shelf and hands me a pair of purple ones with rainbows and unicorns. Fantastic. This is my battle gear.

I shimmy into the scrubs. They fit okay, maybe a little short in the legs. I wince as I'm pulling the shirt on and hope Connor doesn't notice, but he does. "Damn it, Emory, we should call the cops."

I put my hands on his shoulders and squeeze. "We can't do that. Tabitha said no cops, no parents, or she'll hurt Liz. Now, let's get out of here and figure out what we're going to do."

Connor is surprisingly sneaky for a guy over six feet tall. Not only does he get us out of the hospital free and clear, but he even steals an orange bottle of painkillers from some snoozing old guy's bedside. The most moral of things? No, but I'm pretty sure the senior citizen can get more, and it's sickly romantic as he feeds me half a pill before kissing the side of my mouth.

Daylight is burning. Literally, it burns like hell outside in the orange sun of a blistering Florida eve. My feet start sweating in my blue Crocs—because, of course, Crocs were my only footwear option in the supply closet. My internal flaming gay might never recover.

We take a cab ride closer to our houses—closer to the Outpost—and have it drop us off near the big banyan by the Lazy Lobster. Screw it, trees don't scare me anymore. I lean against the trunk in the shade while Connor paces. "Your parents must notice Liz is missing, right?"

I sift back through my drug haze of earlier. "She said she was going out for a nice burger. They probably think she met friends at a restaurant. And it's not like my parents keep a close watch on us anyway."

"They're about to when they find out you bailed from the hospital. Your mother was going to come back later with homemade ravioli."

I tug my hair. "Shit, I'm a fugitive. In unicorn hospital scrubs."

A car whips by on Gulf of Mexico Drive, so Connor steps farther into the shade. He is, after all, my accomplice. "So let me get this straight: Tabitha wants us to buy a bunch of kegs and throw a raging solstice party at the Outpost that ends in a massacre and possibly Armageddon?"

"She didn't mention Armageddon. A demon's just going to be King of Earth."

His mouth drops open as he stares at me.

"Connor, I don't want her to hurt my sister." I hate that my voice shakes, but it has the positive effect of bringing Connor into my arms. He hugs me—gently. I speak into his shirt. "What if we, I don't know, formed a virgin kindergarten army?"

He doesn't laugh, just ruffles my hair. "We can't bring children into this, even if they are virgins. Let's be rational."

"I was once," I murmur, and he's back to pacing.

"First off, tonight is, like, *here*. How can we get a party together by midnight, especially when half the kids on Longboat are scared of the Outpost right now?"

I crouch with my back against the tree because maybe standing does hurt a little, even with the helpful buzz of Vicodin. "Tiffany with a double E."

"Huh?"

"I don't know if she spells her name with two E's. It seems like something a girl like her would do, though. We have her text everyone. We just need to find her number."

"I have her number," Connor says.

My nose scrunches up, and I flash my teeth. "What? Why?"

"Emory, babe, you and I weren't always a thing."

I harrumph.

He crosses his arms and stands with legs slightly spread like a superhero. "So what do I tell her?"

Light bulb. "We're filming a horror movie at the Outpost and need extras. Everyone knows about you and your camera fixation, and everyone wants five minutes of fame. Plus, if we tell them the fictional monster is a blood-eating demon, when we tell them to run, they probably will."

He slumps to a seat and wraps his arms around his legs. "Oh my God."

"It'll— it'll be a distraction, right?" I scoot closer to him over fallen leaves and woodchips. "Remember that time I fell through the floor at the Outpost? Well, I saw Athsaia, as he was, just red eyes. I bet that's where Tabitha is keeping Liz, somewhere near that place. You and your film extras will act as a distraction while I search. Once I find her, you yell run."

He lifts his head. "So we get away tonight. Then what?"

239

I shrug. "One battle at a time?"

"Em, can you even run right now?"

I'm really not sure, but my wounds are bandaged up tight to keep my blood both out of the air and off the ground. So… into battle.

CHAPTER 22

onnor sends "The Text" to Tiffany. Within minutes,
I imagine phones are lighting up all across the
beach of Longboat Key—the telephone equivalent
of "game on!" Despite the nerves and whispers of an Outpost
curse since Duke's death, few kids can pass up the opportunity to be in a movie. Plus, free beer. I really hope we're not
rounding them up for slaughter.

Connor also texts a guy who can get kegs at light speed.
Funny I never realized he knew all these people, had all these
numbers. When I give him a funny look, he shrugs and says,
"I had to fill the Emory void with something."

Getting shit out of our houses is more complicated.

Firstly, because Connor's nerd level knows no bounds, he
refuses to pretend to film using his iPhone; he requires his
fancy digital camera. Secondly, he insists I have a pair of real
shoes if I'm being chased by a demon, although if I'm being
chased by a demon, I don't feel like footwear is going to
matter. If I'm being chased by a demon, I'm probably about
to be dead. He'll hear none of this; he requires we go home.
Well, *he's* going home—to both of our houses.

He shook his head when I suggested I sneak into my own bedroom window. "If we're going to die tonight, it'll be because we're trying to save your sister, and possibly the world, from a monster—not because your lanky ass broke his neck climbing a drainpipe."

So now I sit a block from both the Nichols and Jones abodes, tugging at pieces of beach grass, weighing our options.

I have no doubt I'll be able to find Liz. Our creepy twin thing will act as a beacon. You think I'm joking? I'm not. It's how I found her drunk and making out with her vegetarian boyfriend in the locker room at senior prom. I'll be able to find Liz, but will Tabitha be with her, standing guard? Will Tabitha have that big knife? Shit, I should have asked Connor to bring some kind of weapon.

I'm counting on Athsaia's attention to be at the faux movie filming. I'm counting on him staying out of my head because if he starts chanting, *Kill, kill, kill,* I'm not sure I'll be able to stop myself. No, I have to believe he'll be watching the kids around the kegs, waiting for a scraped knee, a paper cut—blood, more blood.

But what if he's strong already? What if he's walking around the Outpost right now? What if he can grab people, tear them limb from limb, and gobble them up? I bury my hands in my hair and rock forward and back. How many casualties am I willing to incur to get Liz back?

Fine, it's no use pretending I'm of upstanding moral character. I'd let a hundred people die to get my sister back. Same goes for Connor. Who's the monster now?

A sound like a bird whistle makes me respond in kind. With the sun fully set—I caught the final notes of "Amazing Grace" on the breeze twenty minutes ago—Connor is a graceful shadow, although I would recognize that confident gait anywhere, hindered by a bunch of stuff in his arms. He drops to his knees in front of me, and shoes land at my feet.

"Your mother is hysterical," he whispers. "I overheard her from your bedroom. The sheriff was already there. I guess they think you and Liz ran off somewhere together to do God knows what. With me, obviously. No sign of Gerald Krauss."

"Yeah, that's because he's tied up somewhere at the Outpost about to become dinner." I reach for the shoes and notice he brought me a change of clothes too: cargo pants and a dark tee. The better to be inconspicuous, I guess. I stand and tug the scratchy scrubs off, but before I pull on the new shirt, Connor puts a necklace over my head. "What—"

"Rosary," he says.

"Wow, good call." I doubt it'll do anything, but it's worth a shot. I'm willing to bathe in holy water at this point.

Connor politely tinkers with his camera when I take off my pants, junk flying free due to my lack of underwear. I assume he wouldn't be adverse to a quickie considering we might not live to see tomorrow, but I can't even think about it—not with Liz in peril.

Connor reaches a hand into his pants and, huh, is apparently going for it even if I'm not in the mood. But then something dark and metal shines in red outside lights. I take a step back and run into a tree. "Why do you have that?"

"It's my dad's. I grabbed it from my parents' room, and I want you to have it." He holds out a gun—an actual gun.

I cower. "No! I don't know how to use that thing!"

"Point and shoot, Em." He puts the dreaded pistol back in his pocket and takes hold of my forearms. "A kitchen knife isn't going to get the job done. Hell, outside of a virgin, I don't know what scares a demon, okay? I need you to be armed just in case. Please?"

"Yeah, but what if Athsaia gets inside my head and tells

me to kill people, huh? Kill *myself*? It'd be a lot easier with a freaking gun!"

"He can only get to you if your blood is in the air, right? So be careful of rusty nails and sharp corners. Are all your bandages still on tight?"

I nod.

He pulls the gun out of his pocket and holds it out to me again. "Please."

I sigh and take the gun from his hand. Despite the humid, hot temperature, the metal feels cold against my palm. He takes a minute—in the dark—to explain the safety and how it's a double-action whatever. His hands are all over mine as he gives me a tiny tour of my first firearm, fingers running over my knuckles, thumb caressing mine, until he finally goes silent and still.

His hand trails upwards. "You have such tiny wrists," he says. He lifts one and then the other, his kisses warm breaths against my skin.

The gun now "safely" in my pants pocket, he wraps me in a careful hug.

"You have your phone?" he says against my ear.

"Yeah."

"You call me when you have Liz, and everyone runs."

I nod and take a big, openmouthed inhale against the side of his neck. If we live through this, I'm telling him I love him. If we don't, I'll die with the scent of his sweat in my nose.

CHAPTER 23

Connor's text told Tiffany to have everyone meet inside the defunct restaurant at the Outpost because, "We don't want the cops to know we're there." Not a lie, just following Tabitha's rules. There's still a good chance the authorities will find us eventually, what with all the teens and twentysomething's of Longboat Key suddenly disappearing from their rooms. Hopefully, we'll have Liz safe by then.

Although a demon might be walking the earth.

We all make concessions, okay?

I'd been inside the restaurant once before. The structural integrity remains, although the inside is stripped bare. Unlike the Squid Shack, all the tables and chairs are gone, maybe stolen. The stained carpet remains along with a kitschy chandelier that is more ret-gross than retro.

By the time Connor and I arrive, twenty kids already mill about, but more are surely coming. (The busted fence momentarily delayed us because Connor, for all his bravado, wrapped me in a bear hug and refused to let me cross the threshold into the Outpost until he covered my neck in kisses and made me promise to be careful. *Promise, promise.*)

Fat pillar candles light the space, and kids crowd around a keg in the corner, although Tiffany—in a skintight striped dress—notices us and looks mighty shocked to see me. Her pretty painted lips part. "I thought you were in the hospital! Are you okay?" Without waiting for an answer, she pulls out her phone and texts. Half the people in the abandoned restaurant reach for their phones and turn to gawk at me.

I brush it all off with a wave of my hand, even though I took another pain pill not five minutes ago. I chewed it for maximum blood stream consumption considering, right now, I can barely stand up straight—not that I'm going to tell Connor that. He's already freaked enough. "You know the rumor mill." Considering Tiffany runs it. "People exaggerate."

"But," she leans in to whisper, "I heard they haven't found the guy who attacked you. In fact, he could be at the Outpost this very second." Instead of rightfully terrified, she looks thrilled.

I shake my head. "He's probably in Cuba by now." I press my lips together. "But if you, like, see him, you know, run. Because he's a homicidal lunatic."

She shows her teeth in a semi-smile.

"But, no, seriously." I giggle like a psychotic clown.

Connor puts his arm around my shoulders and squeezes. "Is everyone excited to film?"

"Totally." She flips her hair. "I've never been in a movie before!"

"Great, yeah, well, I'm the writer, of course, so, um..." God, I'm so bad at bullshitting. "This is going to be a monster movie." I nod at Connor, willing him to take the reins.

"Right," he says. "I figure I can start by filming kids partying." He lifts his camera and looks through the viewfinder. He waves it back and forth before I leap forward and remove the lens cover. We are terrible at this, just terrible. Connor clears his throat and lets the camera fall back against his chest. "The lighting is great. Perfect spooky ambiance."

"Yeah, so." I put my hands in my pockets but drag them both back out when my finger touches the cold metal of Mr. Nichols's gun. "While Connor does that, I'm going to scope out other locations on the property."

"Right," he agrees.

"Because movies need lots of locations."

"Right."

Poor Tiffany is watching us like we're a ping-pong game.

I grab her by the shoulders. "At some point, Connor might need everyone to look panicked and run. Um, see, the monster is a demon, so if Connor yells, 'demon,' everyone needs to run. And continue to run until you're off the property. Can you be in charge of that? Think mass hysteria."

She nods. "Totally." And smiles like she's won a prize. I'm starting to feel really bad about this.

"Great!" Connor sounds over-caffeinated. He clasps his big hand on my shoulder and pulls me backwards. To Tiffany, he says, "Could you give us a minute?"

"Of course. Let me go tell everyone about the demon."

My laugh continues to be high-pitched and hysterical.

With his hand on my elbow, Connor steers me away from the kids and their kegs and back toward the front door. Once there, his eyes quiver. He's mapping my face, memorizing every eyelash and freckle. He cups my jaw in his hands.

"I'll be all right."

"Yeah." He kisses my forehead. I get it: a kiss to the lips would feel too final, like goodbye. He tucks hair behind my ears and adjusts the collar of my navy-blue shirt. "Okay." His hands drop to his sides.

"Okay," I reply. I have trouble swallowing, so I get the hell out of there.

Outside, I might as well be walking through water. This is the solstice in Florida, summer's official onset. As if it wasn't hell-hot already in June, the temperatures only climb from here until the Gulf feels like a bathtub, and everyone hides inside from one to three. It's coming; I can feel it in the way my shirt sticks to the back sweat that's already there, how my bandages itch and curl around the edges. Pieces of hair stick to my forehead as I hurry away from laughter into the silence of this place. Like a black hole of sound, I can't even hear the beach. Palms dance but don't rattle in a refreshing breeze I don't feel. I take a steadying breath that shakes, so there's nothing steady about it at all, and trudge through humid air, free balling, wearing worn-out Vans, with a huge slice across my abdomen and pain pills in my blood.

Jesus, how am I going to save anyone?

I lean a hand against the nearest building and lean over. I can't breathe. Shit, this is not the time for a panic attack. Breathe, damn it. Breathe!

My head starts swimming, but I'm not about to pass out. It's the Vicodin kicking in.

"Fuck," I mutter and rub my eyes.

I'm no stranger to pain pills. One of the jocks I slept with —a basketball player from Toledo—injured his knee, so we would sit around high on pain pills, sipping his dad's scotch between sex sessions. I'm not, like, proud of this, but I know my Vicodin, okay?

I let the rush overtake me. There's numbness, although not as much as I'd like, and a twinge of euphoria. I can breathe again at least. Riding my counterfeit courage, I keep walking and make my way to the frankly dangerous hole in the ground I fell through one rainy day when Connor tried to kiss me. I eye the nearest empty building, and a side door is open. It must lead to the staircase Connor took to rescue me.

I wince when the door creaks and freeze. When nothing lurches out to grab me in the dark, I wait for my eyes to adjust and stare down a long hallway, covered in dirt and old furniture. Dim light glows at its end. I didn't know the Outpost had electricity, but nothing surprises me anymore. After all, here I am, trying to rescue my sister from a demon. Oh, and I have a boyfriend, so anything's possible.

To my left, there's a staircase going down. I use my cell phone as a flashlight, tiptoe down the dusty steps, and am immediately disappointed. It's nothing but a tiny storage space. So much for hiding Liz here.

A rat screams and scurries across the floor, but I barely budge. Rats are the least of my worries, especially since the little critters have always been nice to me—although now that they've had the taste of man flesh, I should steer clear. I watch the little guy hop up the steps and decide to follow.

On the ground floor, I walk cautiously toward the light. There aren't hotel rooms down here but instead what appear to be big, empty conference rooms that open like midnight mouths on either side of me. When I turn a corner, a row of bulbs lines the ceiling to my left, leading down a seemingly endless hallway of light and shadow. I follow the hallway. It's like walking through pockets of night and day, my eyes constantly adjusting to ten feet of light, ten of dark.

In the midst of a dark spot, my whole body veers right when I get another pain pill rush. I grab the nearest object— a crooked chair—and cuss before leaning my back against the wall. Spiderwebs tickle my face as I feel my pulse beating beneath my bandaged wound.

I hold my breath at the sound of a scuffed shoe—a Louboutin. I would recognize the soft sigh of expensive leather anywhere. I duck beneath the chair and hunch in on myself in an attempt to be as small and invisible as possible just as Tabitha creeps past. Head tilted, her eyes stare straight ahead. Did Athsaia tell her the party started? Has she come to see for herself? Regardless, I assume I'm in the right place to find Liz if her abductor is here.

Before I pass out from lack of oxygen, Tabitha moves off down the hallway. I wait until I hear the creak of the door at the end of the hall to keep going, but I now move with intention. Liz has got to be nearby. When the hall splits in two, I pause.

"Come on," I mutter and wait for that familiar buzz, our creepy twin thing. I found Liz at senior prom, but she once found me in an amusement park when we were seven because, in her words, she "knew you'd be harassing that clown." There's a tickle in my right ear like the sound of static, so I go right, even though that direction smells—not going to sugarcoat this—like rotten meat.

More scuffling up ahead. I increase my speed through the flashes of light, dark, light, until I almost kick a rat and slow down. The hallway opens to what was once a fancy ballroom, and in front of me, the whites of Gerald's eyes glow like bike reflectors. He's tied to a support beam, hands behind his back, duct tape over his mouth. He kicks at the floor when he sees me, but who cares? I only have eyes for Liz, who sits next to him in a similar state. When she sees me, she makes a high-pitched squeaking noise, so I run and kneel at her side.

I rip the tape off her mouth, and she starts sobbing. Based on the melted state of her mascara, she's been doing a lot of that already. "Emory, we have to get out of here!"

"I know, I know." I reach behind her and start tugging at knots.

Gerald keeps kicking his feet, mewling like a horny cat, but I freeze when I hear, "Emily?"

I lean forward and peer over Liz's left shoulder. *"Leland?"*

The old guy doesn't look good. His skin hangs from his face like he's lost weight, and that flesh is pale and almost green. There's old, dried blood on his Hawaiian shirt and what looks like food on his big, white beard.

"She's been slowly feeding the demon his blood," Liz whines.

"Tabitha?"

She nods and shakes her whole body. "Get us out of here!"

I shush her and free her hands before moving to Leland.

"Emily." His big head lolls from side to side. "You gotta get out of here, kid."

"Not without you." I go to work on his bonds.

Behind me, Liz bounces on the tips of her toes. "She's been sustaining the demon with Leland's blood, but it hasn't been enough." Her voice lurches on a sob. "I saw it, Emory, that fucking thing. It's Voldemort floating around, like in Harry Potter movie one, though, like when he's just a floating cape and drinking out of unicorns." She hiccups and sobs and hiccups some more.

"Liz, breathe. I can't carry you out of here if you pass out."

She breathes, but it sounds more like wheezing.

Leland's arms fall limply to his sides once I finally tug the ropes free. "Can you walk?"

He blinks at me, slowly. Even though he's not drunk, just dying, I pretend he's drunk because drunk Leland, I can handle—especially when he says, "I was in Vietnam. Of course, I can walk."

We clasp fists, and I tug him to standing. We both weave a little, but hey, at least we're up.

Gerald's pathetic begging has gone from cat howl to police siren. Liz kicks him right in the thigh, which shuts him up.

She points in his face. "You stabbed my brother, so you're dead!"

"Shit, Liz."

"What?" she hisses at me.

I shrug and look down at Gerald. "I mean, she's right, I'm not untying you, but— shit. Anyway, let's go."

We start walking back the way I came, leaving a screaming Gerald to hopefully rot. I'm about to reach into my pocket and call Connor, tell him I have Liz, so let's get the hell out of here, but a myriad of high-pitched squeaks like a bird migration stops us in our tracks.

Liz hugs herself. "What is—"

Rats. So many rats.

Like furry ocean waves, they syphon into the room and cover the floor. They scream and run, little guys scurrying across my feet. Liz does high knee leaps, and Leland stares, openmouthed, probably thinking this is all an acid flashback.

But then I remember...

"Follow them."

"I'm not following a bunch of rats!"

When Connor tried to kiss me, and I fell and cut my head, the rats stared at me—until red eyes showed up. Then, they fled. They're scared of Athsaia, so if they're running, it means the bastard is coming.

"Liz, follow the goddamn rats!" I grab onto the back of her shirt and shove and drag Leland behind me. "Go, go!"

We join the herd, although it's hard to move with any sort of speed when you're trying not to crush your rodent allies. We follow them from the big room down another thin hallway and into another big room. This looks like a lobby, so we've got to be close to an exit.

As I start scanning the dark, though, the rats halt like they've hit an invisible wall. They make a 180-degree turn and haul ass the way they came.

I turn and watch them rush off in horror and only then notice why I've been smelling rotting meat. In the corner, barely lit, is a pile of disembodied corpses. Arms stack on legs on top of one openmouthed head, but there's no blood. They're like human raisins.

These are the "unfavorable men" Tabitha mentioned, the ones she set up to steal copper from this cursed place, the ones she killed and fed to Athsaia before my family even arrived for summer vacation.

Of course, there's nothing I can do for them now. Nope, I have much bigger concerns—namely rats running away.

Athsaia has circled us. He's here, blocking our way out.

Like a horror movie scream queen, Liz puts her hands to her face and shrieks at the darkness.

There's movement in the shadows, a floating presence—the scrape of something sharp in front of us, then behind. The rats are gone, long gone. I can't even hear them squeaking anymore. As the new, ominous sound comes closer, I try to circle Liz and Leland, keep them protected.

Five feet away, red eyes ignite like candles. They appear at the level of my chest and climb until they're well over my head, looming up at the ceiling. Above the sound of Liz's harried breath, bones click and crack, unwinding. A single sharp claw enters our line of sight and withdraws.

Liz pulls my hair. "Do something!"

"Like what!" *Think, Emory, think.* I pull the gun from my pocket, hand shaking, and point at those red eyes. I doubt this will stop him, but maybe I can slow him down, injure him enough to find some stairs and get above ground.

I close my eyes and pull the trigger, but nothing happens.

The sound of Athsaia's deep laughter shakes the room.

"Christ's sake, Emily!" Leland grabs the gun from me, checks the safety—oh, right—and shoots into shadow.

I hiss and cover my ears, the sound like an explosion.

The red eyes blink and disappear. I'm about to start cheering, but by the time I hear the telltale click of an expensive stiletto, it's too late. Tabitha easily disarms Leland in his weakened state before ramming her pointy elbow up and into the center of my chest.

Since when was the basement vacant of air?

I curl over and tumble face-first into dust and grit. My shirt is wet and warm, stiches torn open. I press my hands to my wound as if they can stop the bleeding and try to see through the salt of my tears.

Above me, Liz cowers as Tabitha wields her big, fancy knife. Leland does his best to fight her off, but he gasps at what I assume is a successful stab. The dropped gun is a foot in front of me. I reach for it and press my trembling lips together, inching closer and closer with one hand still on my bleeding chest.

"Emory."

No, shit, no. My blood is in the air. He can control me if my blood is in the air.

"So glad you came back, Emory."

Tabitha falls limp at my side. Her knife skitters across the ground like another scared rat. I have but a moment to glance up and see a victorious Leland with a brick in his hand—although he doesn't look victorious for long. His arm is bleeding, fresh blood. His eyes take on a hazy, hypnotized look as he drops the brick and stands there motionless. Athsaia has him too.

"Kill them, Emory. The gun is right there."

I cover my ears. "Get out of my fucking head."

"Kill them. Kill—"

You know the end of *Lord of the Rings*? When the ring of power finally gets destroyed and Sauron screams like a little bitch? It sounds a lot like that, but at least my head is clear. I look up to find my sister standing over me with Tabitha's knife in her hand and blood dripping down her wrist.

She screams, "Take that, you stupid demon!" She swings her arm around.

"Kill—"

I wince and curl into a ball, but Liz is there to uncurl me. Hands covered in her own blood, she runs her thumbs across my cheekbones in a mimic of war paint. I watch her do the same to Leland before she again crouches in front of me and says my name. Her blood is all over me, but the more she rubs into my skin, the more peaceful I feel.

"Does that help?" she asks.

Oh, for the love of— "You're a *virgin?*"

"Well." She shrugs. "Yeah."

"But—" I try to sit up, and Liz has to help me. "Bowling Green guy, sophomore year."

Her nose wrinkles. "I made that up. Honestly, I was pissed you lost yours before I did. Shit, I was the cool one."

"Why. The fuck. Didn't you say... something... earlier?" I wheeze.

"Oh, yeah, because I was going to believe a nutcase like Gerald? Maybe he just had a fetish."

I laugh and immediately stop.

Her hands grab both my shoulders. "Emory, are you okay?"

"Yeah." Frankly, I'm glad Connor brought me a dark shirt. I'm pretty sure it's soaked in my blood, and I'd like to keep that under wraps for the moment. "But we have to get out of here. Help me up."

Leland scoots Tabitha's unconscious body out of the way with his foot and picks me up with a hand around my ribs. If he feels how soaked my shirt is, he doesn't say anything, but I'm thankful to be able to put an arm around his neck to stay standing.

"There are doors up ahead." He nods, face covered in swipes of red. Brilliant on Liz's part to think the presence of virgin blood could protect us all.

"What do we do with her?" Liz none too gently kicks Tabitha in the side.

"There's no time. We need to get everyone away from the Outpost."

If possible, Liz's face gets paler. "Oh my God, the summer solstice party. Did anybody show?"

"We might have invited the entire beach to save your ass."

"Aw, fuck!" No longer the whimpering, crying girl from earlier, Liz points Tabitha's knife in front of her. "Follow the virgin, bitches!"

CHAPTER 24

Outside, I try calling Connor as I limp, with Leland's help, across the property, but my phone has no service. Despite the pain, I refrain from popping another pill. Although it's nice to be high for the most horrific night of my life, I should maybe have a clear head. The pain is sure helping with that. I'm alert as a nervous squirrel with ADD right now—although I'm worried the blood loss is going to be a problem pretty soon.

Up ahead, Liz slams through the door to the restaurant and holds it open for Leland and me. At first, no one pays us any mind, too busy play partying as Connor circles people, camera in front of his face.

I yell, "Cut!"

Tiffany, red Solo cup in hand, grins and nods. "Whoa, great movie makeup!"

I sort of forgot we're all covered in my sister's blood.

Connor lets the camera fall around his neck and bounds toward us before reaching for me. "Whose blood are you wearing?"

"Liz's." I nod at my sister. "She's a virgin. We have to get out of here."

"Why didn't you call?" he asks.

"There's no phone service. Let's go!" I stand on tiptoe to see over his shoulder. "People, the demon is coming; we need to get off the property."

There are mutterings about "party" and "beer," but Connor in his big man voice yells, "Get the hell out; cops are on the way."

That'll get a bunch of underage kids moving.

Solo cups drop with hollow, plastic *clacks* as Leland turns to drag me to the door.

"Wait a goddamn second," Connor says.

Half-drunk teenagers mill past. Liz is doing her best to hide the huge, bloody blade under her shirt, although the wound on her arm still weeps blood, while Leland and I tilt back and forth like a boat at sea.

Maybe this is a lot for Connor to take in at once, even if we really do need to get moving.

He points to each of us in turn. "Leland's alive. Liz, why do you have a huge knife? Emory, why aren't you standing up on your own?"

"We'll explain everything later, son. For now—" Leland scoops me up like a bride and hands me to Connor, who supports my weight easily. "—I think it's best we get the hell out of this warzone." He gives his sagging pants a sharp tug and marches for the door like a soldier into battle. Well, a drunk soldier. He stumbles as he steps outside but doesn't stop moving toward the busted back gate.

"Come on." Liz gestures with the knife—I suspect, her favorite new accessory.

I wince when Connor adjusts me in his arms and follows her. "Let me guess: the stitches?"

I lean my forehead against the side of his neck. "Yeah, Tabitha made quick work of those."

"And the demon?"

"I don't know. Let's get out of here, fight another day and shit."

Connor jogs to catch up with the group. If they're as scared of cops as most kids I know, I would have expected them to have sprinted home by now. Instead, there's a crowd by the empty pool and back gate. There is a crowd, but they're silent, which is not possible for thirty horny, drunk kids.

Liz starts shoving them forward. "Go! Get out! What are you—"

She must see it the same time as me—a tall, furry, *pulsating* wall has grown over our usual exit. That freaky wall hugs the back fence of the Outpost, and I suspect the entire property by now. Gerald wasn't kidding when he said he felt Athsaia getting stronger. The demon has walled us in.

I swallow the taste of metal in my throat. "This is why the phones don't work. Remember what Gerald said? Athsaia *is* the resort."

The hysteria starts small, some whispers and whimpers, then soon deepens into screams and sobs. A stoner dude reaches forward to touch the pulsating wall until a girl slaps his hand away, and he sucks his thumb.

Tiffany puts her hands on her hips, considers, and turns to Connor. "Did you do these special effects for your movie?"

I whisper, "I don't think she understands how special effects work."

"What are we going to do?" Liz shrieks.

I don't notice the stoner kid going for the wall again, but I assume he touched it because I hear a choked "Ouch," and the guy's fingers have melted to bone. Staring at his own charred flesh, stoner dude doesn't freak out. I'd like to find the nearest drug dealer, because Jesus, I'll have what he's having.

Of course, after all I've seen tonight, I don't freak either. High on Vicodin remnants and blood loss, I observe the mob mentality as the mood shifts from panic to blame to downright apocalyptic. Two kids I don't know start making out. Stoner guy's girlfriend flaps her arms and walks in a circle—a demented chicken dance. Liz uses her knife like a finger to prove a point in someone's face, and Connor sighs into my hair as if he's ready to give up.

"Goddamn it," I mutter. "Hey! Shut up!"

Nobody's used to me screaming—not the brooding, quiet kid—so they do indeed shut up. I blow hair out of my face since one arm is over Connor's shoulder and the other is fruitlessly holding my insides together.

"How many of you are virgins?"

Liz raises her hand—and no one else.

"This is serious. How many of you are actually virgins but have lied about it because you think sex is cool?"

Nobody.

"People." Again, Liz brandishes her knife. "Listen. There is an actual bloodthirsty demon floating around this resort right now—"

Connor says, "Floating?"

I whisper, "Don't ask."

"But virgin blood will protect you, protect all of us. So if you're a virgin, raise your hand right now, and together, maybe we can figure a way out of here!"

All thirty kids eye each other, and some look guilty. Tiffany, the gossip goddess, is surprisingly the first one to raise her hand, followed by about a dozen others.

I mutter, "Oh my God, I *am* a whore."

Liz nods. "Okay, excellent. Now, you need to cut your

selves so the demon will smell your blood and leave you alone."

"Wait!" I yell. "You have to bleed on the ground."

There's a collective echo of "Huh?" but I only need to make things clear to Liz since she's holding the blade.

"Liz, Athsaia is the resort. Maybe if we hurt him, we can get the wall to come down." I nod at the pulsating monstrosity boxing us in.

"He's right," Connor says. "Have the virgins bleed on the ground."

"Add that to the list of things you never thought you'd say."

He chuckles against my ear.

Some of the kids aren't too keen on cutting themselves, but the stoner kid, who's now singing a lullaby to his fleshless hand, serves as incentive. A couple partygoers are willing to cut their own forearms, but others ask Liz to do it. She does so without hesitation. Yesterday, my little sister would have asked me to kill a bug in her room. Tonight, she's Rambo.

I'm the master of ceremonies, perched in Connor's arms. "Drip blood on the ground near the wall, but don't touch the wall!"

Our confused virgins nod but do as I say.

The effect is immediate.

From somewhere, a creature screams. Ground trembles beneath us as Connor holds me tighter. The wall weakens and begins to dissolve in front of us. I can see Longboat Key. I see houses down the beach with their red patio lights—but then, they disappear.

"Liz, more blood."

She nods and holds her breath before cutting her other arm and joining the whimpering line of virgins who didn't plan on spending the summer solstice bleeding. Once they see the furry wall start to weaken, though, their whimpers turn to cheers.

The demon screams again as a gaping hole opens in the wall.

"Nonvirgins, go first! Go, go!"

I don't have to tell them twice. Rich kids in designer duds roll through sand to safety. Soon, we all start streaming through. Connor puts me down, so I can roll through on my own, but not until I make sure Leland is ahead of me and safe. The poor guy has been through enough. Oh, and Liz. I get Liz the hell out of there, too, before making my way through the momentary weakness in Athsaia's trap.

Connor is right behind me when I hear a muffled *thump*, a big body thwacking into sand.

I look over my shoulder and am met with a terrifying sight. Something is pulling Connor back, back, deeper into the Outpost and away from salvation. Above me, Athsaia's wall is rebuilding. In a moment, it'll burn me in two, but I'm not leaving my boyfriend, damn it.

Liz must sense I've made my choice, because I hear her scream my name—but it's too late. I do a duck and roll back into the Outpost just as the wall again solidifies, and I lunge forward. Connor, still being dragged away, clasps my hand, and I pull until he lands in my lap. Whatever had a hold of him let go. Jesus, I see it. A vine slinks back into shadow.

Connor kicks at his ankles as if something might still be there. When he realizes he's free (and we're trapped), he spins on me, face red and twisted with rage. He squeezes my shoulders until I gasp. "Why? Why did you come back? You were safe!"

He's hurting me, so I shove hard against his chest. "Because I love you, stupid!" So much for waiting to see if we live through this, but hey, it's not looking good.

He drags me into a hug that almost breaks my face on his

collarbone and rocks us back and forth. "We're going to get out of here."

I allow myself a single moment of rest against his chest. My hands cling to the sweaty back of his T-shirt. It would feel so good to sleep right now wrapped in his arms—but nope.

Need to stay alert. Need to fight.

I support myself on his shoulders and stand. "Why'd the wall go back up? We had him. Where did he find the strength?"

Connor stands next to me and wipes what I suspect are tears from his cheeks, although I do not comment. "Tabitha?"

"Some drops of blood from an arm wound wouldn't be enough to beat a dozen virgins."

The wall pulsates in response and must block outside sound because I'm sure Liz is cussing me out something fierce right now.

"Well, what then?"

"*So* close." Tabitha's voice carries like a gunshot.

Connor spins at my side—and promptly retches—but I turn slowly, not quite ready to face the redheaded woman who might be my undoing. Stylish as ever in all black, her hair is a bit mussed from Leland's wicked blow to the head. She has somehow successfully navigated the entire property in her Louboutins, and she holds Gerald's disembodied head in her hand. He seems surprised to be there.

She throws what remains of Gerald, and his head bounces and rolls and stops a foot in front of us. Mouth open, he desperately looks like he wants to sell me something.

"So close, Emory," she says. "Almost got away, but you shouldn't have left Gerald. After all they'd been through together, Athsaia was only so happy to bleed him dry. Gave him the boost he needed to beat your virgin army. Quick thinking there, by the way. It's always the smart ones you have to look out for, even if you are pretty." She winks and reaches into the back of her pants. "You also shouldn't have left *this*." Mr. Nichols's gun is, right now, scarier than any demon because I know she'll use it. She lifts it and points it at my chest. I take a step back even though there's nowhere to go, nowhere to run. "Hmm, actually I think—" She shifts her aim and points the gun at Connor.

Without hesitation, I step in front of him. It's like being at the doctor when they hit your knee with that hammer thing: a reflex. He doesn't fight me, I think because he doesn't want me to have to watch him die first.

Tabitha smirks. "Your sensitivity is showing, Emory. A little late to learn now, but you should never show weakness."

I never did let the bullies see me cry. I kept up a cold exterior for all of high school—a skinny kid with a brain but no heart. Even the guys I slept with never knew the real me. Nice as they were, they ignored the bruises, never asked about my family, my writing, or my day. No one but Connor let me stop being so strong and just be me. I grab his hand.

"People like weaknesses, imperfections," I say. "In fact, they love us for them."

My awkward stuttering, clumsy feet, messy hair, and Barbie doll lips; somehow, Connor loves all that stuff. Maybe I do too.

Tabitha comes close enough to press the gun to my forehead. "You're too young to realize that only perfect people are ever happy."

I don't care that I'm crying now, salty showers that run down my face and drip from my chin. "You don't seem very happy. You're a bullied little girl who became a bully."

Her mouth twitches before I close my eyes, waiting to die, but the earth shakes beneath our feet. She stops pressing the barrel of the gun against my forehead, and I open my eyes to find her smiling. "Here he comes. My master. Dinner is served."

Connor spins me around and engulfs me in his arms. I rest my cheek against his chest but keep my eyes peeled as Tabitha backpedals, grinning like a mad goose. I assume we're about to be scooped up and tossed like peanuts down a demon's throat.

Imagine my surprise when a fist the size of a VW Bug emerges from the dead, dried up palm trees by the pool and lifts Tabitha into the air. The gun falls from her grip. She holds tightly to a huge, dark red finger instead. A momentary Zen descends on her face. I can practically hear her thoughts: *I will sit on his shoulder like a parrot. He will carry me around like a pretty pet. We will maul and murder for all eternity.*

The Zen only lasts a second when the fist starts squeezing. I see the massive fingers tighten, and Athsaia steps forth from hiding. He's all red and covered in muscle with horns and, yes, red eyes—pretty much exactly what I pictured.

When he squeezes again, Tabitha groans; her eyes bug out of her head. She kicks and claws at the giant fist. Then, his voice echoes like thunder in a cave. "Thank you for giving me life."

Tabitha tries to talk, but she has no air.

Athsaia's tongue is a huge slimy slug across his lips. "Haven't you heard? One should not conjure a demon."

"It's never a good idea," I whisper.

I squint when Athsaia chews her head off, keeps chewing, and swallows. His shiny, red demon face takes on a thoughtful appearance. I almost want to ask him if she tastes like chicken, but there's no time. His beady, red eyes catch me watching, and he reveals pointed, bloody teeth.

"Shit," I manage before he drops Tabitha's corpse, and that big fist reaches for me, even as Connor latches onto my shirt and holds on tight. A big, buff quarterback is no match for a demon from hell.

My shirt tears as he lifts me, leaving Connor with a

handful of fabric. Feet off the ground, I don't struggle against Athsaia's grip; what's the use? His hand feels uncomfortably hot. Tears mingle with drops of sweat, which makes him laugh in my face. Ten feet off the ground, his breath smells like smoke and blood.

"Your pathetic tears washed away the virgin blood." He traces my cheek with a claw, and the burn tells me he broke skin. "You are merely a dead hero now, and hero's blood tastes the best."

I close my eyes and hope Connor has started running, escaped somehow, but I'm rudely wracked out of my daydream when I smash into the ground and hit my head. I cover what's going to be a sizeable lump and cuss.

Above me, Athsaia writhes and covers his eyes. Big breaths make his lobster-red chest rise and fall before he growls down at me but comes no closer.

What the literal fuck?

Shirt basically gone, something tickles my chest. I look down, and Mom's rosary hangs across my ribs. "You've got to be kidding me," I mutter.

Athsaia lunges, so I hold up the holy relic. His skin literally steams. He howls like a wounded dog and backs up, away from me. I crawl forward using what's left of my strength and brandish the cross.

I think of *The Exorcist*. "The power of God, uh, compels you?"

By now, Connor is behind me, lifting me by my armpits. I keep waving the rosary at Athsaia, and he keeps shrinking, shrinking. His howls change from a deep rumble to helium high as he claws backwards down the side of the empty pool.

By the time he shrinks enough to slide down the rusty pool grate, Connor and I are both acting like priests with our God and compelling and... I slump forward and stare at the tiny trinket that saved my life.

"A rosary? All this time? Seriously? Oh my—"

Connor covers my mouth. "Now is not the time to blaspheme."

The fuzzy, black walls make a cracking noise as they crumble around us, revealing the Outpost's broken fence and flashing blue lights. A bloody crowd lingers, Liz in front with Tabitha's knife and my parents around her. Other parents hug crying kids, and cops with wide eyes hold guns limply at their sides because there are no bad guys left to shoot.

I finally give way to exhaustion and land with my face in the dirt. Connor is there to scoop me up and into his lap. His fingers feel good in my hair as he whispers, "I've got you."

EPILOGUE

I run past Emory's window at 8:30 a.m. but know he's not there. He no longer sticks his curly head out and waves when I pass. I sort of miss it, sort of don't. His sneaky window watching is a reminder of wasted time, at least two summers of us pining after each other while hiding behind playful pretense and movie trivia. Things are different now.

Liz practices yoga on the lanai as I pass. She's upside-down, standing on her head, but waves when she sees me—and promptly falls sideways into a chair. No matter how different she is from Em, they're similar in a lot of ways—klutziness one of them—not that I'd ever tell her that. Ever since the night she wielded that knife, I've come to realize pretty little Liz Jones is tough. Part of the reason Emory is so tough too.

Mrs. Jones hands me a cup of coffee in the kitchen and smiles. Emory's dad sits at the kitchen table, newspapers spread out. The headlines are varied but all equally dubious.

Demon in Longboat Key?
Mob mentality and teenage self-harm!
Serial killer on the loose?

Sensationalism at its best.

Since that night at the Outpost, Roberta has been our most unexpected ally. Once Leland received medical care—making a full recovery, by the way—he asked her on a date. He said, "Life is too short." He told her everything about Athsaia and Tabitha and the poor copper-stealing bastards she murdered and nobody missed.

According to Leland, Duke was an accident. Athsaia wasn't supposed to eat him, just drink a little, but starving demons aren't good at self-control. Like Gerald before her, Tabitha made it look like a shark attack to keep the attention away so the solstice party could be big as ever—a full capacity massacre to bring Tabitha's master to life. Too bad she didn't watch more horror movies. We all know demons aren't to be trusted.

Roberta, bless her, listened to all this from Leland and believed him. She made a few calls and brought down some rehabilitated Holy Roller ex-gangbangers from her Detroit days. With their crosses, holy water, and frankly bad ass attitudes, they're keeping an eye on things for now, but I think they're planning a trip to New Mexico to check out this Keebler and Crown and put them out of business for good. We don't need another Tabitha on Longboat Key.

You should have seen Emory when Roberta said, "Everyone knows to use crosses and holy water with demons."

Cooped up in a hospital bed, he wrapped himself in a big blanket and pouted all afternoon. "I just finished *Salem's Lot* and *The Exorcist*. Why didn't I think of that? God, I'm worthless. I'm—"

When he gets that way, the only way to shut him up is with a kiss, so I did. I'll never get sick of Emory's mouth.

I sneak into the living room where he's been sleeping since they brought him home. He's still too injured to go up and down stairs. He's still too injured to travel even, so the Jones family has extended their Florida stay. My parents left a couple days ago to head back to upstate New York, but I refused to go with them. I won't leave Emory, not until he's better.

He's still sleeping when I walk in, morning sun painting his full lips and chiseled chin. The couch is too small for him —this summer. His long legs hook over the end; his arms stretch above his head, bent at the elbows. A blanket covers the bandages on his chest, and the thin cut across his cheek will be gone soon enough. His wild, dark curls are a shadow around his head; long eyelashes quiver as he hears me, or maybe he dreams.

I take out my phone. My favorite camera broke the night we almost died, so this will have to do. I snap a picture. The side of his mouth curls before he grins, eyes still shut.

"What are you doing?" he asks.

"Looking at you." I sit in my usual chair next to him and try not to sneak a peek at the open notebook on the floor.

He's been writing something, although he won't tell me what yet. He says talking about new projects makes them disappear, but he does say there's a hero in it who looks a lot like me. I keep reminding him that he's the hero, and even though he blushes and chews his lips every time, I think he believes me a little.

"I bought you something."

His eyes flutter open—shamrock green, mermaid green, some amazing green they've yet to name. *Emory green.*

Every day, I run by a gaudy tourist shop. I've never once set foot in there—until today—because we have to go home soon. College doesn't start for another month and a half. I can't remember being without Emory for two *days*, so I bought something to try and keep us connected, keep me sane. I reach into my pocket and pull out two cheap, matching friendship bracelets of red, black, and green.

He winces as he leans up on his elbows. "How nineties of you."

"Might be eighties even. Give me your wrist."

He rubs his eyes and holds out his arm while yawning. It's alarming how I think everything he does is adorable, like I'm thirteen, hanging with my first crush when, instead, I'll be twenty-one in a month, and I'm staring at the man I love.

For all Emory has grown and changed over the past year, he still has those delicate wrists. I loop the braided material below his pulse point and start tying. "Too tight?"

He shakes his head. "Nope."

I secure a double knot before turning his arm over and admiring the dark string against his pale skin. He didn't get as tan this year as he usually does, what with hunting demons and all.

I hold up the matching bracelet. "Do mine?"

He shifts and folds his legs under him before going to work. He looks so gorgeous tangling strings together, so I kiss his nose. His face wrinkles, but he smiles. "There." He presses his wrist against mine. "With our powers combined..."

I give his ribs a quick tickle, gently. "It's supposed to be romantic."

He slumps back—gently—and fidgets with the strings on his wrist. "Thank you."

A quiet knock on the living room door must be Mrs. Jones. She's nice about giving us privacy, more than Emory's dad who looks at me sometimes like I'm the bad boy taking his daughter to prom. Only sometimes, though. Mr. Jones has known me a while, so it's not like he actually doesn't trust me; it's just that the dynamic is different now that his son is no longer my neighbor but my boyfriend.

"Emory, honey, Sheriff Willick is coming over in a bit. I think he has more questions."

Emory's head tilts back in annoyance, and I subdue the reflex to lick his Adam's apple. Christ, how am I going to survive even five seconds without this guy? "But I've told Tom Selleck everything!"

We have, many times over.

I get it. From the sheriff's perspective, nothing makes sense. He can't arrest a demon, even one that's all wilted and weak and currently being tormented by a bunch of badass Detroit church folks in the bottom of a pool. Even one tabloid's suggestion of a mass LSD trip does not explain Tabitha's headless corpse, Gerald's, well, *head*, or all the body parts in the Outpost basement. That's where the serial killer theory comes from, which—in the grand scheme of life, I suppose—is more comforting than a conjured demon from hell. Then, there are all the Longboat party animals calling Emory and Liz heroes for making them bleed. Yeah, if I were the sheriff, I'd have questions too.

I nudge Emory's knee with mine. "One more time, babe. That's it. I literally won't let him in again."

He puffs out audible air. "Fine."

"Coffee?"

"Not yet, Mom. Thanks." He again fiddles with his bracelet as she closes the door and leaves us alone.

"Want some of mine?" I offer him my mug, but he shakes his head. "Are you okay?"

He shrugs.

"Em, what is it?"

He crosses his arms over his injury. He's been doing that a lot lately, subconsciously protecting what will eventually be a scar. "I was thinking about New York. We'll be away from each other for almost two months, and then we'll be in the big city. What if—?" He presses his lips together, and I think

I see self-doubt coming. He sighs. "I mean, what if I meet all these other hot guys and realize you're not that special?"

Wow.

As I scramble for words, he busts out laughing, eyes crinkling with all his teeth on display.

I kneel on the couch next to him and pull his face back with a hand in his hair. "Holy shit, once you're better, I'm going to kick your ass." I suck his bottom lip into my mouth, and this is how I know I love him: even his morning breath tastes good.

ABOUT SARA DOBIE BAUER

Sara Dobie Bauer is a bestselling romance author and mental health / LGBTQ advocate with a creative writing degree from Ohio University. She lives with her hottie husband and two precious pups in Northeast Ohio, although she'd really like to live in a Tim Burton film. Visit Sara's website to join her newsletter and private Facebook group.

www.saradobiebauer.com

ALSO BY SARA DOBIE BAUER

Abstract Love

Handsome Death

We Still Live

Broken News

He Sees You When You're Sleeping

The Escape Trilogy

Escaping Exile

Escaping Solitude

Escaping Mortality

Other Florida Rom-Coms

Bite Somebody

Bite Somebody Else

CPSIA information can be obtained
at www.ICGtesting.com
Printed in the USA
LVHW111342210521
688017LV00012B/929

9 798727 920145